Flunky

Also by Steve Vivian

A Self-Made Monster

FLUNKY

Steven D. Vivian

Boson Books
Raleigh, North Carolina
2002

Published by **Boson Books**
3905 Meadow Field Lane
Raleigh, NC 27606   ISBN 1-886420-97-1

An imprint of **C&M Online Media Inc.**
Photography & Cover Design by Once Removed

C&M Online Media Inc.
www.cmonline.com
e-mail:boson@cmonline.com

*Boson Books thanks the wonderful Amy Ickes for her
tireless expert technical assistance*

For Theresa
Without Whom
Not

If it's Monday morning, the President will be yelling.

Dr. Don Boyle, the President of West Central College, will crash into the conference room like an errant Scud missile. Then, face reddening, he'll launch into his arm-waving, finger-pointing, full-throttle Monday morning inquisition. I mused that Boyle, like a soprano practicing scales before a performance, rehearses his operatic tirades before the colossal bathroom mirror of the Presidential lavatory. The Presidential water closet, by the way, is the subject of ceaseless rumour. According to the most reliable gossip, it's mauve and blue and boasts a wide-screen stereo TV, phones, sauna, microwave, cappuccino brewer, toilets designed by a leading chiropractor, and a bar stocked exclusively with 1959 wines. These Chicago Irish, I guess, live with zest.

We waited for the President's entrance, clutching our notebooks and grinding our teeth. Nobody talked—we were too busy being nervous. The Cabinet meetings, as the Prez calls them, were always on Monday at 10:00 a.m. and were always frightful.

A slamming door announced his entrance.

Again, I was struck by the contrast of his small stature and large temper. Boyle's barely five foot eight. He's in his later 40's but is teenage thin. He weighs maybe a hundred fifty if you factor in the five pounds of polyurethane he lavished daily on his styled auburn hair. His suits were slightly baggy, suggesting a child in adult clothes. I'm a good six one and pushing two hundred forty pounds; I've often ached to smash Boyle against a wall, battering-ram fashion. But then he starts yelling at everybody. Suddenly you're a ten year old, cowering before your pissed off father. He took his chair, which was upholstered in unborn calf. "To begin," he boomed, "I direct our attention to Dr. Malvick's analysis of spring enrollment figures."

We dutifully thumbed through our pile of papers. I envied Malvick, the Dean of Enrollment. The economy, well into a decade of economic "recovery", had somehow forgotten to produce jobs with recovering wages. The shell-shocked citizenry was enrolling in record-busting numbers, hoping to gain some college credits and earn an employment upgrade. Or just keep the job they had, which might at any nano-second be nuked to satisfy Wall Street.

"What should we think of these enrollment data?" Boyle asked rhetorically.

I was about to praise the figures, but Bruce Herrig—a virtuoso buttock buffer—was the first in line to Boyle's behind. "Wonderful, just wonderful. Up six percent."

We murmured and nodded and grunted, all the while deeply

loathing Malvick's guts. Malvick flashed a self-congratulatory smirk.

"This report is a disaster!" Boyle boomed.

"It doesn't, I mean, I don't understand," Malvick sputtered.

None of us understood. The news was all good.

Boyle snatched a page of Malvick's printout, tore it into confetti, and threw it at his face.

"You're a short-sighted fool!" Boyle declared. His declaration left Malvick blinking through tears and Presidential spittle—the Prez spit when he yelled, so he spit plenty—but Malvick dared not wipe his suddenly damp and ashen face.

"You've cost this college hundreds of thousands of dollars! I have never seen someone so incompetent," he continued, his eyes narrowed to a vicious squint. "So stupid, so thin-spined and dim, and..."

I was grateful to be hung over: I could settle back into my murk and fog as Boyle mauled Malvick. The first flunky always got it the worst because the Prez had the whole weekend to simmer and boil. He tended to fire most of his load at target number one.

But Malvick made a terrible mistake. He talked back.

"I must humbly suggest," the Dean began, "that the report was not as, it's really quite positive."

The President paused in mid-insult, as shocked as the rest of us.

"The report is, it's true," Malvick blundered, "and I—"

"Unghh, ahrabba, ungh!"

"The state board of education could reprimand us for distorting information if..."

"*Flunky!*" Boyle jabbed the air with his forefinger; he looked mad enough to jab Malvick's eyeballs. "I do the reprimanding! Pump up those figures! We must show an overwhelming demand for a second campus."

Yeah, the second campus. It's all Boyle cares about anymore, and he's hell-bent on breaking ground within the year.

"—education is enrollment-driven! Push the numbers!"

"I will, I shall!"

"Get out of my sight."

We flunkies gasped collectively.

Malvick stood as if to leave, then he—

"Out!"

—he dropped to his knees, like a supplicant before the wrathful king, and pleaded with clasped hands and white knuckles. The President scoffed and waved him away, threatened him with the campus police and a lawsuit. The poor Dean, I knew, was scheduled for a triple by-pass next month. And without a job, the poor Dean had no medical insurance. Without medical insurance, he had no reliable pulse.

The Dean kept genuflecting, but Boyle was unmoved. The Prez's secretary poked her head into the conference room. Boyle nodded, and in thirty seconds the campus cops arrived to remove Malvick.

The cops grabbed Malvick's feet and dragged him across the deep pile carpeting. "I can't lose this job!" he wheezed. "I have health problems, I..." His head struck the doorframe.

Malvick's pleas faded down the hallway. We stared straight ahead, our faces betraying no emotion.

Boyle paused for several gulps of coffee, and he scrutinized us over the rim of his stein-sized mug. He had us. If we didn't jump through every hoop, we could face mortgage foreclosure or medical disaster within the week.

As for Malvick—what? You think he'll sue? No, that's comically naive. Don Boyle's got the goods on Malvick, you can be sure. Hell, everybody knows that Malvick's been boffing his half literate and fully stacked secretary for the last six months. The secretary is a patronage employee, and she knows where her bread is buttered. If told to, she'd march into court with a headline-grabbing tale of sexual coercion. Never mind that she'd be lying her plush buns off; patronage sometimes requires perjury. No, if Malvick wants even the slightest severance, he'll shut up or the college's goon squad of lawyers will make him run the gauntlet in court, in full view of Malvick's wife. His three daughters. His pastor.

The meeting resumed. Boyle, face animated with tics and grimaces, interrogated each of us. Herrig, the Director of Public Relations, was currently on the rack.

"—didn't we agree that the new color pamphlet would have five colors, not four colors. Didn't we? You *failure.*"

Herrig didn't bother to defend himself because defense was impossible. Last week, Boyle wanted four colors in the pamphlet. Now he demanded five. Boyle changed his mind about everything continually. He was addicted to those pop business bestsellers like *Vlad the Impaler's Strategy Secrets* and *Dare to Dream, Dare to Scream.* He called his thought-flips the "Flexible Proactive Goal Management Method of Chaos Driven Decision Making."

My thoughts turned to Lydia Fairview, sitting three chairs to my left. Lydia could lose a few pounds, true, but her red dress was tight in all the right places as she took notes. I caught her glancing about the room and smiled, but she returned to her notebook. See, Lydia pretends to hate me. Last year during the Christmas party, she drank six Bloody Marys and fell during the hotel bar band's Neil Diamond medley. She rose, flapping and braying, jugs liberated from their prescription-only brassiere.

I shoved aside her shocked samba partner and offered my assistance.

She was indignant, complaining that she didn't want help, but I insisted with collegiate clutches. She kicked me. Now it was my turn to hit the floor, clutching my bruised shin. But that's just her way, I think. Lydia, I'll bet you, likes some violence with her sex.

I was recalling the heft and hang of those hooters—rendered exotic by the dance floor's blue and green lights—when a Boyle bombshell struck my bunker and brought me back to the present tense, er, tense present.

"Deyme, brief me on our political action caucus."

"Huh?"

"Don't let me."

"The progress is, it's, it's coming along nicely, Dr. Boyle."

"For example?"

I tried to review my notes on the political action caucus. This was difficult because I'd forgotten them. "We've met lots of times. At least twice."

Boyle's nostrils flared.

"And we've got volunteers to cover the precincts with leaflets a month before the Board elections. And I've got some contributions to buy coffee and gas money for the volunteers."

"Speakers lined up for the Rotary and Township meetings next week?"

Uh oh.

My peripheral vision faded. I could see only straight ahead, as if I were looking through a tunnel. At the end of the tunnel was Boyle's ruddy and muscled face. I got light-headed, and for a nanosecond I thought I was going to faint into Herrig's lap.

"Yes, I have speakers lined up."

Please, God, please. Please don't let him ask who my speakers are.

"We all know how very important these Trustee elections are for us. To think this guy Drock could get elected to the board..." Boyle chewed on his bottom lip for a moment, then turned to somebody else.

Herrig loudly cleared his throat. I offered him a quick and smug smile, then slipped back into the sludge of my hangover for the meeting's duration.

Welcome to my life. I'm James Deyme (as in "dime," as in two nickels), but I prefer the less formal *John*. All the James's I knew as a kid were cross-eyed freckled bookworms. So just call me John.

I am Associate Vice President of West Central College, one of several community colleges in Chicago's sprawling suburbs. If you're unfamiliar with the intrigues of higher education, you might be impressed by my title. Don't be. As my name-choice reveals, I'm ironically less than comfortable with books, with learning, with smarts.

As one of today's Education Professionals, I didn't study language or math or science or any other actual subject. I studied a mushy discipline called "Education." We Education majors slogged through courses in bulletin board design and Affective Interpersonal Relating and esteem repair. Oh yeah. We play acted too. You know, we acted out roles like the Sickeningly Cheery Teacher and the Pistol Packing Student who flunked the spelling bee. What the hell. We education majors often score near the bottom of the SAT yardstick. What else are we supposed to do?

After getting my teacher's certificate, I further enfeebled my intellect with a "doctorate" in Educational Administration. Educational Administration gives bullshit an irredeemably bad name. In one class, we studied campus organizational charts: a box here, a rectangle there, even the occasional rhombus, all connected with elaborate lines and arrows. The course's climax occurred when I created my own organizational chart composed exclusively in triangles, which illustrated, I claimed, "synergistic dynamic responses to challenge."

Upon hustling my doctorate, I resolved to conquer corporate America. For two years, I managed one of those Rumpus Room Teaching Centers...you know, the chain outfit that closed because half the "teachers" were child molesters. None of the sickos, fortunately, had infiltrated my particular Room. Thank Christ, because I was pretty slack in the interviewing process.

When the Rumpus Rooms closed, I was on the dole for six months until I crossed a picket line at a local high school and got a job teaching social studies to some unbelievably sullen sophomores. The bureaucrats seemed to like my spirit though, and when the job at West Central became available, they put in a good word for me.

God damn did I luck out! No way could I find another job that paid seventy-one grand a year, plus bonuses and benefits. That's the thing. All those private sector money men walking the flimsy high-tech high wire of today's information economy...well, sure money's been made, but taped to their PDA's are micro-thin cyanide pills....at any moment, they could be mortally downsized. Me? I'm savvy enough to sniff after the surprisingly impressive lucre of the higher-ed hustle.

At West Central, we flunkies are paid very well to endure Don Boyle's rants. Snorting and belching at the public dollar trough, we have little cause to complain—though we still do. But, telling you the truth, I'm thrilled to be here. I think I'm working for a genuine genius. That talk about Boyle one day being a U.S. Senator, that's not just bullshit: I can picture him on C-Span haranguing and pleading and cajoling.

Boyle's genius is probably in the genes. His father was, as a young man, a Catholic priest whose taste for the good life—attractive women, unblended whiskey, expensive poker nights with Chicago's Irish establishment—convinced the Church that he was better suited for a lay position. He became a prized Catholic school administrator. He had a rare grasp of politics and was appointed city comptroller, where he mastered the high wire art of Chicago patronage. The old man never forgot his roots, and the Chicago diocese was all too pleased to accept the wave of "charitable donations" in return for its political clout. Donald Boyle got a free Catholic education all the way through graduate school, and he too became a patronage pro. He'd even run a few Catholic high schools, but he got sick of that damned separation of church and state. Boyle hungered for the tax dollars of public higher education. Now he had them.

By eleven thirty, I was ready for an early two-hour lunch. I wanted to leave immediately, but it looks better if you wait for a few other bureaucrats to leave first. From my smudged office window, up on the second floor, I could see colleagues heading for the parking lot. I waited five minutes and left.

"Have a good lunch," called Barbara, my alleged secretary.

"Make sure to call Herrig and Johnson and all those other guys," I said. "I need to line up speakers for the Rotary and, and whatnot."

"But I do have a report to type this afternoon," she reminded me.

"So make your calls during lunch!" I politely snapped.

On Mondays, the nearby Chinese restaurant has an All You Can Eat buffet. I can eat a lot, as my burgeoning belly and bulbous butt graphically attest. I was shaking with food fever. You've seen the food fever shake: it's the shake of the starving stray dog that discovers a squirrel carcass mashed into the road. His tail, his butt, and his trunk shake. His limbs tremble. That's me, shaking and belching as I mug my heap of chicken wings and fried rice.

After my second plate, I wowed my fellow diners by imitating a flatulent otter. Chastened, I hurried into the can and went at it. The fish sticks I had for breakfast hadn't agreed with me. I finally finished the job, though I would have been grateful for stirrups.

Back at my office, a message from Boyle was on my voice mail: "Call me immediately."

Rheena, Boyle's fawning secretary cum surrogate Grandmum, announced my call. Boyle didn't greet me with a curse, which encouraged me. "Listen, I forgot to find out this morning. Who've you got lined up for that Rotary meeting day after tomorrow?"

"I've, I've got Herrig lined up."

"And for the west Cook county Democrats meeting next week?"

"...Herrig."

"What, is he a good speaker?"

He was awful. "He's outstanding."

"Okay then. But I want you to get different speakers for the Republican crowd. I need a speaker who can talk about lower taxes and high standards and all that, you know, all that bullshit. Just in case any of the Republicans gets elected—we can't alienate that crowd."

"Very wise, Dr. Boyle."

"We could cope with any of them but that bastard Drock. If he gets on—Christ."

Drock was a Republican of the far right variety, and he was stumping for one of the three contested Board of Trustee seats. Drock had a mini-empire in area computer stores, and he was promising to bring abhorrent "fiscal responsibility" to West Central College.

"That bastard Drock," Boyle complained, "has been saying that West Central administrators are the highest paid in the state! And he says that the second campus is just a patronage front for Democratic contractors."

"That's really irresponsible!"

"Demagoguery!" Boyle hung up.

Damn it, I had to get to work. What would it take to persuade Bruce Herrig to make some speeches for me? Cash, of course. I flipped open my battered wallet and sighed. Ninety-two bucks surely wouldn't be enough. Then the phone rang.

Boyle eschewed niceties such as "Hello" or "Another thing."

"If Drock wins this election," he growled, "I'm in a tub of boiling fat. And you're there with me."

Bruce Herrig told me to meet him at Ralph's, a restaurant and bar a few blocks from campus. Herrig was smiling in a corner booth, his seemingly polished bald head a beacon in an otherwise dark dining room.

I pushed my gut past the intrusive table corner, and Herrig helped himself to one of my Arctic Blast menthol cigarettes. "I don't know why I'm helping you out of your little jam," he teased. "Lying to the President like that."

"You have a stake in this too," I reminded. Alfred Rochinni, Boyle's confidant and Board Chairman, was up for re-election. Drock had been especially harsh in criticizing Rochinni's patronage hirings. Drock even started a whispering campaign among local pols that Rochinni's string of liquor stores had ties to organized crime. Rochinni called Drock a racist interested only in smearing Rochinni's Italian heritage.

Herrig dismissed my fears. "Either way, it's okay for us. Hey, Republicans are pro-management, and they hate unions."

Indeed. Drock had fought off unionization in his Chicago chain of Big Byte computer stores. He'd even gone to court to stop the distribution of union propaganda sheets. His suit failed, but his fervor impressed the local Republicans, who are always trying to get a foothold in Chicago.

Herrig rubber-necked at our approaching waitress, who wore a black sequined slingshot. He ordered another pitcher of Behemoth Dark, then made me pay for it.

"So, do you hate Boyle as much as me?" Herrig demanded.

"Sure."

"No you don't. I, you're the biggest ass kisser in the college."

"You're just pissed because Boyle yelled at you for ten minutes about your stupid pamphlets. Hey, it's better getting yelled at than getting canned like Malvick."

"God, look at those."

Herrig nodded toward our waitress, who stood in profile at the bar. Her gravity defying tits threw a shadow across the faces of two sputtering drunks. The drunks, two retirees in checked shirts and Brylcreem, complained she'd short-changed them. Finally, after a lot of hair-splitting explanation and earnest assurances, the waitress escaped.

"Hey over here!" Herrig called.

She returned, smiling warily. Or wearily.

"We'll take another pitcher," Herrig announced, "and my colleague will pay for it." The waitress dutifully returned with fresh beer, its rich head flowing luxuriously over the pitcher's rim.

"Join us," Herrig urged.

"I'd love to, but I'm still working."

I was about to hand her four dollars, but Herrig pushed my mitt away. He didn't want the waitress to leave.

"Did you know," Herrig inquired, "that my friend and I are employed at the fine nearby college?"

"I'm the Associate Vice Tresident, the Vice President of Liberal Arts," I interrupted. "My colleague is just a Dean."

The waitress tried to look interested.

"I'm the reason that we have regained our fine reputation," Herrig interrupted. "We're on the bleeding edge of computers and of, of educational things."

"Forgive him," I said sonorously. "He just can't stop the P.R., even after business hours." Whoa...I was suddenly feeling much better, exhilarated by the wonderful beer and wonderful boobs. "Did you ever tell us your name? What's your name?"

I don't remember what her name was. I do remember that my chair began to quake and shimmy, as if its rocket boosters had suddenly fired. See, all the Behemoth Dark was violating the laws of gravity and motion. Still, I kept talking, though the escalating G-forces had mashed my mug against the suds-sopped table. "Now c'mon. What's your name?"

"My name's Bruce Herrig."

"Why don't you let her talk?"

"She left five minutes ago. Did you pass out?" Herrig didn't wait for my answer. Toward me he pushed a shot glass filled with an innocent clear liquid. "Drink up."

I drank up. The Ouzo's volatile fumes escaped my slack mouth, and I wondered if Herrig's cigarette would catch fire. After heroically swallowing his shot without a flinch, Herrig agreed to deliver a couple speeches for the paltry sum of three hundred dollars. I squawked only halfheartedly. Herrig was helping me; he could have begged off and enjoyed my desperate attempts to round up speakers, then come in and demanded even more money.

"The West Central political action caucus thanks you," I croaked.

Yeah, Herrig was all right. As the drink flowed, we bonded as flunkies do when alcohol taps our mother lode of anxiety. At one point, I even offered motherly sighs of sympathy as he revealed his hair problems: He'd tried a rug, but it looked like an unruly shrub atop his squat and pocked face. He'd tried Rogaine with Monoxidil and grown a bumper crop of peach fuzz—but the fuzz died the next week. He'd tried Assertiveness Training with Positive Self Imaging. Now he was trying the removal of all mirrors from his apartment. I'd never before been struck by the plight of a relatively young man—Herrig was 34 last month—with a nearly nude scalp. I'm blessed with few attractive facial features, but I do have a thick curly bloom of black hair.

"You don't know how lucky you are," Herrig accused. "If you die, you've got to will me your hair."

Herrig had touched my heart. We hacks have so little esteem-support during the workday: the President yells at us, and the faculty dismiss us as illiterate parasites. I felt bad for Herrig. Hey, imagine being a professional mouthpiece, trying to put the best face on a bogus college. You're blathering about "quality education", armed with glossy pamphlets and your bored audience is thinking, "That guy's a cue ball."

The afternoon surrendered to evening. Herrig kept hustling the waitress. He even tried to kiss her hand. She quickly withdrew it and disappeared. By now, Herrig was crocked on Ouzo and lust; he mistook our packed ashtray for his glass and sipped a mouthful of butts. A wave of crimson began at his scalp and traveled across his face to his neck.

Then he did the big spit under our table.

After a lot of woeful gagging, Herrig stumbled out, though he managed to leave his business card with our appalled waitress. An old codger led him to the door and Herrig, now sobbing, gave the codger ten bucks.

I slyly disassociated myself from Herrig by moving to a table across the room. With the assistance of anonymous steadying hands, I made it to a new table without incident in five minutes, though the thirty-foot journey drained me. By now I was too drunk to do anything but drink and make frequent zigzags to the stall. Finally, around 9:00 or maybe midnight, I bravely ordered a cheeseburger. Miraculously, it stayed down and my head cleared. The euphoria of food and drink, however, surrendered to the existential dread of a new hangover. Or maybe it was the same old hangover refreshed by the booze.

I was minding my own business, content to smoke and burp and evaluate chicks. One hot number inspired me to do a leering 180. But the chick's hulking husband or bodyguard told me to fuck myself. Dejected, I tried to cheer up by deciding to take tomorrow off.

"Hello, James."

For the love of bleary Jesus...Boyle. He pulled up a chair opposite of me, a glint in his eye. He motioned at the waitress for a drink, a gold pinkie ring accenting his gesture.

"Have a drink, James. Or some coffee."

I tried, as drunks do, to look sober.

"Looks like you've had a few."

"Sure, whatever you say, Dr. Boyle." I winced as the hangover delivered its first punishing blow to my forehead.

"Don't apologize to me. I had a few too many myself last night. It's just white wine for me." Boyle leaned forward, intimate and candid. "I'm glad I found you here, James. I've been meeting with some of the county Democrats, firming up commitments and so on for the board elections. I came here just to have a quick drink, to relax, and I find you here. Now I don't have to drink alone."

"That's why I came here too, to not drink alone. But Herrig left, and I've been trying to leave for hours." I lighted still another Arctic Blast. My demoralized lungs accepted the heat and poison without protest.

"I need your help, John. Your help with something very important." Boyle gently patted my hand.

All this male bonding! I almost sprawled across the table to hug him.

Boyle's smile revealed his alarmingly white teeth. "What I need you to do...it's not illegal. Really, it's just good old American political hardball." Boyle paused meaningfully. "Hardball."

I listened to Boyle's plan as carefully as I could. Paying attention was hard: Boyle kept ordering this invigorating white wine, and the wine and my hangover waged a battle for my drinking soul. In the end, the wine won.

Boyle explained the plan, then asked me to repeat it. Quietly.

After a few false starts, I repeated the plan and Boyle nodded his approval. "The faculty zealots will give you a hard time, but pay no attention to them. Just proceed with the plan." He rapped the table. "We are the college's guardians. Faculty troublemakers are not. Management takes the risks, so we'll take the rewards. Don't you agree?"

"Risks," I nodded slowly. "Reward."

"Come through for me on this one," Boyle half-whispered, "and your future could be much brighter."

"—Thank you," I faltered. "I'm eager to, uh, to do really well and—."

"Don't let me down, James." Boyle ordered a pot of coffee for me and took his leave. I scorched my tongue on the jet-black java, but I was all smiles: Boyle had offered me a one-way bus ticket out of obscurity. Now I'd board that bus and commandeer the driver's seat to run roughshod over West Central's halting herd of timid toadies.

After a final restive session in the can, I wisely called a cab. Upon arriving home, I struggled with the door key—after all this boozing, it was belligerent and kept fighting its way from my grip. Finally I made it inside my rented duplex and collapsed on the rented living room couch. Of course, I had to piss within three minutes. I ignored my bladder's stabbing demands as long as possible then struggled to my feet, lamenting the long trip up the creaky steps. Screw it. I grabbed a sixteen ounce pop bottle and gave it new life as a urinal.

Getting comfortable, I considered my rising fortunes. Within a year,

I'd probably be out of my cramped duplex, freed of its asthmatic furnace and noisy pipes. I was keen on a new townhouse development in exclusive Hinsdale. The townhouses were oh-so-chic, all polish and pretension, and the clubhouse's two kidney shaped pools seemed terrific cocktail party sites. I imagined myself sipping mint juleps as a chick— Lydia Fairview?—massaged my shoulders and congratulated me on my latest bonus.

All this luxury was within the grasp of my nicotine-stained fingertips: I needed only to persuade Patrick Drock to drop out of the West Central College board of trustees election.

The morning arrived incredibly fast, as such mornings do. Why are post-drinking mornings so impatient? I lay there and marveled at my headache, which had acquired a physical heft and provided a light show of red and white explosions on the back of my eyelids. On any other morning, I would've been trembling and swearing under a scalding shower. Not today. I took my sweet time calling in to my secretary. I wouldn't be in today, I informed her. I asked that she call Patrick Drock at the Big Byte computer store on 170th. Tell him that Dr. Deyme of West Central College would be seeing him.

As I drove to meet Drock, I hoped that a revitalized career would revitalize my love life. By now, almost anything would be a gratifying improvement.

Joan, my ex, was my last steady sackmate. Ah, Joan. My college senior year steady who I married the day after graduation. In school, she'd always been so affable as I tossed back beers and blew joints. But her smarts grew during our schooling, and continued to after our marriage, and I guess she might've grown a teensy bit bored with me.

Our pillow talk gradually degenerated into her monologues about my widening waist and stalled salary. And Christ, she learned how to stick in the knife, and when to twist it. Like when I was canned from Rumpus Room. I came home that afternoon barely able to utter, "I got laid off." I stood bloody but unbowed in the doorway of our modest suburban ranch waiting for my wife's defiant, "Screw them, they've lost a great manager," or brave declaration, "James, I know we'll make it somehow." Instead, I got a sarcastic, "Does this mean we're not getting the new refrigerator?"

Joan was immediately absorbed in schemes for winning the best divorce settlement. She was a paralegal and hired her boss, who stuck me with his towering tab. I got clobbered. Joan and her boss selected the good old "abandonment" argument. True, I hurt my own cause by getting drunk and AWOL for a few days, so she had a good case: the loser husband gets canned, then he gets lost for 36 hours, then he finally washes up on the front lawn, snoring and flat broke. She woke me by dropping my suitcase on my head. But you understand, don't you? I was crushed: first by Rumpus Room, second by my wife.

So, sex isn't part of my day-to-days. And when I do indulge...well, things get weird. Like last month. I met a chunky Clairol blonde—a dean of Nursing somewhere—at a conference in Toledo. She seemed a little flaky or a little high, but I didn't care because she loudly encouraged my cocktail hour advances. By eight-thirty, she was naked on my hotel room bed, save for her Just My Size knee-highs. As I smoked her skinny designer cigarettes, she warmed up with a girlish finger fuck. She made me watch because she was an aspiring performance artist who hoped to open her own regional theater. The play's the thing.

The aftermath was less giddy. She was, it turned out, a manic-depressive who bitterly complained that she'd "lowered her standards to screw a tubby guy with stubble."

"Your standards?" I studied my pear-shaped torso and hunched shoulders in the dresser's mirror. Compared to her, I was petite.

She pointed at me. "Dirty man! You make me feel dirty!"

"Then shag your big ass out of here!"

"Dirty man!"

I dragged her from my room by her thick ankles. I refused to let her back in, opening the door only to pitch her shapeless appliqué dress at her.

Sex with Joan was less humiliating: at least she didn't point at me and cry afterward. But it was still like fucking your wife, you know? A wife who sees you only as a paycheck.

After the divorce two years ago, Joan got the house and quickly sold it. And now that I have a paycheck again, the court ordered that Joan receives a portion. A big portion. I wanted to fight it—Christ, she wasted no time in dumping me, but my lawyer advised me to shut up and live with it. Joan, she always makes out—she's even latched onto some spoiled sap down in St. Louis whose dead parents left him a bank-breaking trust fund. Meanwhile, I retreated here to my duplex, with the dusty couch downstairs and tiny john upstairs. The Korean family in the neighboring unit is OK. There must be at least twelve of them in there, and they often cook greasy pork.

Now you can see why I'm eager to perform well on this Drock deal. It's a chance to thumb my nose at Joan and start getting laid a lot more. I mean, it's goddamned awkward. I'll be 38 next spring, and I shouldn't have to bring a date back to this dump, with its weary furniture and scuffed squeaking floors.

Chapter Three: Hardball

My cabby dropped me off at Ralph's. In the far end of the parking lot waited my faithful Slug. The Slug hadn't had the best of evenings, apparently: a long painful scratch, probably from a key, marred the driver's door, and the passenger door window suffered a long crack.

Some fashion-oppressed teenagers had mugged my car. The youths probably mistook my boots in the back seat for high-tech athletic shoes, then signified their disappointment with the key—or a knife blade or pistol barrel—against the door. I patted the Slug's roof, apologized for being absent in her moment of crisis, and headed toward Drock's store.

The traffic was, as usual, a sentence thanks to the junk food joints, discount strip malls, and factory-sized grocery stores that relentlessly lay claim to any remaining acreage. The smudged and squinting drivers abuse both accelerator and brake pedal. They cut you off at fifty miles an hour for the privilege of beating you to the interminable red lights. Why are they so impatient in their rusting cars, their hoarse heaps? Most don't have the cash and credit to justify such high-profile traffic stunts: the bed-ridden steel and auto industries have seen to that. More and more of the folks spend their working hours bagging groceries or building burritos or snarling behind cash registers or changing your car's vital fluids at Oil Pit. The drivers' children might end up at my college. Some gifted and resolute children will prosper. Others will quickly exhaust money and willpower. I don't condemn them. What's the point of studying when you know that a "job" around here awaits you only at Burger Stud or One Size Fits All Shoe Emporium? Otherwise, drag your undereducated ass to the north side and ride out the economy until it crashes.

As I pulled into Mega Mart, I guessed that Patrick Drock wasn't doing much better. How can he compete in such a cutthroat business?

An overeager sales woman approached me. "Yes sir! How may I help you today?"

"Patrick Drock, please."

"He's on the phone with a customer—"

"He still has some?"

"—Yes."

"Tell him, if you could, that Dr. Deyme from West Central College is here to see him."

Presently, Mr. Patrick Drock strolled toward me. He had an Irish barrel chest and a gut to match. His big hand was extended, and a lock of white hair dropped across his fleshy forehead.

"A pleasure, Dr. Deyme. Your secretary called me. How may I help you today?"

The saleswoman loitered nearby, pretending to fiddle with a printer.
"May we talk in your office?"

Sighing, Drock looked skyward, as if asking the Deity for good luck. Inside his paneled cubicle, I was handed a cup of coffee and offered the boss's chair. I took the coffee but sat on the plastic-covered couch. Boyle had urged me to be polite but direct: no hemming and hawing, no bullshit.

"Mr. Drock, West Central College is interested in upgrading its computer capabilities."

"A fine idea."

"—and your name has been mentioned by colleagues as someone to see about this matter."

"You're thinking of me as a source of—" He cocked his head, not sure of how to continue.

"Of expertise, of support, of the best deals on computer equipment." I whistled a bar of music from his radio ad, ubiquitous last year and conspicuously absent this year.

"I'm flattered by your interest, and I do want to help you."

"Of course. I understand your problem." I leaned forward, making the couch's plastic wrap crinkle. "You're thinking of running for the college board this November."

He too leaned forward, and fleetingly I pictured us as opposing linemen, reading to do battle. "I am indeed thinking just that," he whispered.

"We're flattered by your interest in West Central College. We want you to contribute. Perhaps you could best contribute by becoming our new supplier of computer equipment and service."

"I'm genuinely pleased you thought of me. But I can't run for a board seat if I contract to supply the college with computer equipment." He clasped his hands earnestly. "It's a clear conflict of interest."

"Most clear." The fish was refusing the bait. He waited for me to make the next move; I waited for him.

"Another cup of coffee?" he asked.

"No, thank you."

I stood and tossed the cup into the wastepaper basket. Now was the fateful moment: the moment to impose my will, and the sooner the better. You've seen such moments in marital melees and boxing matches. Somebody's got to suck it up and take command. The other somebody's got to give in.

"Not the best of mornings, Mr. Drock." I pointed at his show room. "Your store is empty. I'll bet your other stores are empty. You can't compete in this business climate."

His rectangular jaw hardened.

"And the not-so-good times keep rolling. Did you hear that Titanium Computer Inc. just laid off another four thousand employees? But of course you did. You know that profits in this business are razor thin." I leaned over and laughed in his flinching face. "At least you're in the high-tech rat race a bit longer. Perhaps another month."

"I have my integrity."

"Your integrity will be a big help when you go bankrupt."

"This is a pointless discussion, Dr. Deyme." He stared at me, eyes narrow and unblinking.

This guy was beyond belief. Here I was, walking into his store like the patron saint of lost causes, and he's talking about his integrity.

"Do you know why I want to be a board member?"

"Tell me."

"I will. But before I do..." He closed the leveler blinds of his cubicle window, then scooted backward in his office chair to his desk. A virgin bottle of Old Bushmill's emerged in his big mitt. "Have a drink, Dr. Deyme."

"I really shouldn't." But I did. I sipped then gulped as Patrick Drock told me, with a soaring rhetoric and a conductor's flourishes, why he wanted a board seat. His parents, he explained, were poverty-toughened Irish immigrants who arrived here in '40. The senior Mr. Drock opened a hole-in-the-wall bar in Chicago's teeming Southeast side. The family's dingy apartment was above the bar. Wife and young children suffered the indignities of being awoken at 2:00 a.m. by frequent fistfights and broken bottles. Senior Drock persisted. He gathered enough money to remodel the bar and even offered nostalgia-inducing Irish imports for fellow homesick Irishmen.

The three children were sent to boarding school, then college. The old man even hung onto the bar into the late '60's, well into the white flight. But after many smashed windows and several robberies, the old man lost the place in a fire that, it was rumored, was started for the insurance.

Mom and Pop Drock moved to Florida and made it to their eighties; Patrick's siblings were in California and New York. "Education made it all possible," Patrick intoned solemnly. "I was the very first in my family to attend college, Mr. Deyme. Education is the key, and your board needs someone who made it because of education."

Now, this was all stirring stuff. But I wasn't impressed. Hey, my parents came over here from no-so-jolly Leeds, England to dream the American Dream, too. Worked in the auto factories of Flint, Michigan. You know, when Flint actually had jobs. I too was the first in the family to attend college. Fine. Let's get on with it, already.

Drock kept orating through half the bottle. He often glanced at me to gauge the power of his performance, but I offered only yawns. Then he began revealing the real reason he wanted on the board.

"My old man was a Democrat, like most the Chicago Irish were. And are. He even contributed money and got a patronage job on the side, in the stockyards. But that patronage, that's a prison because those Democrats owned him."

I stared at my watch.

"In my fifty five years I've never taken a patronage job. I want freedom."

"You'll be free and out of business."

"Not if I get on your board." His bright blue eyes widened. "The county Republicans are finally serious about competing with the Democrats, and I want to help them. And they want to help me."

I considered him anew. Perhaps the whiskey we shared became a psychic medium. At any rate, I suddenly grasped his thoughts and motives as clearly as if I'd read his diary. This was all bullshit. He was just posturing, trying to get the best deal he could.

"You want a big piece of patronage pie, don't you? Your father had only crumbs."

"You're perceptive," he mocked.

"You want to hand out the jobs and get the kickbacks and have your flunkies kiss your ring."

He slammed the desk with his glass. "I'm going to help the Republicans get a foothold in Cook county. For Christ's sake, more and more big cities are going Republican except Chicago. Chicago's still in the stone age." He poured me another drink. "We'll win at least one of the three vacant seats, maybe two. From there on in, it's all ours. If things go well, Dr. Deyme, I could one day be your boss." He winked and ordered me to drink up.

"Mr. Drock. What's the best contract you've had in the last year?"

"The last year, we've just broken even. Mostly renewed maintenance contracts. No big purchases, hardly any upgrades."

I let him have it. "Western Central College is interested in a purchase of, oh, in the range of eighty thousand or so."

"It's not enough."

"You're drunk."

"So are you. And it's not enough."

"All that talk of integrity and immigrants and your Republican stalwarts." He slapped his big knee and laughed. The negotiating had commenced.

We haggled and sputtered and swore and drank. During one sticking point, I grabbed Drock's glass from his hand, drained the glass in a prodigious swig, and threatened to walk out. I even paused to pick my nose with pornographic candor. Yeah, it's gross but it's dramatic. It makes a statement.

"We'll take our chances," I said. "And if you lose, we'll get your name blackballed with every Democrat in the suburbs. Hope your Republican friends keep your business afloat."

"Make it two hundred thousand."

"A hundred fifty."

"A hundred eighty."

"A hundred seventy."

"Agreed."

We shook hands and toasted one another's health. Then I grabbed Drock's phone and called Boyle. Boyle groused a bit—he'd wanted to keep it at $120,000—but he approved.

"So, what do you need these computers for—"

My belch silenced him. "Sorry." I belched again. "Sorry. Anyway, I don't know what stuff we'll buy yet. See, there's this committee that's supposed to decide, but last year the committee decided against any more computer equipment for another, uh, 18 months. So this'll take a while to sell."

Drock frowned. "Perhaps I'll remain in the race."

"Stop with the threats, already," I laughed. "I'll just make out the purchase order and handle the committee later."

He handed me yet another drink. "Here's to purchase orders."

All this freewheeling negotiating had inspired me, and I came up with some sweet icing for Drock's cake. "One more thing, Mr. Drock. You'll have to join the Democratic Party."

"Balls."

"The current board isn't fond of Republican contractors."

He pretended to be perturbed, but I just mocked him and his talk of principles, patronage prison, etc., etc. He soon agreed to join the Democrats and even ordered out for a couple large pizzas from Mulligio's, the elderly owner of which had a legendary career as Chicago Democratic precinct captain and ballot box stuffer. I congratulated him for his sudden good sense.

By three o'clock, Drock was snoring in his chair, his beefy arms dangling at his sides and his shoeless feet on his desk. I wrapped the five remaining slices of pizza in toilet paper and traipsed toward my car. Halfway home I started in on the pizza—you know how it is when you're driving drunk and there's pizza in the car.

I committed only one drunk-driver indiscretion: I misjudged the approach to my driveway and broke the Slug's left headlight on the edge of the duplex. My poor mistreated Slug—it beseeches me to cease drinking. The Korean family immediately came to my aid, assisting me up the front porch stairs and opening the door for me. I couldn't understand what they were saying to me or to one another, but I dramatized my gratitude by giving the grandmother ten dollars. She stared at me, momentarily uncomprehending, then burst into grateful tears.

Inspired by me, this stumbling generous American, the entire family joined the love in. I fought to stand under the crush, staggering to the left then the right, then helplessly tipping left again as the children began piling on. I felt in the middle of a rugby pile-up. Finally I imploded. There was alarmed chatter as they pulled me into my duplex and left me on the couch, a greasy pillow under my sweaty scalp. All the booze and excitement and human contact moved me. I wept.

In fact, I was so stricken by their squawking affection that I gave the father a twenty-dollar bill. Now it was his turn to burst into tears. He fell atop me, rubbing my head and squeezing my neck. I wasn't ashamed to be weeping in the clutches of another wet eyed male, but I needed room to breathe. I bucked him off me and offered mime-like gestures that I needed sleep. He finally understood and, with a face-splitting grin, tiptoed out of my duplex backward, a hand in the air to quiet his cheering tribe.

Chapter Four: Three Thorns and One Lily

For the next few days, I was high on hubris. I talked breezily with colleagues about investments in the information superhighway and rebuilding rare autos and weekend gallivants in Vegas. When Herrig assured me that his speech to the local Democrats had gone well, I patted him on the shoulder and recommended that he keep impressing me. He grunted at my condescension, but he understood the rules of the game. He understood power.

On Thursday, Boyle beckoned me to his office and ceremoniously opened his oak humidor, stocked with Cuban cigars. As I accepted the flame of his gold-plated lighter, Boyle poured on the praise. Thanks to negotiating aplomb, Patrick Drock was no longer a threat.

Boyle's sunny mood and generosity had to be basked in fully; at any moment, he might erupt in a profane explosion. That was Boyle's managerial secret: he ridiculed and threatened you, only to turn around and offer you more candy and a bigger allowance. His mercurial, yin to yang mood swings unnerved the flunkies, but the bottom line was: it worked. Bi-polar Christ! He kept you on your toes.

My swelling ego made for a swelling libido, too. I contrived to drop in on Lydia Fairview in her office. I casually remarked that, in the light of my inevitable promotion, the college would need a new Associate Vice President. She'd probably be a candidate, yes? Her features clouded with suspicion when I suggested we get together for lunch, but she nonetheless nodded and agreed to a lunch "sometime soon." I departed with a stiffo and a smirk.

Whistling a chipper rendition of "On Green Dolphin Street", I returned to my office and offered my secretary a hale hello. I directed her to call all members of the Computer Committee for a meeting at 1:00 p.m. Friday. Counting myself, the committee was composed of four administrators and four faculty. Now, how exactly that mathematical disadvantage wormed its way into the faculty contract, I don't know, but I'd promised Boyle that I'd seal the deal with minimal fuss.

But aside from Dwayne Derrickson, a weak-kneed pushover, the faculty on this committee would be real pains in my ass. See, they were union zealots suffering from savior psychosis. They fancied themselves the guardians of higher education, stalking and slaying the slightest administrative fiat or contract fudging. I feared the militants would twist the arm of their weak sister, Dwayne Derrickson, to vote down the computer purchase.

At least I could rely on my fellow flunkies. My fellow yes men would rise to the occasion and vote "yes."

Friday morning, I was up early, fretting about the meeting. Psyching myself, I stood before the dresser mirror and modeled various power accessories: crimson power tie, fake gold power watch, black power wing tips. Adding to my anxiety, my choicest sport jacket callously reminded me that I'd put on several pounds over the summer. I threw back my shoulders and sucked in my gut. Well that's better, I thought, admiring my improved form for a minute. And a minute was all I could endure. With my gut sucked in, I couldn't actually breathe, so I grudgingly let my gut resume its sloth-like hang over my belt.

Uncertain that I'd have time for lunch, I toasted a quarter loaf of rye and slathered on the peanut butter. I also downed a pot of coffee and blitzed several ciggies while watching the morning news. Hmm. Yet another fresh-faced network news fox. Christ, look at her: a team of dentists must buff her teeth during each station break. And check out those deep-dish tits, so appetizing beneath the crisp white blouse.

I've heard that her senior colleagues don't like her because she majored in cosmetology rather than journalism. To which I sneer: So What? I mean, the whole point of chicks on TV is to look good. And she looks good. Besides, she's not reporting news. She's just reciting horror stories off the TelePrompTer.

Last night in New York, said the news fox cheerfully, a mass murderer's career ended when he got caught at a Burger Stud drive-through. The nut case opened the car door for his strawberry shake, and a victim's head rolled out of the car. Adding to the chaos, one of New York's addled Home-and-Foodless was scavenging about the dumper. When he saw the head, he grabbed it and ran several blocks before an overwrought cop shot him.

Meanwhile in Chicago, a pimp was murdered by his crack-addict sister. Sis was peeved that her ingrate brother forced her—at gunpoint, for Christ's sake—to hose ten dicks in twenty minutes. Later, as little brother enjoyed a heroin blackout, Sis shot off his face.

And in "entertainment news", washed up movie star Hawkins Breed checked into a top-dollar dry-out hospital. Frankly, I'm just a tad suspicious. He's needed good press ever since his last three movies bombed. He'll get a synthetic septum, a personal trainer, and a space-age hairpiece. Then he'll revive his career on the talk-show rounds, tearfully confessing his sins before scandalized and star-struck housewives. Still, I empathize with the Hawker. When you've got no talent, you need a scam. And knowing the world is filled with no talent jerks like Hawkins Breed, it cheers me. I mean, if he can hit the jackpot, why can't I?

Once on campus, I frittered away the morning thinking of how to run the meeting. A cardinal rule for the ambitious bureaucrat is to control meetings. Right from the start, you assert your institutional muscle. One method is to arrive late. If everyone's waiting for you, then you're important. I waited until ten after one, sucked in my gut, and headed downstairs.

What with my gut sucked in and my shoulders squared, my back was again sore by the time I arrived in the conference room. But I didn't let on. Any hint of distress could hurt my battle plan, and make no mistake, a meeting of administrators and faculty is a battle. We've each got our axes to grind, to sharpen, to wield, and we look forward to letting blood even as we fear bleeding.

I was indeed the last to arrive. My fellow administrators nodded with that telling combination of respect and resentment. The bureaucrat Busy Body Club had disseminated the gossip at computer chip speed: I had staved off Drock, the Republican juggernaut. With a casual smirk, I took my proper place at the head of the conference table.

The faculty glared at me, plainly unimpressed, and I suffered that familiar pang. Despite my best attire and practiced arrogance, the faculty unnerve me. Sure, I think they're often jerks and ingrates—but I concede that they're smarter than me. I mean, they know things. They know about Aristotle or leptons or the id/ego/superego ordeal. It's awful when I must actually talk, must discuss things with them. But at least Dwayne Derrickson the preternatural wimp was here. He could be the swing vote.

"Thanks for attending this meeting on such short notice. The President has asked us to consider the purchase of computers, for..." Christ, for what? I knew I'd forgotten something: I hadn't yet come up with a plausible explanation. "—for computing."

"For what?" Steve Luken, an English instructor, grinned with hostility. "Before we begin, may I ask why we're here? Didn't we agree last spring that the college had enough computers and software?"

"That's true, but the President has, he's asked us to reconsider."

"Why?" asked Sheryl Farella, a psychology instructor. "What's changed between now and last semester?" She adjusted her quaint wire-rimmed glasses and awaited an answer.

"Our enrollment has really gone up," offered my good buddy Bruce Herrig. "If the enrollment keeps going up, we'll need more computers to, to meet the students' needs."

To meet the students' needs. A wonderful cliché, an all-purpose cover that has justified more administrative spending binges and patronage than anyone can calculate.

Jim Pouris, the third faculty fuck, piped up. Pouris teaches math and he's always piping up. "Unless there's been a dramatic change in enrollment, and unless the dramatic increase continues for several semesters, there's no need that I can see for new computer equipment."

With his waffle-stomper boots and jeans, he looked ready to milk cows. And Pouris really owns cows. He's a nutrition nut, one of those natural food neurotics.

George McCarthy, a long-time low-level do-nothing, did his best to defend the idea. His best is about anybody else's worst: he's a year or two from retirement and always seems in danger of slipping into a coma. He sniffed about the need to look forward to tomorrow's needs and maintain our cutting edge, but McCarthy is way too burnt out to spout those clichés with conviction. Even my fellow hacks yawned.

Dwayne Derrickson had been swallowing nervously, really working that Adam's apple. He's the type who bites his nails bloody and suffers crippling anxiety cramps in the midst of confrontations. Therefore, he's your ideal faculty member, a sheep in sheep's clothing. He's most fulfilled when he's submitting to the powers that be, so I played my hand.

"Dwayne," I asked, "isn't the business department having a hard time providing computer time for all its students?"

"Sometimes."

"Wouldn't new computers help?" I persisted.

"It might."

"Wouldn't the students have more access more often?"

"Maybe."

—Dammit! If I could get this guy alone for a minute, I could really—

"Where might we get these computers?" Steve Luken asked. Then he winked at Jim Pouris. "From Patrick Drock?"

My face was instantly hot, and I heard myself sputtering about preliminary price checks and bid invitations. But all along I just wanted to punch that jerk.

Now Sheryl Farella was jawing at me. For a moment I watched her lips form words, but I didn't hear her. My hate for Luken deafened me. If I ever see him in a bar, and I'm stoked with a few whiskey and waters— well, maybe not. He's pretty stout, actually, and his messy long hair betrays a hostile personality, a guy aching to split open my face with head butts and beer bottles.

"—not comfortable *suggesting* it," Sheryl was saying. "But we've all heard the rumors."

"What?" I reached for the pitcher of ice water in the table's center and shakily poured myself a glass. "I'm sorry. You were saying...?"

"It's hardly news," Sheryl continued, "that Drock was going to run for the college board. Now he's going to contract with us for computers?"

"You're becoming quite the wheeler dealer," Luken smiled.

Careful! I warned myself. Already the meeting had gone south, but I couldn't lose my cool. "It's a question if we really don't need them. The computers." I fired a power-glance at Herrig. He responded instantly, as a flunky should.

"My office has done a survey recently," Herrig began. "This survey, it revealed that community interest is interested in computers. Further, it said, the survey revealed that some evening students don't feel they have sufficient time to work on the computers."

"You can get a survey to say anything," Pouris remarked.

"Are you accusing Mr. Herrig of writing a self-serving document?" asked Pete Jones. Jones, the Dean of Institutional Wide Impact, had been barely attentive, his double chin cradled in his fat hand. But Jones despised Pouris, and he was happy to argue.

"I might be."

"That's really uncalled for," Jones continued. "You haven't seen the document, you know nothing of it—"

"Nobody's seen the document," Luken observed. "Are you sure it exists, John?"

"Of course it does," I barked, though of course Bruce was making up the whole damn thing.

"The point is," Pouris snapped, "that if the survey isn't carefully done, if its questions are leading, the results aren't reliable."

Jones and Pouris fenced for a few minutes. Jones did well, adopting the crucial administrative blend of arrogance and condescension. My hopes soared. Then Jones stupidly let Pouris force the discussion toward statistics and reliability and verifiability and whatever, and Jones was reduced to petulance and whining.

"The reliability of a study is often an untested assumption built into the survey itself," Pouris was saying. Or I should say, lecturing. He leaned forward professorially. His stern stare and bewildering phrases soon had Jones reeling on the robes, looking for a way out of this mismatch. "And the assumption of its reliability, if incorrect, can skew both the questions and the interpretation of the questions. For instance..."

As Pouris professed, I glanced about the room. Sheryl Farella was listening carefully, pretending to understand Pouris. I don't know, maybe she did understand. Steve Luken, that smart ass, fixed his attention on Jones. Each time Jones harrumphed, or admitted ignorance, Luken smiled. I really wanted to hit him, let me tell you.

And I wanted to hit my fellow administrators too. McCarthy and Herrig had tossed in the white towel at the first sign of trouble. They didn't care about this computer purchase. They wanted only the meeting to end, so they could retreat to their offices for coffee and gossip. That's their fatal flaw, I thought contemptuously. They had no ambition, no drive. Unlike me, they were content with their little offices, their lazy secretaries, their long lunches and yearly bonuses. But what really angered me was their impotence in the midst of Pouris's assault of a fellow flunky. They didn't try to help him.

Yeah, OK. I didn't try to help him either, but it wasn't for a lack of effort. I just didn't understand a goddamned thing Pouris said. Pouris finally shut up, and I took action.

"Let's try to get back to the issue at hand," I insisted.

"This is the issue!" Pouris insisted.

"Then what is the issue, Dr. Deyme?" Luken grinned.

"The issue...?"

Then Sheryl Farella made a motion to table the issue for further study, and I couldn't navigate in my fog of fatigue and umbrage. Everybody but me voted for the motion.

Abruptly, the faculty rose in unison and left, leaving we administrators to blame one another. "If you'd just challenged his math a little." Herrig was starting in on Jones. "I came up with the survey idea and the rest of you just let it sink."

Jones wasn't impressed: "I'm the one that got beat up here." He snorted. "Thanks for your help. All of you." He lighted a cigarette and sucked violently. It was instantly reduced to ash, so he lighted another.

"Gimme one," I ordered. Jones sourly complied. Soon we were all smoking and complaining and commiserating and wondering what to do next.

When Jones's cigarettes were gone, everyone took their leave. I trudged toward my office, growing nervous. The meeting had flopped, and Boyle wouldn't be happy.

On a hunch, I called Derrickson. His line was busy and I slammed down the receiver so savagely that the handset cracked. Then my phone rang, and I'll be damned it was Derrickson. He surprised me by coming right out with his price for a "yes" vote. He would vote "yes," he asserted, if he could be guaranteed the business department chairmanship next fall. I told him I could probably—

"Probably' won't get you the vote," Derrickson said hotly. "You're the Associate Vice President, and you make the recommendations for department chair. Do you know how many times I've submitted my name?"

I did not.

"None! You barely knew I existed. Now you know I exist, and now you know what I want—Mr. Wheeler Dealer."

The twit! I imagined his eyes blinking excitedly behind filmy spectacles. This lily, he really drove a bargain. What the hell. Give Dwayne some power and he'll become an ally to me and another weak link in that goddamned faculty union.

That's the thing about it, about power. When you don't have it, you want it. When you get a taste, you really want it. Derrickson, I knew, would be a most cooperative stooge, and all for a two-dollar tin nameplate that proclaims him the business department chair.

Chapter Five: Making Friends

The five o'clock news was more grim and more stupid than usual. Aside from the usual arson antics, cannibal orgies and UFO abductions, there was more slaughter in Detroit: the Big Three automakers announced still another round of downsizing. Downsizing: an exemplary double-talk word. Kinder & gentler, I guess, than "layoff" or "bloodletting." Anyway, another 10,000 of the U.A.W.'s finest will soon languish in the unemployment lines. I didn't think there were 10,000 autoworkers left in the country; I figured they were all in Japan and Korea and Mexico. Much worse—a traitorous act, really—was the kiss off of another 5,000 white-collar workers. Christ! My private sector managerial brothers are in the toilet with the stinking union riffraff.

"Payroll adjustments are temporarily painful," a rumpled economist expounded, "but overall the economy continues to show strength. Jobs continue to emerge in the service sector. There's continued volatility in the tech stocks, but retail and service growth is..."

All these economic war stories, they usually depress me. As a flunky, it's a blunt fact that I'm expendable. You're expendable, too. Yes you are: just like those former auto industry employees, you could soon be marking your time with soap operas and generic cigarettes. You could be another victim of our bi-polar economy, and your pleas and whelps wouldn't be noticed.

But I wasn't depressed today. It was a good day after all. True, the meeting with the faculty fucks was a bust, but my deal with Derrickson was a rousing comeback.

Exhilarated, I'd stopped by Lydia's office and suggested an early dinner. She accepted. Over at Ralph's, we enjoyed veal and a few carafes of blush. Lydia's usually distant demeanor—the guarded smile and averted eyes—warmed to my charismatic presence. I kept ordering more wine and reminding her that I might soon be a full Vice President. By the third carafe, I was admiring Lydia's plush bod through the luster of wine and testosterone. Lydia's got no slump or slack on her frame. She's firm, built for comfort.

"Too many administrators," Lydia was saying, "don't understand that their own career depends on being a team player."

My mouth full of wine, I nodded.

"You've understood that, James. You've seen that with no team-building, you can't get ahead. None of us can."

"Yeah." Yeah, Lydia's really stacked.

"And when one person prospers, the whole team prospers. That's what Boyle understands."

I wondered: was she a screamer?

And I'll be happy to be part of your political committee. Where do you want me to give a speech?"

"Wherever. How about another carafe?"

"I really shouldn't," she teased.

"Yes you should."

We drank happily and then—yeah, you've guessed it, haven't you?—then I spooled Lydia.

It's really wonderful, isn't it? The food/wine/spool ritual? Lydia's fond of it, too. We came back to her two-level condo and had a couple shots of brandy. After the second shot, my head bubbled and hummed, and I chased Lydia's powerful hams up the stairs. These career babes, they're so forward. She had my clothes off before she removed even her wristwatch. We fell onto her bed, which was adorned in riotously colored quilts and over-sized pillows. Lydia, breath sweet with brandy, pushed me onto my back and told me to relax.

What a life, eh?

An expert driver, Lydia treated me to a terrific stick shift routine: first gear was slow but powerful, all torque and growl. Second and third picked up the speed, really got my engine revving. Then she popped my clutch and we were in fourth, then fifth. We were in overdrive. Blood pounded in my ears and my gasket threatened to blow.

Then at the crucial moment: "Could you get on your knees?"

"—Uh?"

"Come on my face, James."

"Ung...!"

"Hurry."

"Don't you just love coming on someone's face?"

"Well, not just anybody's"

"I read somewhere—in a book by Andy Warhol, I think—that it's good for your pores. Semen really tightens up your pores."

Andi Warral...wasn't she one of the Brady Bunch sisters? Christ, now she's doing porno. Man, my neck hurts.

"You've got a sore neck?"

Now I remember. Andi Warral is that syndicated TV junk journalist who reports live from prison electrocutions and S & M resorts for rich pervs.

"I'll give you something better than aspirin." With a heave, she rolled me onto my gut and dug her fore knuckles into my tender neck. After a few crude and ineffective digs, she paused and laughed huskily.

"What?"

"You've got a cottage cheese butt."

"Cottage butt what?"

"A cottage cheese butt. Lots of curdle-shaped fat."

I could hardly disagree, but her candor was just too candid. I mean, here I was, bluntly and unglamorously naked. And without the benefit of diffuse lighting, smoke and mirrors, booze, or a stiffo, there was nothing to distract Lydia from my thick face, burly gut—and my cheesy rear.

"I used to have cottage cheese, but not anymore." She rolled me back over and made me study her fat free rear. "Just look. See any cottage cheese?"

"No."

"It's all exercise," she boasted. "Speaking of exercise..." She winked most adorably.

I woke to find her scribbling in a notebook. She abruptly capped the pen and pushed the notebook under the bed. "Finally you're awake."

The bedside clock read 8:30 p.m. "Sorry to be such poor company."

"Not at all." She snuggled beside me.

"What were you writing?" Was my performance being duly recorded, analyzed, and cross-referenced?

"Ideas for my speech to the Suburban Business Consortium."

Wow...what a rousing work ethic!

We talked hardball politics until well past midnight, periodically pausing for colas and popcorn and cigarettes. As flunkies, we knew that a hostile political wind could suddenly blow us out of the college and into the unemployment office. But the board elections, we agreed, should be all right because that troublemaker Patrick Drock had been bought off.

As our discussion become more intimate, I recounted for Lydia, with expertly dramatized details, my victory over both Patrick Drock and Dwayne Derrickson. Don Boyle's management style, I revealed, had taught me that very few folks will turn down a payoff. Nay, most are eager to abandon their "principles" for some cash.

"You really are a take charge kind of guy." Lydia winked.

"I'm learning."

"And I always thought you were just a blowhard."

"I've barely opened my tool chest," I harrumphed.

Inspired by all this career talk, we spontaneously agreed to form a private, two-member consortium: our purpose was to advance our own careers, and of course to offer one another a helping hand whenever possible.

"We're buddies," Lydia smiled, kissing my face.

"Buddies."

I slipped out of Lydia's around 7:00 a.m., mumbling that I had a terribly busy weekend ahead of me filled with long postponed chores.

Back at the duplex, I wondered if I should go to bed. I actually had no long postponed chores. Dismiss me as a spoilsport, but I loathe standing in a strange shower stall and drinking unfamiliar brands of coffee. And I especially dislike eating the runny eggs and margarine-soaked toast of the Morning After.

In general, other people's kitchens unnerve me. I'm a slob in all household habits except kitchen cleanliness. I couldn't care less if your cat pees nightly on your living room carpet, or if a moldy slice of pizza festers under your couch. The cigarette burns on the recliner? So what! The heap of spoiled underwear in the corner? You'll get to it. Just don't let me see your dirty kitchen.

My kitchen is the cleanest anywhere. I'm not kidding. The tile floor is waxed monthly. Yeah, and the self-cleaning oven self-cleans weekly under my stern eye. My refrigerator's cheery interior is as spotlessly white as the day I bought it. The breezy blue valance over the kitchen window is replaced every few months—nothing is worse than a drab kitchen window!

Since my wife left me, I guess I pour all my domestic instincts into maintaining a germ-free kitchen. The rest of my living quarters—which resembles a frat house, really—can go to hell.

I don't remember falling asleep on the couch. I do remember waking, though: the family next-door, the imports from Korea, were squabbling. Again.

Kim, their oldest daughter, is causing problems because she's becoming an American teenager. Like many other young American females, she might at any moment announce that she's three months pregnant and in love with the greasy-haired, greasy-clothed, unemployed and unemployable father of her fetus.

A few nights ago, I was sitting on the porch enjoying a cigarette and the mild September air. Kim came stumbling up the sidewalk with another girl and a couple boys. They'd been busy drinking and were now busy groping. Kim saw me and dropped her beer bottle out of fright.

Consternation. Then, after an anxious moment of peering and whispering, the teens deduced that I was not Father Kwang. Kim bid her friends good evening and skipped past me into her humble home.

As soon as she shut the door, round one commenced. Soon Kim's shrill complaints rose above all other voices. The door opened and Kim nearly ran over me as she escaped the familial wrath. Mr. Kwang began to give chase, but stopped when he saw me sitting on the steps.

It was tense for a moment: his breathing was sharp, as if performed through clenched teeth. Not moving, I offered only my big rounded back and shoulders as he stood over me, struggling to control his temper. Finally, he diffidently cleared his throat.

"Mr. Deyme. May I bother you for cigarette?"

I was a little irritated—I had only ten left—but he needed some neighborly support. We sat and smoked, savoring the warm sweet breeze and the big orange moon behind the elms. Eventually, he asked me if I had children.

"No. Not yet anyway."

"Children are, they are blessing." He lowered his head and chuckled. "Except seventeen year old girl like Kim."

I knew he was, in his uncertain way, asking for advice. But I'm the wrong person to ask for life-advice, for strategy smarts. I could only offer vacuous reassurance that American teens are often a pain in the ass. Well, I didn't say "ass." I just said "pain."

He smiled sadly, his face lined and older in the moonlight. He asked for another cigarette.

The weight of this fatherly grief was alien and unsettling. I'm responsible only for myself, and that's all the responsibility I can bear. The problems in my life are purely, narrowly mine. And yet a father's problems...they're his and so much more.

"I brought my family here for opportunities," Mr. Kwang noted. "But my daughter has wrong kind of opportunities."

"Yeah. American opportunities."

He laughed as if I possessed actual wit. My wit isn't often appreciated, so I instantly took a liking to Mr. Kwang. We talked a bit more, and his daughter came tiptoeing up the sidewalk. Mr. Kwang sighed and simply waved her to come into the house. She silently obeyed. Mr. Kwang patted my knee, thanked me for the kind company, and retired.

The truce was evidently short-lived. Kim's squeal of anger now rose like a siren. I heard commotion and banging, as if a wrestling match had broken out. Then a ringing crash, like broken glass. I got off the couch and peeked out the front door window. Kim sprinted out of the duplex and in a heartbeat was up the street and out of sight. I re-retired to the couch. In a minute or an hour later, banging again startled me. But the banging was coming from my back door.

It was Kim, tears brimming over her large onyx eyes.

Kim coyly blew her nose a few times, then sat politely at the kitchen table. I served coffee in my spotless white china cups, with some very nice coffee cake on the side. Kim thanked me and for the tenth time asked that I forgive her sudden intrusion.

"It's not a bother," I lied. I don't like unannounced visitors: the kitchen might not be clean enough.

"I, I know that you don't know me. But father says you're very kind and intelligent."

A bit embarrassed, I pretended to be busy buttering my coffee cake.

"I just don't understand why father has to be so strict." Her little fists hardened. "I am sheltered, but he thinks I do too much. Sometimes I, I'm so mad that I want to punch him."

"He's just worried about you. You know, hanging around with kids. With boys. Boys with beer and cars. He just wants you to—" Well, father Kwang didn't want daughter Kwang to come home with a smoker's hack, beer breath, and her skirt on backward.

"He wants me to be..." She glanced upward, searching for the word. "To be chaste."

Chaste. Only an import could use such a word without sarcasm or irony.

"So what's wrong with chaste?"

"Nothing." For the first time, she smiled. "But father thinks that having a beer and walk with boys is not being chaste."

She had a point. These days, a mere beer and grope are what parents pray for. Hey, you know the sad facts. Today's hip teens bide their time with six packs, waiting for their chicklet or toy-boy to arrive with more booze and a fresh pack of condoms. Of course, they don't bother with the condoms. After a few beers, high school sophomores are as brazen as the rest of us.

With surprising ease, Kim and I talked for about an hour. She readily admitted that she loved and respected her father. She just wished he would trust her. I marveled that, as pissed as she was at Dad Kwang, she still spoke highly of him. Finally, she looked at me steadily and asked if I would like to visit the Kwang household for dinner.

"That's awfully nice of you. But I can't impose."

"No, please! It will help father. He needs to be around more Americans, to see that Americans and America is not so dangerous for teenagers as he thinks."

"Okay. But I don't think that my visit will convince him to let you stay out with your boyfriends."

"Thank you so much." She rose and shook my hand. "Come over tonight at seven o'clock. Father is making beef and noodles. You'll love it."

Chapter Six: Like a Good Neighbor

I filled the remaining morning and afternoon with cigarettes, a baseball game and a few beers. The dull baseball game and delicious beer encouraged my thoughts to wander back to last night's fun with Lydia. Everything had been fine until her throaty request for an impromptu facial: it made me feel uneasy, even a bit queer, I guess. I mean, I'm teetering on my knees and she's fumbling to keep her hair from getting—

The phone rang. Rising from the couch, I kicked over a fresh bottle of beer. I answered the phone cursing under my breath.

"That's no way to greet the President of your college."

"President Boyle. What a, a pleasure."

"Certainly. Listen, James. I've heard that there was a little problem with your computer committee."

I imagined my skull being centered in his psychic cross hairs. In a moment, my career would be splattered all over my living room. "Just the smallest amount of trouble, really. I've already—"

"I know what you did." Jesus, he was talking so quietly. It was unnerving. "You practiced a little quid pro quo."

Prid cue what?

"Most of my administrators would hesitate before coming to such terms with a faculty member. Nice move, making Derrickson the department chair. James, I like it when my people take charge."

Yes!

"After Drock dropped from the Trustee election, so did his partners. The election is all but over."

"I'm glad it's gone so well."

"It has. Cancel your speeches and fold the tents of the political action caucus now." Boyle took a deep breath, then announced, "You are now one of my starters, James. You're on the first string. I need you to work harder than ever for the college's continuing success."

"—Whoa!"

"The college faces a few challenges that need immediate attention. I think you can help. See me Monday morning before the Cabinet meeting."

Me! The first string: Boyle's hand-picked pack of fearless flunkies. Flunkies who possess Boyle's favor before all others. The first string fills Boyle's need for hatchet men and human flack jackets. Currently, Boyle's first string consists of two high-level administrators: Dr. Douglas and Dr. Olsen. Up until last year, a certain Dr. Martinez had been a first-stringer, but he'd been booted out after loudly and drunkenly declaring at a college function that Boyle had snubbed several Latino building contractors and "gone along with same old crew of Irish." Right there, before several chagrined trustees and startled bureaucrats, Boyle challenged Martinez. Boyle pointedly asked if he, Martinez, wasn't one of the most highly paid bureaucrats on campus. And did he not receive two merit bonuses last year? Martinez, instantly apologetic and instantly sober, anxiously agreed. Seething, Boyle loudly declared Martinez an ingrate and a race-hustler hypocrite. The next day, the Board of Trustees acceded to Boyle's demands to dump Martinez, sans golden parachute.

Martinez threatened a suit, but one of the Board's fire-eating attorneys—a Latino, of course—promised to bury Martinez. Martinez slunk off, never to be heard from again.

The first string, it's a very mysterious institution. The other administrators petulantly note that first-stringers are excused from Boyle's sadomasochistic Monday morning Cabinet meetings. Instead, the first stringers huddle with Boyle at various times during the week, whenever a crisis breaks: a sticky faculty grievance, a hostile story in the press. Douglas and Olsen walk with a superior stride, their electronic pagers ever alert on their hip.

Intriguingly, one of the first stringers—Dr. Michelle Olsen, Executive Vice President of Academic Programs—is a chick. You know, female. Good looking too, with a fulsome figure and rock 'em sock 'em rear. She's one of those early fortyish women who never appreciably age, blessed with some mysterious reserve of skin-preserving moisture and bust-preserving tone. Predictably, she's not well liked. The women don't like her because she's good looking and at the top. The men don't like her because she's at the top. She also talks too much and often laughs raucously at other's suggestions. Some flunkies peevishly suggest that she's got something on Boyle: proof of marital indiscretion, or maybe evidence of a narcotics hobby.

Dr. Fred Douglas is not quite the lightning rod of flunky loathing because he's not a woman and he's not loud. Dr. Douglas, the Executive Vice President of Community and Business Relations, is virtually invisible: short, dull dresser, no fuse-breaker. You notice him only because he's totally bald, save for a few greasy blonde hairs atop his pate, and he wears bifocals the size of your car's windshield. He's rumored to be Boyle's idea man, the brain behind the mouth. Could be. He spends hours each day locked in his windowless office, allegedly reading conspiratorial-minded books about the JFK assassination. Herrig swears that Douglas often wears disguises and moves from apartment to apartment every six months.

So, we have loud Dr. Olsen and mysterious Dr. Douglas. And me. Big John. I completed the administrative triumvirate. I could already hear the fevered gossip and bitter speculation about our relationships, our salaries, our expense accounts. Why Deyme?, they'd complain. Because I'd proven myself, dammit. I'd taken a risk with Drock and won. The other flunkies, terminally timid, never would've tried. Hey, I'm not smart. But I'm not shy, either. And Boyle would now reward me. There'd be abuse and humiliation along the way. But that's okay. Boyle always loves the ones he hurts.

To celebrate, I popped a bottle of champagne that I'd meant to present to my evening's hosts, the Kwangs. What the hell. I'd just run out and snatch up another bottle. The champagne soon imbued the afternoon with gaiety and effervescence. The sunshine through the window was golden, festive. The baseball game grew hilarious—when a Detroit Tiger struck out with a slapstick swing, I laughed so hard that I spilled the champagne on my lap. The fizzing, it tickled. Stupid with whimsy, I cried out to myself for another bottle, then drove to the Liquor Factory and picked up three more bubblies. Back at my duplex, I wandered about my messy bedroom searching for suitable duds. The Kwangs...they're nice people. I really should bring them two bottles of champagne. But I couldn't—I'd finished off all but one.

Christ! Time to go. I clutched my remaining bottle and was halfway down the stairs when I noted that I had no pants on. Maybe they wouldn't mind—you know, I'm just the casual neighbor who shows up in his underwear with a bottle of fine spirits. No. Better not. I forced myself into some jeans. Man, Lydia's right. My ass is cottage cheese.

Anyway. Here I go: John Deyme, rising star.

Boy, that sure went well, didn't it? I can see why Father Kwang would want to invite me, the model American, to dinner. I was such a friendly and frolicsome guest. No, I didn't get into a fight, or insult the grandmother, or vomit the noodles and beef. But I, I—I fell a lot.

The floor plan didn't help. The Kwangs' duplex quarters are just like mine—sort of. See, my apartment occupies the left half of the duplex, while theirs is on the right. Everything is reversed: it's like passing through the looking glass. My kitchen is in the back—you take a left. Their kitchen is in the back—but you take a right. And so it is with everything.

After the bubbly, the sudden and complete reversal was a challenge. Almost immediately, I crunched my big toe against the leg of a chair. Oh yeah, did I forget to tell you? I arrived shoeless—see, I'd removed my shoes when I put my jeans on, then forgot about the shoes. I wore only black socks. No holes, though. After I crunched my big toe, I whooped and careened about on one leg. Or rather, I tried. My balance was as drunk as the rest of me. I fell against a table and a very nice table lamp crashed. All of this in the first ten seconds of my arrival.

Somehow, I managed to hang on to the bottle of champagne. My determination to save the bottle impressed the Kwangs. They all assured me that no harm was done. Sporting a two-toned red face (one tone for pain, the other for embarrassment) I insisted upon paying for the lamp. The clan shook their heads and waved away my offers, then Mrs. Kwang—charming in her powder blue dress and tiny gold broach— gently led me by the arm to the dinner table. I was famished. Drinking on an empty stomach, it's not filling. I heaped my plate high and wide and ate noisily, my chewing often interrupted by soggy, primordial burps. Slowly, my head cleared. I became aware of more than my rumbling stomach and swimming popping head.

"Jae, please don't interrupt," Mr. Kwang was saying. A little girl, maybe seven or eight, nodded. "You were saying, John?" Mr. Kwang asked.

"Was I?"

"About your parents?"

Yeah, I have parents. Oh yeah. "They're from England. Leeds."

"You don't have an accent at all," Kim remarked.

"No. I got the American accent at school."

Mr. Kwang exchanged a nod with his wife. Mr. Kwang suggested that my parents must have been very wise because American assimilation brings American success.

"Your parents," Mr. Kwang continued, "came here for opportunity, just like we did." He seemed pleased, as if the decision of my parents fifty years ago validated his own immigration.

Mrs. Kwang refilled my coffee cup. Hey, when did I switch from alcohol to caffeine?

"All their hard work paid off," Mr. Kwang beamed. "And that's why I brought my family here." He turned to Mrs. Kwang. "I can't believe it has been..."

"Ten years," she smiled.

"And we have some good news to celebrate, John. I have purchased a restaurant in town. We will be open for business in two months!" His broad face was made even more broad by his smile. Mrs. Kwang bolted from the table and returned noisily with a bottle of champagne in both hands. Here we go again.

"You were so kind to bring a gift," Mrs. Kwang told me. "It's a family tradition here to let the guest open the bottle and have the first drink."

I accepted the bottle and corkscrew. With a cheery *ka-pop!* the cork ricocheted off the ceiling and into the living room. Everyone applauded and I filled the glasses of Mr. and Mrs. Kwang, then mine. Kim asked if she could sample the stuff, and Mr. Kwang sternly shook his head.

Mr. Kwang cleared his throat. "John, you have been so kind to us."

I smiled, but was a bit confused. I'd distinguished myself by arriving drunk and breaking their lamp.

"Do you remember driving your car into the porch?" he continued.

I nodded. The landlord, did I tell you? He charged me three hundred dollars for repairs.

"We helped you in, and you gave my mother ten dollars."

I dimly remembered giving money to somebody.

"Then you gave me twenty dollars."

Christ, what next? Did I give Mrs. Kwang a fifty and Jae a hundred?

"I was so ashamed yet so grateful. I had no money that week at all. All my money was tied up in the restaurant. My daughter Kim wanted pretty blouse, and I couldn't—" He glanced toward his daughter. "And I needed that money. I thought you were sent by God!

"From God!" Mrs. Kwang asserted.

"And so I had this money," Mr. Kwang continued fervently, "that you gave us out of your generosity. I had been so depressed that, that week. I got Kim a new blouse and my wife some detergent."

Detergent? This was depressing.

"And you got Jae that little doll," Kim reminded.

These imports sure know how to stretch a dollar. I was so moved by this family pathos that I wanted to give him another twenty.

"The next morning, bank called and said loan is approved," Mr. Kwang recalled, almost shouting with excitement. "We were so joyful. I am on phone hearing that I have money. Kim was just coming down stairs in her new blouse and Jae playing with her doll."

"And I was finally doing the wash," Mrs. Kwang laughed.

"I said, this is so wonderful. And it all start with our neighbor. I don't believe in magic or other nonsense. But your generosity, it was like a, a—"

"A symbol," Kim suggested.

"It was like a turning point," Mrs. Kwang added.

"John, you will never pay for food at my restaurant," Mr. Kwang declared, voice growing thick. "You are always guest. Always your meals will be our pleasure."

At that moment—I don't know. I guess it's just the sentimental slob in me. The booze probably contributed, too. But here were these imports so grateful for a lousy thirty bucks. They reminded me of my parents, the awe-struck tones in which they reminisced about coming to America with me, a five year old, in tow. About earning a legitimate living, free of that crass class system. We ended up in a rusted trailer in Flint. Yeah, in a trailer park. In Flint. Lots of yahoos with yellowed teeth and blackened mouths lived there, in the days before trailer parks became miniature ersatz subdivisions with sidewalks and street lamps. In those days, it was one step up from a tent city. Sounding "snooty", Mum recalled, didn't go down well with the nasal-twang banjo-busters who filled their front yards with treadless tires and blasted pickup trucks.

Anyway, all this grateful talk of finding one's fortune in America really got to me and...Yeah, you guessed it. I started blubbering. The Kwangs' eyes got a little moist, too. We finished off the champagne and Mrs. Kwang hurriedly opened another. Then another.

With my immigrant family's heart on my sleeve, I shared the news of my escalating fortunes at West Central. "You see?" Mr. Kwang shouted. "Opportunity. Opportunity!"

Everybody warmly congratulated me, and I was really moved. It struck me that the Kwangs were the first real friends I'd made in— Christ, in too long. We chattered for hours. Eventually everyone but Mr. Kwang retired. Soon Mr. Kwang broke out some wine—pleasantly stout red—and we clicked glasses. Mr. Kwang holds his liquor pretty well, though the booze didn't leave him unscathed: he kept putting the lighted end of a cigarette in his mouth. Never complained once. These Asians, I guess, really are inscrutable. Or maybe like me, they're just impervious to cigarette burns and barked shins after a night of booze. By now, Mr. Kwang was talking in Korean. Weirdly, I understood. No, not the words, really. Rather, I deeply understood the emotions and the impassioned rising voice and charged hand gestures that proclaimed, *We're going to make it!*

Mr. Kwang stood to make an especially crucial point, arms waving and eyes blinking. I excused myself to visit the can. My visit took longer than expected. As I've explained, the Kwang floor plan was the exact opposite of mine. At the top of the stairs, I took my habitual right turn and collided with a wall. The collision, in conspiracy with the red wine, tricked me into peeing on my feet and snagging my prong in my zipper. The drink, thankfully, was an excellent anesthetic. I didn't want to risk another prong-pinch, so I descended the stairs unzipped, my shirt tail serving as loin cloth. Mr. Kwang never noticed. He was still standing, yakking at the ferns beside his chair.

Alcohol does more than cross-wire your limbs and tongue-tie your brain. It does something to time. Time stammers and spills its drink, stains its new shirt. Time loses track of time. My watch whimsically informed me that the time was a preposterous 3:30 a.m. Kwang was really rattling, insisting on pouring yet more drink. I kidded him by talking some pig-Korean, you know, some fast and nasal "kwing soh how!" Crippled with laughter, he dropped the bottle. His merriment infected me, and I was soon laughing and choking on phlegm or a fur ball. Finally, after plenty of chortling and gagging and snorting, I told him that I would clean up the glass of his broken bottle. Once again, the floor plan fooled me. While searching for a broom, I broad sided the kitchen cabinet. As I was falling, I silently thanked Kwang for serving so much drink. Hitting the floor, I figured, wouldn't hurt too badly.

My bladder woke me. I crawled out the front door and peed off the porch, growing gradually aware of the crystal-like dew glistening on the dappled morning lawn. A pair of love-birds—cozy robins, actually—cheerfully pecked at my lawn for the morning meal. A crew of kids, eyes bright and smiles wide, glided by on their fluorescent blue and green bicycles, and I closed the barn door just in time.

What a beautiful morning! The air was fresh, the sky cloudless, and the morning sun rendered the streets as enchanted as Dorothy's yellow brick road. The cheerful a.m. filled me with hope: for a moment, I believed I might escape the misery of a roiling hangover. I took a cautious deep breath. So far, so good. I exhaled and took another breath, more deeply and confidently. Hell, I'd be fine.

Then I gagged: my lungs, fouled by last night's three hundred cigarettes, rebelled at the prospect of actual oxygen.

Then I threw up.

Fortunately, I scrambled onto my side of the duplex's porch and performed the sorrowful heave ho onto my arthritic shrubs. After several dreadful propulsions, I wiped my trembling lips with my trembling hand and crawled into my dingy quarters. My body was so angry that, for a good hour, it would not let me sleep. Instead, it assaulted me with a bellicose headache and boiling bellyache. Man, I overdid the celebrating.

All this success could be my downfall. Finally, after a smoke to calm my lungs and a few swigs of stale cola for mouthwash, I slept.

Chapter Seven: Rat Fucking

Don Boyle pointed out his office's newest ambiance upgrade: a two hundred gallon aquarium. A school of neon fish jetted exuberantly through lush seaweed and the labyrinth-like nooks and crannies of a miniature sunken ship. Little green and blue track lights rendered the tank festive, like a theatre stage.

"It was a three day job installing this baby," Boyle explained. "The physical plant boys had to tear out several studs to cut the hole in the wall." Boyle settled into his ergonomic titanium-and-leather office chair. A mug of freshly-ground cappuccino steamed on his oak cherry desk. I was about to sit on the straight back chair in front of his desk, but he shook his head.

"Please, sit on the couch."

The couch, upholstered and hand stitched in the finest leather, comfortably supported even my big ass. Boyle explained that the couch was "a little thank you" from the contractor hired to revamp the college's courtyard.

The Prez handed me my own mug of java. "Nothing better than a little thunder in the morning."

"Nothing better."

"John, welcome to the first string. I know that you'll perform well, and I know the college's board will reward you well." He winked with an easy humor I'd not before witnessed. "The board has complete confidence in my administrative ability and my institutional vision. If I tell 'em that a certain member of the team merits a bonus, I have their total support." He cleared his throat meaningfully. "Now. Let me lay out the game plan. The first string serves as my collective right hand. When a problem comes up, they drop everything." Already a bit caffeine manic, Boyle sharply slapped his desk to emphasize everything.

The caffeine was getting under my skin too, and I reminded myself not to grind my teeth. I accepted another cup. This stuff, it was pretty good.

On occasion, I may need you after normal hours. Sometimes the first string meets at seven or eight in the evening. Maybe later. Do you understand?"

"Yes."

"For example. Last month. I needed the first string to meet at nine in the p.m. Dr. Olsen was giving her two young children a bath, and the husband was upstairs in bed with the flu. Or the cramps. She didn't want to leave the children alone, of course, but she's on the first string and that's the way it is. She kissed the kids goodnight and was out the door in five minutes. Of course, she drained the bath water so the little pistols wouldn't drown."

"Huh."

"The husband understood completely."

"I don't have children, so—"

He raised a palm, and I fell silent.

"But if you don't have kids"—the silencing palm fell—"then you have other things. Paperwork. A late night dinner. A one night stand. Indigestion. Bunions or bloody hemorrhoids or, uh, perhaps a dead parent." He shrugged. "I'm just making a point here John. The first string comes first." He glimpsed at his watch. "Enough of the small talk, don't you think? Let's join the others."

Dr. Douglas and Dr. Olsen were sitting in the conference room adjacent to Boyle's office. They were surrealistically polite to Boyle, with lots of hale wishes for a good morning and heart-felt hopes that his weekend was wonderful. Douglas even remarked to Boyle, "Hey, you're looking wonderful today." This struck me as strange, but it was apparently common courtesy, for Douglas additionally complimented Boyle's chic sport jacket—"All natural fibers, right?"—and Olsen stacked superlatives on Boyle's haircut.

Boyle nodded curtly then took his place at the head of the conference table. He had a new chair, apparently custom-made. It stood at least a foot taller than your standard office fare and featured a headrest, armrest, and mug holders on either arm. With his dark blue jacket and crisp white shirt, Boyle looked like a jet pilot.

"I think you'd be best served by merely observing today," Boyle told me. "If anyone has a question for you, they'll ask."

None of the others looked at me. Fine, I thought. It's better this way—I can ease into my new duties gradually.

And then, with his first question, Boyle approached the real reason for today's meeting: "What are this college's greatest challenges?"

A full two seconds passed without an answer, so Boyle slapped his forehead with feigned impatience. "My friends, there used to be two truly crucial issues facing this college. But since our friend Patrick Drock dropped out of the race thanks to Dr. Deyme—"

I felt the other flunkies' collective resentment, but they didn't dare look away from Boyle.

"—there is now one crucial issue: the upcoming faculty union elections." He wriggled out of his sport jacket and carelessly dropped it on the floor. "The faculty election, it's now on the front burner for us, people."

Dr. Olsen cleared her throat, her hand on an enormous note book.

"Go ahead," Boyle urged.

With a theatrical flourish, Dr. Olsen opened the notebook. "In anticipation of our discussion of the faculty elections, I have gathered some preliminary information."

She paused for a moment to assure that all attention was fixed upon her. Then, she shared the fruits of her research. At first, I had trouble following her report. Her boobs. They're so fit. Not really large. I mean, they're not jugs. But they're really toned. I instantly knew that, even sans brassiere, they remained round and wrinkle free.

Anyway, as I was explaining, I had trouble following Olsen's report. Eventually, though, I noticed a pattern. Several times, the name "Sheryl Farella" came up. Remember Sheryl? Yeah, she's one of my three faculty butt sores on the computer committee. She and Jim Pouris and that insufferable Steve Luken. Just the other day, Luken stopped me in the hallway and said that all my strenuous thinking was paying off because my forehead looked ten pounds lighter.

"—and I have it on very good authority," Olsen continued, voice rising, "that Jim Pouris will be a candidate for faculty Vice President."

Boyle massaged his temples. "Pouris, he's a pain."

Olsen nodded sympathetically and resumed her report. Pouris, it seems, was sharing a ticket with Farella. This could only be trouble: Pouris and Farella, they're practically anarchists. With religious zeal, they appear at board meetings and blab to the press about patronage, huge administrative costs, do-nothing bureaucrats, etc. Last month, they even told several reporters that Boyle's fringe benefits surpassed that of U.S. Senators.

"I have here," Olsen proclaimed, "a draft of the Farella and Pouris campaign statement."

With a thespian's drama, she recited a particularly damnable excerpt: "Let us ponder the etymology of the word college. A college is, in the strict sense, a collection of colleagues who gather to discuss academic matters, to discover and to disseminate hard-earned knowledge. Nowhere in the classical paradigm is there room for the modern administrator. Today's college administrator, as seen on our own campus, is a careerist, grasping, nap-prone and academically deficient bureaucrat who has, for far too long, exploited the politically naive academic. Exploiting the good will of the naive academic, the modern administrator amasses power and influence. Therefore, the modern flunky spends public money on anything and everything but instruction. The modern administrator builds his own empire and is accountable only to a low-I.Q. board of trustees that is, sad to say, more interested in mawkish flattery and in snaring contracts for friends and relatives than ensuring quality education. Furthermore..."

"Jesus," Douglas whispered.

The radical rant continued. During one especially inflammatory section, Boyle began rubbing his back against the chair, as an itchy grizzly rubs against a tree trunk. Soon he was reaching down the back of his shirt, crudely scratching his shoulder blades. When the Farella/Pouris hate sheet described Boyle as "a four-faced mediocrity interested not in education, but feather-nesting and union-busting", Boyle yanked off his tie with a two fisted grip and dug at his chest.

Boyle's face became a pissed-off palette: crimson cheeks and forehead, white splotches, dark greenish crescents under suddenly bloodshot eyes. Then hot little pimples or rash-stars bloomed on his neck and face.

"—and the challenge facing the union is clear: restore the integrity of the faculty by claiming governance of this college, or watch the current administration turn this once fine institution into a patronage sewer and academic laughing stock."

"Enough!" Boyle suddenly stood and, most unfortunately, bashed his knee against the table's corner. He managed to stifle a yelp and hurried from the room.

I imagined the other first stringers pointing at me, screeching, "It was Deyme's fault!" Presently, Boyle returned with a giant mug of java in one hand and a stinking, filterless cigarette in the other. He took a few gulps with his eyes squeezed shut.

I surveyed my fellow first stringers. For the first time, they returned my glances with something that approached camaraderie. Douglas even held a forefinger to his lips, indicating that nobody should speak.

"That's the most irresponsible garbage I've ever heard from this union!" Boyle finally said. "Goddammit! If I could just find a way to fire Farella and Pouris!"

"Perhaps we can look into a lawsuit," Olsen suggested. "Slander or—"

Boyle shook his head violently, like a coyote shaking prey in its jaws. "Freedom of speech protections, etc. We get government money and that damned first amendment applies...Besides, I can't risk World War Three by suing union candidates. They'd get sympathy votes." Boyle resumed his candid scratching, this time roughly thrusting both hands down his pants."

I have an idea," Douglas soothed. As if gathering profound thoughts, he glanced upward at the fluorescent lights. "Though I may be speaking too boldly—" He looked to Boyle, who croaked "Continue!" while rubbing his itchy palms against his pant legs.

"—I suggest that we form a committee." Douglas lowered his voice, and we all leaned forward to hear him. "The committee will see to it that the faculty election has an outcome that's favorable, if you will, for the

Flunky

college's administration."

"How can we do that?" Olsen asked.

"Misinformation. Bonuses, say, for selected faculty to vote against Pouris and Farella. Most importantly," Douglas intoned, "we must discretely sponsor credible opponents." He smiled knowingly and allowed the rest of us to digest his strategy.

Douglas, I saw, was one very clever bureaucrat. For most of the meeting, he'd been silent, satisfied to let motor-mouth Olsen be the star. Then he stepped in at the crucial moment to grab the spotlight.

"Explain the sponsorship angle," Boyle said.

"Does anybody remember a guy named Donald Segretti?"

Yeah, I thought. That rookie who pitched a no-hitter just last week.

"Donald Segretti was one of Nixon's boys," Boyle recalled. "He sabotaged Democratic campaigns."

"Exactly. He sent out fake campaign literature. You know, stuff like Scoop Jackson had illegitimate children and Hubert Humphrey was a drunk driver. The Republican dirty pranksters called it 'rat fucking.'"

Boyle brightened. "I was a Young Republican until Watergate. I switched to the Democrats to look clean."

Douglas chuckled. "So did I."

The tension drained from the room. Boyle congratulated Olsen and Douglas on work well done. Olsen profusely thanked Boyle and assured him she would "keep interfacing" with her sources. Douglas quietly sat back and lighted his pipe. Smoke and schemes wafted above his head.

"What about the credible opposition?" Boyle asked. "Any suggestions?"

Olsen loudly made several suggestions, but Boyle reflexively dismissed them as "not what we're looking for."

As the others fell silent, I tentatively suggested Dwayne Derrickson, the faculty wimp on the computer committee.

Olsen laughed. "That little man with the greasy glasses."

I wanted to boast of the little deal I'd cut with Derrickson, but I held back on the boasts. "He's reasonable. And I don't think he likes Pouris and Farella. He voted against them and with me."

"Maybe he's just what we need," Boyle reflected.

Olsen quacked again about how "little" and "funny" Dwayne was. Nobody joined Olsen in her ridicule—I could sense Boyle's impatience, and Douglas seemed bored—yet she energetically continued. Funny, isn't it, how some people are so oblivious? I mean, Olsen just kept talking, and nobody said a word, but she didn't notice. Or care.

During some portion of her soliloquy—she was now reminding us that Dwayne was short, and so probably suffered from episodes of "height anxiety"—she paused to breathe.

At that very moment, Boyle announced the meeting was over. He would meet with us later in the week to discuss the rat fucking strategy.

Douglas quickly departed, leaving a faint trail of aromatic smoke in his wake.

Olsen crisply gathered her notebook. "Nice meeting you, John."

I thanked her. I was about to leave when Boyle asked me to help him figure something out.

"Anything you need, Dr. Boyle."

Boyle began unbuttoning his shirt. "C'mere John." He shrugged his shirt halfway off. "Reach in and, uh, and scratch these hives on my back."

Chapter Eight: Success Flatters Me

I'd been avoiding Lydia all week. She'd leave a message on the office voice mail, alternately demure of voice, then all husky and suggestive. A couple times, she contrived to stop by my office, but my door was closed and I'd left ironclad orders to my secretary to turn away all visitors.

I was being less that sporting to Lydia, I knew. But I just couldn't bring myself to care. With my power surge, with my soaring status, my fledgling relationship with Lydia suddenly seemed, well, almost pointless. Lydia was suddenly several torsos below me on the college's tribal totem pole, and it was just good career policy to keep our relationship under control. Now that I'd passed her up, I didn't really need her help. Call me a callous careerist, but I'd had a thought-flip regarding our pact. Our little affair would be inevitably charged with political intrigue, and Lydia had everything to gain. She might well try to sleep her way up the ladder, but I had no such commensurate advantage. Sure, I like string-free fucks, and I find myself easily disarmed by her sudden laugh and relaxed company. But I had to be careful. I had a wonderful thing going here at West Central, and I had to heartlessly protect it.

On Friday, I was sneaking out for an early lunch—my stomach was demanding a down-and-dirty showdown with some burritos and beer over at Esperanza's—and I nearly crashed into Lydia as I rounded a corner.

"Hey!" I sputtered. "Watch where you're going."

She wasn't sure how to take this and offered a quizzical smile. "Leaving a little early for lunch, aren't you?"

I blustered that I'd had only dry toast and low-cal, no-caffeine herbal tea for breakfast.

Lydia's eyes widened. "You really are going to lunch! At 10:30!"

I held a silencing finger to my mouth and nodded for her to follow me.

"I can't leave this early."

"Yes you can." I was quickly entranced by her ample cleavage, deep and mysterious beneath today's blue blouse.

Giggling, she followed me out of the building and to my car. Why not, I asked myself? Why not some mid-day T & A?

Why not indeed?

I just couldn't say no to her good company and guilt-free coupling. She was unusually fun-loving, even liberated, in the sack. Lydia's really liberated. I mean, here we were in the middle of a mid-day wild thing. I was doing something that—No, I can't tell you. You'd think I'm a perv.

Okay, I'll tell you.

She was on her hands and knees. What with my gut-heavy thrusts, she had trouble staying upright on her over-stuffed bed. She looked over her lightly freckled shoulder at me, urgently mouthing words. But I couldn't hear her. I was watching TV with headphones on.

Yeah, spooling to the tube. We had a porno in the DVD. I suppose this reveals me to be a wanker at heart. But don't scoff until you try it. The tape gives you ideas, gives you energy, gives you inspiration. On the screen, for instance, a skinny guy—Christ, he had no ass at all—was atop an Asian gymnast or circus contortionist. Though pinned on her back, she drew her knees to her chest, then managed to slip her legs past the guy's arms and grip his sweaty face with her feet.

Lydia yanked the headphones off me.

"What's wrong?" I asked between burning gasps for oxygen. This video-accompanied spooling, like video-accompanied exercise, it was work.

"Let's try that."

"You're kidding."

On the screen, the Asian had the guy on his stomach and she was...Christ, that has to be faked.

"It'll hurt!"

He was yelling. She pushed him onto his side, grabbed his bobbing prong with one hand and, with the other, slowly pushed a pink pseudo-prong into his rear. The scrawny punk looked both pained and transported. Whooping, swearing, and weeping, he spoke in tongues like a Pentecostalist high on scripture and angel dust.

Absorbed by this spectacle—even by porno standards, its candor and debasement were remarkable—I noticed too late that Lydia had a dildo in her hands. Its alarmingly large head was poking at my suddenly shy rear.

"Hey!" I barked. I scrambled away and, with my foot, pushed Lydia onto her back. Then I was on top of her, eyeball to eyeball, and I wrestled away the dildo.

"Two at once?" she challenged, one eyebrow cocked.

I accepted her challenge. Flesh in front and rubber in rear was Lydia's fevered fave. Her freckles were thrown into high relief on her sheened face. She tore scratches on my love handles that would have implicated a mugger. Eventually I was totally deflated and had to rely on my artificial friend.

Finally she surrendered and rested her head on my heaving bosom. Jesus, was I bushed. Yeah, bushed and tingling with that porn amalgam of titillation and embarrassment. I'd had similar pangs of mixed emotions as a kid, when I'd come across Dad's wanker rags and retreated to the bathroom, the flushing toilet and gushing faucet serving as audio-cover.

"Do you think I'm a dirty girl?" Lydia punctuated her query by plucking a few of my chest hairs.

I laughed. This was terrific: the dirty girl your addled pubescent imagination burned for. I was thirty eight, and my teenage wish had arrived. But my relatively advanced age was a plus; now I really knew how to take advantage of my good carnal fortune.

"You're *really* dirty."

Our post coital pillow chat turned to campus politics and office intrigue. Lydia again surprised me with her nonchalant attitude toward my power ascension. She didn't try to take coy advantage of our relationship, which relieved me. But it disappointed me too. The petty part of me, the biggest part of me, had looked forward to rebuffing any attempts to parlay our relationship into her professional gain. See, I was getting laid exclusively on my terms.

"We're involved in some faculty distraction at the moment," I remarked. I explained that Boyle was bent on getting Dwayne Derrickson elected as the faculty president.

"He is sort of a wimpy guy," Lydia agreed. "He'd be easy to deal with."

I rambled on a while about our rat fucking project. Then Lydia surprised me by politely announcing that I would have to take my leave.

It was only 7:30, and a Friday night to boot. A bit hurt, I asked her about her evening's plans.

"Don't sulk, dear heart." She kissed my wrinkling forehead. "I'm meeting some friends for drinks. You'd be welcome to come along—"

"Sounds good."

"Except it's just us girls. No guys allowed." Already, she was sitting up and brushing her hair.

Driving home, a feeling of cheapness dampened my spirits. Is that how you women feel, when your Significant Other casually reminds you that he has a life apart from you? I stopped at a Zippy convenience store and bought three burritos and a longneck beer. I downed the snack in five minutes. Then I got hungry, so I stopped at the Burger Stud's drive through for a Stud cheeseburger six pack.

My primal urges satisfied, the evening's remains had little purpose. Once home, I thought about reading a book. I kept thinking about it for fifteen minutes—five of those minutes with impressive concentration—then turned on the TV. Armed with my remote control, I scanned dozens of stations and drank a few more beers. Eventually, I settled on *Homeboy Video*, an offering by one of those cable channels that sprout weekly. The show was composed of clips filmed by viewers with their own video equipment. The subject matter—grimily filmed violence and chaos—was shrilly deemed "the bleeding edge!" by its pimple cream and teen clothing sponsors.

Each week's collection of videos had a theme. Last week's theme was called "The Good Times Are Killing Me." Highlights included a bungee jumper hopping from a hot air balloon. His cord broke and he splatted all over a grocery store parking lot as horrified shoppers shrieked and fainted. In another clip, a homemade roller coaster crashed into a tree, killing both occupants.

This week's episode was "Young Death." One segment featured a barn in high flames and oily smoke. For just a moment, I wondered what the point was—big deal, it's a burning barn, artily filmed against an autumn night sky with an orange harvest moon. Then a chorus line of synthesized trumpets announced this video's star: a beanpole teen fled from the barn, his black T-shirt aflame. A screaming teen aged girl galloped after him. I guessed she was simply trying to douse the kid's flames. Wrong. She was trying to kill him. As an obese sheriff ineptly interfered, the girl cornered the still burning kid and repeatedly struck his head with the bucket. The soundtrack goosed the action with a crashing snare drum roll and skull-splitting guitar.

The last segment was alarming even by *Homeboy Video*'s standards. In the middle of a rubble-filled city lot, a posse pulled the football jacket off a struggling kid, then knifed him. The camera man, allegedly hiding behind an abandoned car, delivered a shaky but graphic close up of the knife slashing the kids face and hands. Upbeat dance music with a chorus of "Take It! Take It!" blared, and the image flipped upside down then went black as the posse ran away with their prize jacket.

I was stunned that the cable station aired the posse segment, but I also admired their broadcasting balls. It was all the talk during the week. And the major networks—no doubt alarmed by *Homeboy's* high ratings— carried hand-wringing commentaries on "our depraved society." And of course, each network saw fit to include clips from the posse segment. For a few days, there was even talk of a congressional investigation, but key Senators discretely lost interest. Seems that the CEO of the show's major sponsor heartily contributed to the Senate minority whip's re-election campaign. The Republicans steadfastly denied, of course, any wrong-doing, righteously hiding behind red-faced homilies to patriotism, Jesus Christ, and capitalism. Meanwhile, *Homeboy Video* was the most discussed show on television.

Encouraged, the cable network and sponsor went on the offensive, claiming that a reformed former gang member mailed the notorious clip anonymously to the station. The network solemnly defended the clip as a public service that illustrated the horrors of inner-city America.

The following Monday, even Boyle made *Homeboy Video* the topic of discussion. In the middle of our first string meeting, Boyle abruptly stood. Pounding the table, he preached the Gospel of Boldness.

"What gumption! Don't you love that!" he bawled.

We reflexively nodded.

"That network glorified—hell, it celebrated first degree murder. And nobody will call them on it. The Senate pulled a bigger scam by swearing no connection between the network and Republican PACS. I love it."

I guessed that Boyle detected some kindred spirits in the Senate—his political aspirations were looking ever more promising.

"The GOP won big," Douglas agreed. "Expert rat fucking."

"That's the thing we draw from it." He nodded violently. "That's our lesson."

"What is?" Olsen ventured, a tad rattled by Boyle's manic enthusiasm for *Homeboy Video*.

"Boldness, dammit. We can't be wallflowers and expect to get, to do the big things." Boyle turned toward me. "That show reminds me of you, Deyme."

Uh?

"You don't just sit at your desk, waiting for payday to roll around. You're not afraid to roll the dice."

"—thank you."

"Take charge!" Boyle implored us.

"Of what?" Olsen asked.

"Whatever! Like the, uh—" He snapped his fingers, searching for the words.

"Elections," Douglas reminded.

"Take charge of it." Boyle pointed at me. "Rat fucker!"

Then he dismissed us and disappeared into his office. Olsen arrogantly ignored my friendly wave of departure. Fine, I thought, roused by Boyle's attention. Sit on the sidelines, Michelle, because I'm taking charge. My upbeat mood stayed with me the entire week, and I was especially virile that night with Lydia. Success, it really flatters me. I mean, look at me. Don't I look happy?

The next first string meeting wasn't so gratifying.

So far, I'd contributed nothing to the faculty rat fucking campaign. Enthusiasm wasn't the problem: believe me, I'd love to stick it to that damned faculty union. But the ideas, they just weren't flowing. But Douglas! He seethed with ideas. True, some were pretty flaky: all those JFK conspiracy books, I guess, has twisted his thinking. Still, Douglas possessed an impressive intensity of purpose, and he did have a gift for schemes.

In fact, Douglas brought in news so wonderful that Boyle nearly wet his pants with joy. Seems that Douglas, in his low-key style, had casually "dropped by" the Business Department to chat with Dwayne Derrickson and suggested they go out for a drink. Plying Dwayne with a few beers and plentiful praise, Douglas convinced him to run for the Presidency of the West Central College Faculty Union. Dwayne protested, confessing that he had no ideas about how to serve as faculty president. Douglas assured Dwayne that the office ennobled its occupant. The ideas would come. Besides, Dwayne could always turn to Dr. Douglas for honest, discrete assistance.

"The ideas will come!" Boyle repeated gleefully. "I love that."

Additionally, Douglas stated that lil' Dwayne had asked for help in drafting his campaign materials. Douglas obliged Derrickson and wrote the entire paper.

Boyle erupted with a staccato laugh and drum-roll on the thighs. "Brilliant! This is what successful administration is all about. Just last week, I was reading in a, a book—an article?—about forging creative liaisons between management and labor."

I was fully pissed at Douglas. People like him, they put you on the spot because they're so damned clever. Olsen's characteristic smirk was a little curdled, too.

My petulance, however, was soon swallowed by fear. Hands clasped behind his back, Boyle looked at each of us meaningfully. If he calls on me...! After three—no, four!—weeks on the first string, I'd contributed nothing but tail-wagging agreement and the occasional coffee errand.

Big mouth Olsen, bless her heart, saved me by asking Douglas a pointless "clarifying" question. Douglas coolly answered. Olsen, still hungry for the limelight, continued with more banal squawks and farts. I'm going to make it, I thought, I'm going to make it...

Then Boyle faced me. "Sounds terrific, doesn't it, John?"

Huh? I nodded stupidly. For all I knew, I'd just agreed to scrape and paint Boyle's house.

"So you'll help out with the details?"

"Absolutely!"

Boyle gave his cuffs a crisp little tug, then smiled. "I'm pleased to hear that you're immersed in the fine points already. Could you tell us which details interest you?"

One thing I've wondered...why does my mouth hang open at such moments? "The details that, those that we discussed. About the election."

"We'll work out the specifics this week," Douglas said cheerfully. Bless him! He's running interference for me—!

Oh boy. Boyle gave his cuffs another tug, as if preparing to explode. Then he grinned at Douglas and snapped shut his black leather brief case. "Colleagues, I've gotta go."

Olsen, forlorn that she'd been denied her fifteen minutes of Presidential attention, tried to take the floor: she volunteered to help write phony campaign literature in the names of Pouris and Farella, the two faculty malcontents.

"What if I were to—"

"You'll do fine, I'm sure. I've got to look at some—Wait a minute. Don't forget about tonight's reception for Dr. Jo Ann Staulen, our new Dean of Academic Diversity. Damn I'm late."

Back in my office, I ordered myself to come up with some faculty rat fucking ideas. I stared at my blank notepad. My notepad stared back, mocking me. After a good five minutes of hard thought, I told myself to slow down—I mean, if I thought this hard all day, I'd be exhausted—so I decided to clean my desk.

Strewn on my desk were some surveys that I'd sent to the faculty a few weeks ago. We bureaucrats are big on questionnaires and surveys: they give us something to do. I suffered a small pang of professional obligation and decided to actually read a few surveys before burying them in the coffin of my filing cabinet. I'd distributed the surveys to all one hundred fifty one full-time faculty. Judging by the thickness of the pile, about fifty had replied. I was pleased: at least a third of the faculty took me seriously enough to respond.

My pleasure was short-lived. The first respondent was obviously a crank. To the question, "How might West Central College improve our image to the public at large?", the respondent answered, "By firing you in a well-attended public meeting."

I flung the sheet into the wastepaper basket and read the second sheet. Dammit! The second respondent answered the question in exactly the same way! So did the third...a ring of angry sweat soaked my collar. Christ All Mighty, sheets four through thirty four had the same answer! Then, upon closer examination, I saw that they were all photocopies.

Some jerk had merely made thirty-three copies of a single sheet. Probably Steve Luken. His day isn't complete unless he's mocked me...yeah, or harassed me with that sullen stare, his deep-set eyes shadowed by his beefy Cro-Magnon forehead.

Response number thirty five was not a duplicate, but I wasn't cheered. The respondent offered this collegiate gem: How may we improve the college's image?

By hanging you and your ilk from the most prominent tree on campus, in full view of the press, students, & faculty. Pictures at eleven!

Worked into a primitive hunger—I mean, getting this pissed off burns plenty of calories—I went earlier than usual to lunch. I pulled into Rossetti's Pizza Palace at 10:55 a.m. Rossetti's has a terrific pizza and salad buffet. I soothed my anger with pizza, beer, and salad. My mood quickly improved, and my thoughts turned toward moving into more suitable digs.

I pulled out some shiny brochures for several hip new condo developments and enjoyed my dessert of beer and cigarettes. I ordered another pitcher, then a third. This lifestyle quest, it's really enjoyable.

The afternoon slipped past in a haze of cigarette smoke and beer foam. I really shouldn't have ordered that fifth pitcher. Driving home, it wasn't easy. I even sat on a milk-crate under the shower for an hour, wondering where the day went. 4:30 and I'd already thrown up in the car.

Time flies, doesn't it, when you're acquiring a lifestyle? I'd driven home with my right hand on the unruly steering wheel and my left clamped across my outraged nose. Even in the most optimum condition, the Slug's interior never smelled of a rose garden after a gentle spring shower. Now it smelled like a fouled septic field on a muggy Alabama afternoon.

Halfway home, I almost passed out from the stench. I violently rolled down the window—busting the handle in the process—and weaved home hanging half-way out the car. What a sight I must've been.

No wonder those spoiled teens burned by in their 'Vette and saluted me with jeers and raised middle fingers.

It made perfect sense, really: Imagine you're a rich teenager. It's an unusually warm September day with all the desired colors: the blue of a perfect sky, the yellow of a cheerful sun, the green of easy money from your rich parents. You're test-driving your mint-condition '65 'Vette, and your wholesome blonde date, her cheeks flush from a day on the beach, is administering a four-barrel hand job. As a bonus, you see me: a sickly-green fat guy hanging from of his asthmatic Slug.

Clearly, duty calls.

You answer the call and flip me off.

Okay, so I'm a bit envious. I wish my own youth had been brightened by such class-conscious displays of arrogance. I really missed out, being born working-class.

After my shower, I pulled on my least-soiled cotton shirt and pants, topped off with a very sharp, light gray jacket that I'd never worn because it had, until now, been too big. Not now. It fit like a glove on a corpulent hand. Man, I've got to stop eating so much. And at times, I have stopped eating so much. But then my stimulus-starved mouth demands a commensurate amount of drink. This Oedipal Complex conundrum...is it real? I'm stuck in the oral stage. Christ, last night I awoke with my thumb in my mouth.

Chapter Ten: Getting By On Charm

The college's newly-renovated theater lobby was the site of tonight's affair. The lobby's drab old ceiling had been torn out and replaced by a high-tech, glass enclosed silo that housed exotic plants from around the globe. The effect was pretty dramatic: You looked up and imagined climbing the vigorous vines skyward, just like Jack on his beanstalk. Two full-time horticulturists patrolled on cat walks and attended to the plants, trimming and watering, feeding and fussing. What with the constantly blooming flowers, the place always smelled terrific.

I made an end-run around the crowd at the entrance and headed straight for the refreshments. And there he was, frowning with a plastic cup in hand.

"Bruce..." I smiled uneasily.

Ol' buddy Bruce Herrig was silent. He just stared at me longer than polite society recommends, then swallowed his wine in one angry gulp. Bruce'd been avoiding me. He probably felt awkward around me, blinded by the glare of my rising star. You know how it is when one friend eclipses the other—the guy left in the dust feels a bit, well, emasculated.

I decided to show the depth of my character with a warm greeting: "You're almost completely bald."

"You're fatter."

Ouch!

We stood eyeing one another. Finally, I extended my hand. He refused, so I gripped his skinny forearm and led him to a corner.

"What's with you?" I demanded.

"I could ask the same of you," he sulked, "but I suppose that would be insubordination. You're such a big shot now."

Okay. I confess. I'm the one who threw cold water on our relationship. But dammit, I just can't schlep with people who can't do something for me. You should never network with an inferior. What's in it for you?

"I've been so busy."

Bruce grunted. "Save it for people who don't work here. Everybody knows the first string is a breeze."

"You're wrong," I whispered harshly.

"Fine. I'll see you later."

Feeling like a jerk, I patted his shoulder. "Let's get another drink."

He grunted, I cajoled, and finally the ice broke. We gossiped and bitched for a while. He was intensely interested in the sexual politics of the first string. Was it true, for instance, that Boyle and Olsen did it on his desk?

"I really don't think they're an item."

"They have to be," Bruce insisted. "Why else would she be on the first string?"

"Well, I'm on the first string and Boyle doesn't ball me."

"Not yet."

We traded a few more friendly insults and accusations. Then discussion turned to this evening's star, Dr. Jo Ann Staulen, the Dean of Academic Diversity. She was causing quite a stir. Last week, the hot rumor was that Jo Ann was related to a Trustee, maybe Rochinni. Rochinni flatly denied it in a brief press story, but the gossip persisted in slightly altered form: Jo Ann was related to Boyle.

But the real news isn't Jo Ann's genealogy; it's her politics. Bruce heard she's a testicle-twisting radical feminist who alienated everyone at her previous campus. She'd even outed a female prof who went on a diet. Staulen mobilized a battalion of sign-wielding students to boycott the dieter's office, her home, and grocery store's low-cal freezer section. Diets, Staulen argued, were metaphors for rape: diets were merely hostile patriarchy imposed on the subjugated female. Makeup was rape, too. So were perfume, creme rinse, and mouthwash.

I was baffled by her arrival at humble West Central. "From an Ivy League school to here. Isn't that kind of a step down?"

"I heard what her salary is."

"And?"

He told me. I thought he was kidding, and only after solemn assurances did I believe him.

"That's a helluva lot more than what I make!"

"Get used to it. She's a big name in her field of, the field of diversity."

Bruce complained that the local press, sometimes suspicious of Boyle's gleeful spending, would have a field day with Jo Ann Staulen. "Any bad press is my fault, of course," whined the beleaguered Director of P.R. "He expects totally positive press, and I can't—Hey, here he comes."

Armed with fresh wine, Bruce and I drifted to the back. Boyle, his chiseled hair gleaming under the lights, was in his magnanimous mode: blinding smile, vigorous handshakes, brief intimate asides with a few Trustees. Boyle was especially pleased to see Democratic Senator Harry Zcigelwitcz. Hallway gossip contended that the Democrats were coaxing Boyle to run for the U.S. Senate; the pols were dazzled by Boyle's patronage savvy and peerless political instincts. This lobby's modern-day hanging garden of Babylon, for instance, was constructed by a company that contributed mightily to the Democrats. Only the hopelessly naive doubted that some of these dollars made their way to the Democratic coffers.

Now behind the podium, Boyle worked the crowd. He thanked various big shots for their continued support of "West Central College's quest for excellence."

"We'll never sacrifice quality," Boyle insisted. "The students, the community, and the state entrust their dollars, their energies, and their hopes in this college. Excellence is our mission. And for that excellence, I want to again thank West Central's marvelous and committed faculty."

I heard a voice behind me. A voice I hated.

"He's really slicing up the baloney," said Steve Luken.

I turned half-way toward my tormentor. "Glad to see you dressed for the occasion." Christ, he was wearing a faded Hawaiian shirt and jeans.

Luken's mouth widened in mock offense. "You forget that I'm just a faculty member, so my salary is appropriately low and I can't buy nice clothes. Teaching's just an afterthought here. An administrative inconvenience."

"Save the quips for contract negotiations."

Presently, Boyle introduced his "hand-picked" Dean of Academic Diversity. "It's my pleasure to introduce Dr. Jo Ann Staulen."

Applause accompanied Dr. Jo Ann Staulen as she made her way in tiny steps to the podium. She was a slight woman, and her white cotton blouse was helpless to flatter her washboard figure. Her appearance was utterly forgettable except for the hatchet sized nose that dwarfed her pale, humorless face. What a schnoz.

Then she started talking. I forgot about her nose.

"The penis," she proclaimed, "is our societal metaphor. This must not surprise us, as ours is a patriarchal society that ruthlessly, if sometimes unconsciously, dismisses elements that are not conceptually phallic. It is this relentless phallocentric episteme that snuffs the matriarchal voices. This is a point that Foucault understood only too well. The penis..."

"What's this all about?" Herrig whispered.

I shrugged. Lots of mesmerizing ten-syllable jargon. Lots of long pauses, as her gray eyes coldly regarded her confounded audience.

"...so the diversity of society is only one victim of the penis. Of course, we are acutely aware of this hegemony in academe. Our traditional academic phallocentric disciplines are hard, they are strict, they are erect. The reliance upon theory, with its rigid frameworks and rigorous supporting exemplars, embodies masculine oppression. This is a most demoralizing realization. Initially, theory was advanced as the best hope of..."

Boyle was sitting right up front, and I tried to gauge his attitude toward Jo Ann. But I couldn't. He was uncharacteristically still and seemed absorbed.

"...response is typically hostile. 'You'll destroy the great disciplines!' cry the Rotting Dead White Males as they spin in their phallic shaped caskets. But these complaints must be answered by any means possible. For too long, diversity has been a callow and shallow cliché. We have had few victories, for the reactionary guardians, the disciples of the Rotting Dead White Men, have ridiculed and dismissed academic diversity as a reduction of standards. But whose standards? The standards of the Rotting Ones, of course. Derrida teaches us to challenge these patriarchal standards and their accompanying logocentric epistemology. The gynecological voice in literature must be heard; the vagocentric voice in science must be attended to. Even in physical science, we are shackled by phallocentrism. We need new standards. We must ask ourselves, 'What if women were the early scientists?' The laws of physical science, we must concede, would be revealed as phallocentric constructs in service of a patriarchal capitalism that has so savagely decimated indigenous and Third World cultures. The so-called laws that govern our physical existence are merely ideologies, a kind of prejudice against alternative forms of..."

Steve Luken tapped me on the shoulder. "Can you follow this?"

"Sort of."

"No you can't."

"And you can?"

"She's saying that gravity is just a conspiracy made up by some dead white guys."

"That's old news." I turned away. I didn't understand more than three or four goddamned words of this crap. But I was sure as hell not going to let Luken mock me.

Dr. Staulen prattled for a while longer. The shock effect of hearing "penis" had worn off, so Herrig and I paid little attention. Christ, when would she shut up? I looked about, trying to spot Lydia and wondering what she'd make of all this talk of dicks and such.

"...irony in our project is that only consensus and dialogue will produce diversity, a diversity that we can all respect and share in." She paused for a long sip of ice-water, bracing herself for a grand conclusion. "There is more at stake here than the banality of a new college catalogue or petty fights over course content. The penis-heavy ideology of academe—so oppressive because we are so unaware of it—must be interrogated, and this interrogator is the clitoris—"

The audience's collective eyes widened.

"The *clitoris*," she boomed, "is our new model for a diverse academe. Because the clitoris has so long been ignored or patronized as a second-rate penis, it becomes the ideal subversion. Academe needs a clitoral consciousness!"

A woman in front of me stared downward toward her lap.

"Vagocentrism is the next wave. We must ride this wave or be avulsed by a society that is far more diverse than even the most liberal among us would dare dream. Vagocentrism is fully accepting. We must each be just as accepting." She said "accepting" with a tone more appropriate for a death threat. "I look forward to working with you. Thank you."

Everyone sat there for a moment, marveling at her forceful pronunciation of clitoris. Huh...I'd always thought the second syllable got the emphasis.

Boyle jumped up applauding. For the first time, Staulen offered a smile. It was a rusty smile, one not well practiced, but a smile nonetheless. Board Chairman Alfred Rochinni, attired in an ill-fitting suit out of the 'fifties, stood and applauded with abandon. He even turned to the audience and motioned that we stand. I'd never seen the old prong so excited.

I found Lydia up front and fetched us some wine.

"Some talk, eh?" she remarked with a small smile. Then she whispered, "Here comes the codger."

"Nice to see all of you fine people," barked Rochinni.

Lydia shook his hand.

"Wasn't that just a wonderful discussion?" Lydia asked shamelessly. Yeah, she kisses ass just like the rest of us.

"I think she's a great addition to the team! Her ideas are, are, they're actually quite..." His voice trailed off as Mrs. Rochinni approached. Boy, what a prize she is: a refrigerator with legs, a blue-white bee-hive atop her powdered and pinched face.

She ignored everybody. Everybody, that is, except her husband, whom she kept on a short and stern leash. She glared at ol' Alfred until he muttered a feeble "Good evening." Then, arm in arm, they took their departure.

Lydia giggled. "What a battle ax."

I wondered how a man could endure marriage to such a woman. I mean, the thought of her naked.

"I think Alfred got turned on by all the talk of penises and clitorises and scientific constructs," Lydia offered.

Herrig, who'd been standing to the side, now laughed. "Maybe she got turned on, too."

And here he came, the walking hemorrhoid, Steve Luken. "Good evening, everybody."

Herrig and I grunted.

"We were just saying," Lydia said cheerfully, "that Rochinni got aroused by tonight's talk."

"Yeah," the buttsore smiled, "I thought the old duffer was walking kind of funny. Maybe he raised it."

"For the first time in years," Lydia agreed.

Lydia's rapport with Luken really pissed me off. I mean, the guy constantly ridicules me, but she's yucking it up with him.

"All that aside," Luken continued, "I know the real reason our new Dean is here."

I made a big show of looking at my watch, but Lydia was all ears.

"She's just a favor returned," Luken announced.

"How so?" Lydia asked, accepting a fresh drink from Luken.

"I think Boyle's paying somebody off by hiring her. Somebody who did a favor for him."

"That's ridiculous," I snapped.

"That's standard procedure," Luken noted.

"Who?" Lydia urged.

"I don't know," Luken confessed. "But somebody pretty high up for Boyle to take on Jo Ann Staulen. I mean, I can't picture Boyle buying into this stuff."

"Maybe it's just his wives who can't," said Bruce, alluding to Boyle's six marriages.

"Radical feminism is getting a foothold in many colleges," Lydia observed. "Boyle knows it's good for his image." Luken chuckled. "Victim status is all the rage, especially with higher ed hustlers like Jo Ann. Poor Jo Ann's being exploited at West Central at $90,000 a year!"

"That woman is making $90,000 a year?" Lydia exclaimed. "I've been here for eight years and—" Her voice trailed off into silent irritation.

Luken nodded happily. "I heard it direct from the high priest of patronage himself."

"I heard it was $78,000." I glared at Bruce. "But my sources are worthless."

We flunkies looked at Luken, this weird dressing guy with the gall to ask Boyle, point-blank, about Jo Ann Staulen's salary. He returned each of our gazes individually, as if saying Yeah, you wish you had the brass. For we flunkies, frank and public talk of salaries was a terrible blunder, like entering a meeting with your pants around your ankles.

Lydia's eyes hardened as Boyle passed our group. "He's setting himself up for a mighty hard fall."

Luken agreed. "This college is a patronage house of cards."

Bruce and I snorted in disagreement.

"It'll be probably be just a little thing," Luken predicted, "like ticking off the wrong person. All this patronage work, all this bed hopping with politicians, all on the taxpayer's dime. He thinks he's insulated himself. Which means he's ripe for the picking."

"Save it for your fellow union fanatics," I smirked.

"You may be on to something," Lydia remarked to Luken.

"See you folks around the old salt mine," Luken smiled. He finished his drink and strode across the room to talk with Pouris and Farella, his union comrades.

I stood there seething: "He is such a prick," I half-whispered.

"You're just pissed," Herrig charged, "that you got stuck with his glass."

"Uh?" In my thick hand was Luken's empty wine glass. He'd thrust it at me when he left and, caught off guard, I just took it. I shoved the glass at Herrig, who accepted it with a downtrodden silence.

"Have a good time with the press," I told Bruce.

I met Lydia for a drink at Ralph's. I downed a few whiskey and waters, not pausing to taste them. Predictably, my mood went from sour to surly. I tried to pick a fight with Lydia about being so goddamned friendly with Luken. She parried my jabs with good-natured laughs and venom-free teases. But that whiskey, it quickly inflamed me.

"I thought you handled him very well," Lydia murmured, her hand lightly touching mine. "You got by nicely on your charm."

My charm? I mused, studying Lydia's cautious eyes.

You've got to hand it to mean drunks. We can find offense in the most well-meaning statements. It's what sets us apart. "I'm glad you approve of me," I snarled.

"James..."

"Feel free to screw him if you think he's so goddamned terrific. Really. Maybe he'll let you wear those, wear his stupid Hawaiian shirt afterward."

Lydia's blue eyes became even bluer in the sudden wash of tears. She withdrew her hand and pretended to study the menu.

I yanked the menu from her hand.

"You drink too much," she said, voice heavy with resignation. She slid quickly from the booth and hurried toward the door, but I was right behind her, swearing all the way. I stood there in the parking lot, legs uncooperative but spirit willing, and kept cursing as she drove away.

After her car's tail-lights were out of sight, I returned to my booth for a nightcap. The foul-mouthed fool in me, the heavy-lidded drunk, was satisfied.

Christ, it feels good, doesn't it?

The waitress approached warily. "Another drink, sir?"

I wanted to answer, but my throat was balled up with regret and I just couldn't seem to stop crying. Whew, this is humiliating. I waved the waitress away and stayed hunched in my booth's shadowy corner. After several thick nose-blowings—they sounded like a crass car horn—I slunk out.

Time really dragged. Big surprise, huh? I mean, my scene-stealing turn as John Deyme, foul-mouthed pig, made the rest of the month anti-climactic.

I couldn't even enjoy Alfred Rochinni's victory. Yeah, he retained his Board Chairmanship. He ran unopposed—thanks to my hardball buyout of Patrick Drock. Bruce reported that Rochinni and Boyle celebrated at a goose and duck soirée. Senator Zcigelwitcz attended and delivered a brief address on the "profitable ties" between education and governance.

Everybody's blithely forgotten that I got Drock to bail out by waving big cash before his reddening face. Bruce hasn't mentioned it once. Boyle even canceled the week's first-string meeting, where I would've had my fifteen minutes of fame. Frustrated, I longed to call Lydia and do some post-election boasting. But that's the downside of becoming a hostile drunk: people just aren't up to praising you.

At night, I moped around the duplex: small talk with Mr. Kwang and TV with menthol cigarettes. Thursday night, I confessed to myself that Lydia had been correct: I've been drinking a tad too freely. Right on the spot, I vowed to drink only white wine. See, white wine really doesn't count.

Thank God for my kitchen hygiene. A germ-free floor became my emotional anchor. Every other night, I was on all fours scrubbing the tiles with scalding water, my hands lobster-red and peeling.

One night Kim stopped in to bum some cigarettes.

"It's funny to see a man cleaning the floor," she remarked. "My father, he'd be embarrassed to be seen doing this."

"So roll up your sleeves and save me this embarrassment," I joked.

"Forget it! Hey, how do you like this vest Father got me? Maybe there's hope for him after all?" She pirouetted to model her new attire. Kim had really turned into an American teen, an expert in high priced fashion. Her studded denim and leather vest—seemingly designed by an effeminate cowpoke—must have cost a hundred bucks.

Kim kept yammering—she had a dance on Friday night, her very first—and I nodded politely. But I wasn't listening, and I was relieved when Kim finally left. I ripped open yet another pack of Arctic Blasts and watched TV with the sound off until midnight.

Late Friday afternoon, I stopped at a bookstore and purchased a volume of revenge tactics: you know, M-80's in your neighbor's muffler, bogus paternity suits sent to philandering husbands, subscriptions to queer wanker magazines for the blue nose neighbor. I stayed up until midnight, actually reading the thing from cover to cover. But it didn't help. I still had no ideas for the faculty rat fucking project.

I tossed the book behind my bed and tuned in the jazz station. My Dad got me interested; he'd play records for me every night. And now, wouldn't you know it, the DJ played a classic cover of "My Foolish Heart" by the Bill Evans Trio. Man, that is not what I wanted to hear...those first ringing piano notes, those mournful bass lines.

I hummed the first few bars and felt sorry for myself. Yeah, you guessed correctly. I was brooding over Lydia.

Without question, I'd treated her terribly. Yet I couldn't bring myself to apologize. Call me a Neanderthal, but apologies open Pandora's box. Lydia, so unfailingly sweet, would accept the first apology, especially if I heaped on the bullshit about first-string stress, my private demons, etc. But apologies can lead to big trouble later on: see, you've apologized. And once you start—well, soon you're apologizing for that innocent glance at a tube-topped teen. And then for the empty Styrofoam coffee cups in your car. And your breath mints.

Of course, this isn't a one-size-fits-all strategy. The cow would jump over the moon before my ex Joan apologized. But with women like Lydia, it's best to be cool. Sure, she'll be pissed for a while. But that little self-deprecating voice inside her starts suggesting that maybe it's not all my fault. Soon she's on the phone, hoping like hell you'll take her back.

I was distracted from my musings by Joe Henderson's cover of "Lush Life." That tune always evokes images of elegant, long-limbed women and bracing, ice-cold whiskey and waters. I suffered a stab of booze-thirst. Telling, isn't it, how jazz paints alcoholism as a romantic avocation?

The phone rang. Ha! Lydia was making the first move! Let the phone ring a few more times. I imagined her lonely in her bed with an extra-large bowl of fudge swirl ice cream.

I finally answered.

"Meet me at Ralph's immediately," Don Boyle barked.

"Immediately," I repeated, glancing at my watch. A skull session just before midnight?

Boyle hung up sharply and I couldn't help but imagine the worse. Boyle once ordered a couple flunkies to a 1:00 a.m. saloon meeting, made them buy him a few drinks, then suggested they resign. And were they shocked? Defensive? Combative? Hell no! Boyle granted them a month's severance pay, so they bought him a bottle of the establishment's best bubbly. Now, I didn't think I was about to get axed...not yet, anyway. He usually foreshadowed firings with a prolonged harassment that unnerved victim and bystanders alike.

Still, I had to come up with something for the rat fucking project. By the time I pulled into the parking lot, I'd sussed out a quarter-assed idea for painting Sheryl Farella and Jim Pouris as hate-mongers who would gladly demolish the college to ruin Boyle's reputation. Pretty promising premise, actually. The details were a little thin, but I was under a lot of pressure here, and I—

A throaty car horn sounded behind me. I turned to see an idling stretch limo. I approached the black ship, which gleamed arrogantly under the parking lights. A rear window descended.

"How about a little pleasure cruise?" Boyle called.

Settling in, I accepted a flute glass from Boyle as the chauffeur eased us onto the road. "I'm glad you accepted my invitation," Boyle said, pretending I'd had a choice. "We have some exciting things to discuss."

The omnipresent Dr. Douglas smilingly filled my glass, and I quickly got comfortable. The limo's passenger quarters were a sunken living room on wheels, with a plush maroon wrap-around couch, stereo TV, and recessed 'fridge.

"I really shouldn't be drinking," I said, sheepish. "I've been tipping a little too much of late."

Boyle rolled his eyes. "Would you lighten up? I pick you up in a limo and you don't want to imbibe?"

"You're right," I said crisply. With a raised glass, I saluted my riding companions. We tabled shop talk for the time being and silently glided into the city. Exiting at Adams, we trolled South Halsted through Greektown. Presently, the limo driver paused in front of Rodity's.

The restaurant door opened and a skinny Greek kid in white shirt and black slacks hurried to the limo with several brown paper sacks. The chauffeur lowered the smoked glass divide and handed Boyle the fresh pasticcio, flambé, braised lamb, and two loaves of impossibly aromatic bread.

"Isn't this the good life?" Boyle asked, eyes mirthful. I heartily agreed, and insisted that the next Greek meal was on me.

Boyle revealed that Greektown always fascinated him; the neighborhood, he noted, was a textbook contrast of haves and have-nots. Indeed. Inside the packed restaurants, cheery haves engorged themselves and called for yet more wine and bread.

Standing on erratically lighted street corners, mere yards from the haves, were the have-nots: stubble-faced, dog-eared, bone-weary. Several layers of dirty clothes bulked up their stooping shoulders. Four grimy old men stood on the littered corner of Adams and Halsted, passing around a bottle of wine or mouthwash. When one geezer took a long pull on the bottle, the others pushed him onto a pile of crushed boxes and litter. Boyle lowered his window and lobbed a loaf of bread at the squabbling quartet. Two of them demanded butter.

"It's a bit eerie, isn't it?" Boyle asked. "The line that separates us and them is so thin." Boyle nodded at the scores of street denizens, shuffling up and down Halsted. "Maybe one of those bums worked for IBM a few years ago."

"Or Sears," added Douglas. He pointed east to the monolithic Sears tower.

"Or went crazy. And then lost their jobs and their medical insurance. And, of course, no pension." Boyle lowered his head to ponder a private thought.

So. Even Boyle isn't free of flunky fears. Even he suffers the midnight nerve eruptions, the anxiety-cramps behind the locked bathroom door. I guess nobody can avoid economic angst, not these days–that roaring economy is just as happy to crush you as enrich you.

Boyle looked for a long moment into his flute glass, then turned to me. "James, you won't mind my saying that you haven't been the most productive member of the first string. Have you?"

I lowered my head.

"In fact, I'm getting pissed off. I hope you won't mind that I talked it over with Dr. Douglas."

I glanced at Douglas, who offered only his enigmatic smile.

"I don't mind at all," I said quietly. I felt oddly detached from this conversation—me, just sitting there, the object of a discussion I did not attend.

"But don't worry," Boyle said. "You're a team player. If you're a team player, you can contribute. In your case, actually, it was Dr. Douglas who worked it out." Boyle lighted a cigarette. His gold lighter's flame briefly illuminated his face in a sinister fashion.

"This is the role we've worked out for you," Douglas began. "My use of the word 'role' is deliberate. We're creating a drama of sorts, and you're the protagonist. Along the way, naturally, protagonists collect antagonists."

"Antagonists," repeated Boyle cheerfully. He was getting a little sloshed, his drink spilling on the car seat.

"Your role," Douglas continued, "is that of Most Hated Administrator. Your name will soon be anathema to the college faculty. The mention of your name will produce a chorus of swearing, and they—" Now it was Douglas's turn to spill his drink. On my lap.

"Goddammit!" Boyle yelled in mock anger. "Pour him, open him another bottle."

"Within a month," Douglas predicted, "faculty will be in a line to kick your ass."

"What are you feelings about this?" Boyle asked.

I didn't feel good about it at all, let me tell you. I couldn't guess what sick scheme Boyle and his lieutenant had in mind for me. But what the hell. I had no choice.

"My ass can take a lot of kicking."

Douglas's broad smile revealed a seemingly infinite number of small sharp teeth. He slapped my knee good naturedly. Growing whimsical, Boyle punched my shoulder as a bully punches his favorite victim.

Douglas carefully explained the plan, though he often paused as Boyle added excited emphasis. At one point, Boyle exclaimed that the seed of this plan came from a pop-business book: *How To Kick Ass Without Wrinkling Your Suit*, by Samuel E. Fronkweistersteikerst. Remember? That publicity-mad speculator and securities guru who...yeah, that guy. He allegedly ordered the execution of an entire jury that was about to drop the legal hammer on a former business partner. Fronkweistersteikerst's gaggle of defense lawyers argued that such a media-famous person wouldn't dare dream such a slaughter. But a defense strategy was thoroughly unnecessary. The Fronkweistersteikerst trial jury was obviously terrified of the accused and found him innocent.

Boyle was nuts about the book: "I, you—this guy, Frankenschnitzel, it's savvy. I, you...He—"

Douglas explained that a chapter called "Let Somebody Else Kick Ass" was especially suggestive.

"It's just the old henchman routine," Douglas said, "but written in an unusually enthusiastic style."

"He loved to kick ass," Boyle roared. "And ever since he built that children's hospital in Harlem, his stock, it's sky high. Boldness, Goddammit. Remember that Deyme."

Boyle, horsing around with another bottle of bubbly, allowed his face to enter the cork's line of fire. *Thwack!* The cork cum missile bloodied his nose. But Boyle was a genuinely happy drunk, not the surly bastard you'd expect. He jovially washed the blood from his nose with champagne and a napkin.

Boyle, I saw, was like a series of Chinese boxes nested in one another. He wasn't just an ambitious academician and courted pol. No, he was also a carefree bohemian and charming drinking pal who enjoyed nights out with limos and chicks and champagnes. All on the taxpayer's dime too. Impressive.

"It's simple," Douglas continued. "First, we turn you loose on the faculty. Yelling, bitching, hassling."

"You *prick!*" Boyle roared happily.

"Then Dwayne Derrickson kicks your ass. He's a hero, and he wins the faculty election in a blowout."

Boyle tossed an envelope at me, then turned to Douglas. "Hey get that, get another bottle for me."

I peeked inside the envelope and counted five one-hundred dollar bills. "You're pretty much on your own as far as being the faculty scourge," Douglas said.

"What it is, you've gotta follow your instincts on this," Boyle urged. "Be authentic."

"How so?"

"Just do it man!"

"That's right," Douglas half-whispered. "Be Zen."

Ralph's parking lot was deserted by the time we returned. I bid an effluent good evening and, climbing out of the limo, whacked my head on its low roof. I stood there rubbing my skull as the limo made a dignified turn onto the street.

I was in a peculiarly divided mood, both exquisitely drunk and quasi-depressed. I loitered in my car for a few minutes, trying to figure out the evening.

Without question, many good things had transpired. First, I was five hundred dollars richer. What easy money: ride around in a chauffeured limo with top-tab champagne and Greek food. But my self-esteem, never really high, had been hammered down several steps. Boyle and his evil little assistant had sussed me as no more than a big-assed bull's eye.

Maybe it was the champagne. They say that booze skews your judgment. I agree—after all, that's the point of liquor. But tonight, the champagne only washed away illusions. I sat there in the car, a stale and stinking cigarette in my mouth, and admitted it: I really am an ass. Boyle knew it. He was simply making use of it. Douglas knew it too.

And Lydia.

3:15 on Sunday morning isn't the best time for romantic reconciliation. But there I was, heart full of repentance and a hand full of dirt and flowers that I'd borrowed from the adjacent condo's garden.

I knocked softly, then loudly, on the front door. The porch light came on but the door remained locked. Was Lydia eyeballing me through the button-sized peephole of her reinforced steel door? As if preparing for a snapshot, I ran my peat-coated hand through my hair and smiled.

Then the light went out.

"Lydia c'mon I just wanna talk!"

A neighbor's door opened. A busybody poked her head out and told me to be quiet.

"Fuck off." I rapped again on the door.

"James be quiet!" Lydia repeated, stepping onto her porch.

"Whataya doing there?"

"I live here."

Then who lives behind this door? I asked myself as the police arrived.

Two patrol cars, red and blue lights flashing, screeched to a dramatic halt at the curb. Officer Friendly, thick hand gripping his night-stick, told me to follow him to his squad car. Officer Friendly's partner, Officer Unfriendly, grabbed my arm. Then he thrust his foot before my stumbling gait.

I fell.

Officer Unfriendly yanked me to my feet, called me a drunk, and shoved me into his cruiser's rear seat.

Boy, was I demoralized. A couple hours ago, I was sitting in a hermetically sealed limo, eating lamb and cheese. Now I was hunched in a squad car listening to Officer Unfriendly loudly recite the riot act. The most depressing element, I think, was the cage: you know, that black fence or barb wire that separates a squad car's front and back seats. The cage was really offensive—I mean, I was a harmless drunk, not a tattooed liquor store thief or sweaty bail jumper. I protested the officers' unjustly low opinion of me, but Officer Unfriendly told me to shut up.

Then Officer Friendly—maybe envious that his partner was :having all the fun—joined me in the rear seat and mashed my face against that wire barrier.

I couldn't help it. I cried.

The cops were, I think, just a bit taken aback. They'd wrestled this grass-stained, loud-mouthed lug into their car, and he limply weeps under the slightest duress. What a weak sister.

Fortunately, a most unexpected sight distracted the cops: Lydia, wearing only a blue terry cloth robe, knocked on the car window.

The cops got out of the car to huddle with Lydia. Soon the neighbor lady joined the curbside symposium. She complained bitterly about the fat drunk that trampled her garden and clobbered her door. By now, several nosy neighbors had stepped outside. They looked holographic, illumined by the squad cars' flashing blues and reds.

The meeting soon broke up. Officer Unfriendly even assisted me to Lydia's front door. Lydia let me inside, took the now-crushed flowers from my hand, and pushed me onto a hard and narrow couch.

"Thank you, Lydia."

Halfway up the stairs, she paused. "Why were you crying in the police car? Did they hit you or something?"

"That's not why I was crying."

"Oh."

"I'd come over here to apologize."

"For what?"

"For everything. For me." I pulled the envelope of money from my shirt pocket. "Being a jerk, it's all I'm good at. I'm so good at it that Boyle pays me." I tossed the money on the coffee table and started to explain the evening's misadventure, but stopped when I heard Lydia close her bedroom door.

Chapter Twelve: Am I a Romantic?

A kettle-drum headache woke me, and I reached for a cigarette, the first step in blunting the pain of a drinker's Morning After. See, you must confront a hangover with discipline and character, in paramilitary fashion. None of that prissy convalescing in a bubble bath with a flower-patterned ice-bag on your head. Instead, I torch several cigarettes in a row, drink a pot of prescription strength coffee, and gulp four aspirin. Of course, a stomach buffer is mandatory; otherwise, this concoction will peel the lining from your stomach just as turpentine peels paint from a wall. A brick of cream cheese atop a toasted bagel works best.

Halfway through my first smoke, I noted the lack of an ashtray. Being a guest, an unwelcome guest, I couldn't just rub the ashes into the carpet or couch. I sat up, coolly butched out the inevitable coughing storm, and searched for a butt bin. No luck. I hurried into the sunny kitchen, drowned the now tiny cigarette in tap water, then pushed it down the drain. What the hell. As long as I was in here...guided by my preternatural kitchen instincts, I instantly located the coffee and drip-brewer in the smallish cabinet beneath the white enamel oven. I also found an old-fashioned ashtray, the type that resembles a palm-sized beanbag.

Now I interrogated the refrigerator. I didn't approve of the haphazard arrangement of breads, fruits, and cheeses. No bagels were in stock, so I settled for cream cheese on rye. The first helping woke my appetite, and I consumed half the loaf of rye and all the cheese.

Refreshed, I returned to the living room and saw a note on the coffee table. The note, composed in handwriting of near-calligraphic quality, stated that Lydia had plans for the day. I could help myself to breakfast. Would I lock the door on the way out?

Of course I would. But in my own sweet time.

It's mischievous fun, isn't it, to snoop through someone's home when they're gone? On my previous visits, I'd been too horny and/or loaded to be nosy. Armed with my barrel sized mug of java, I scrutinized Lydia's living room. The brash room contrasted interestingly with its diffident owner. Lots of vibrant, vitamin-injected house plants, brimming bookcases, buoyant throw rugs, and pricey reproductions of seascape paintings. I paused to examine one of the seascapes: the artist's brush-stroked signature read "Monet." French. Ugh. The French, my father had claimed, are obsessed with the ridicule of mental midgets, of undersized intellects. I knew they'd make fun of me.

I paused before the four tall bookcases. Lydia was, it seemed, a fine art addict. She had dozens of big art books. I removed one—the paintings of John Singer Sergeant—and examined the dust-jacket flap.

Strangled Christ! The book cost eighty five dollars! This art hobby isn't cheap.

Conspicuous in its absence was a TV. No boob-tube, no cathode ray...no idiot box. A nuanced portrait of Lydia was emerging; she was more than a modest career gal whose sole distinguishing feature was a taste for cheerily dirty sex. No, she was well-read and cultured, selective and discerning. Hell, maybe she was even a closet bohemian, one of the artsy intelligentsia who reject stultifying middle-class life for the life of the mind.

I'd just sprayed down the living room and kitchen with air freshener—Lydia surely would frown on my smoking—when the phone rang. I stood in the kitchenette and waited for the voice to come over the answering machine. But nothing happened. I squatted to find the volume knob. As soon as I touched it, the machine squalled and hummed. Startled, I dropped the machine and tangled its various cords. By the time I separated them, Lydia's caller was long gone.

I was pissed. I mean, I'd spent an hour investigating Lydia's living room and kitchen. I naturally wanted to eavesdrop on Lydia's phone friend. The hell with it. I pressed the play button:

"Hello, Lydia," a familiar male voice began. "I—we want to thank you for the wonderful contribution. I'm sure we have things wrapped up, but you never know. My tiresome old colleague George Prescott is holding out on some money, but—" A phlegm-clotted cough. "Oh my! Excuse me. Anyway, I'm sure I can persuade him. See you at the next gathering."

I rewound the tape, listened again.

Then I was sure of the caller's identity.

I was so indignant that I resolved to wait for Lydia to come home. She was really putting one over on me: working on some project with board chairman Alfred Rochinni!

Camping out on Lydia's tiny back porch, I killed time and abused my mouth and nervous system with more coffee and cigarettes. I was trembling by 3:00 p.m. All the caffeine and nicotine, all the deceit and hurt. You just can't trust people any more. No, you're on your own.

By 4:30, time was dragging its ass. My adrenals were dried up and pleaded for me to end the punishing parade of stimulants. But with no TV, I didn't know how to occupy myself. Well, she did have an old black and white in the spare bedroom, but I can't stand black and white. I rifled through the 'fridge, hoping to cadge the stray beer, but no such luck. Only diet soda.

By 6:00, my indignation had spent itself. I was limp and embarrassed. If Lydia returned, I'd be hard-pressed to explain my loitering. What if she yelled at me? I might start crying again. This crying habit, it's awkward. And scary. Maybe I'm really screwed up.

All this worrying...it worried me. I developed anxiety cramps and retreated to the bathroom. Pants bunched around my ankles, I took note of the spotless vanity mirror, feminine pink towels, and tiny flower-shaped soaps.

Sudden pounding on the bathroom door startled me. I grabbed for my pants like a wanker caught in the act. Trouble was, my gut was so big—did I forget to tell you that I ate several peanut butter sandwiches?—that it took several attempts to get buttoned and zipped.

"Are you all right?"

Standing there in the bathroom, the overhead fan roaring and the water running, I studied my reflection. I looked awful. The jowls, the red nose and sinking chin—only my hair, my ever-healthy hair, has retained its youthful sheen.

"James?" Lydia asked, more urgent. "Are you OK?"

"Go ahead," my reflection lip-synched. "How else will you explain why you're still here?"

"James!"

I dampened my mug with a handful of water, then slowly opened the door. "I'm—I really apologize. I—"

"You look terrible."

So was the bathroom odor, judging by Lydia's wrinkling nose.

"I've been ill. I started to leave, and—"

"Why don't you take a shower?"

"As soon as I get home," I promised.

"Take one here."

She went into the kitchen to put away groceries. What a dope I am— I hadn't noticed the half dozen grocery sacks on the kitchen counter. I belatedly insisted on helping her with the chore, but she shooed me away, claiming that it's easier to put groceries away by oneself.

With feigned reluctance, I turned and ascended the thickly carpeted stairs. Yeah, a shower. I was feeling better already.

The hot water and soap were a tonic, and my spirits soared. Scalp full of lather, I even risked hoping that Lydia would pull back the shower curtain. She'd be nude, save for her rubber shower-cap, and she'd remove the slippery soap from my hand, place the hand on her breasts and...of course the image evaporated. Not even Lydia's that forgiving.

I trotted down the stairs feeling much better: no stomach cramps, no fleeting nervousness, no tinges of suspicion. Hell, I told myself, Lydia has a life of her own. If she's working on something with senile Alfred Rochinni, more power to her.

I entered the kitchen in time to hear Alfred Rochinni's recorded message, which Lydia was just getting around to. I tried to look neither interested nor uninterested.

"Alfred's such a funny old man," Lydia remarked. She rewound the answering machine's cassette tape, then sat at the kitchen table. "Here. Have a glass of pop."

I hate diet pop—it tastes like watered down dish-soap. I don't know how chicks can tolerate it. Still, I accepted the fizzing swill and joined her at the table.

"Alfred's all gung-ho about the art gallery expansion. I didn't tell you? He wants to double the size of the college's art gallery. Maybe even triple it."

"No," I answered lightly. "You hadn't, uh, I hadn't heard about that. I didn't know Alfred was cultured."

"He's not," she smiled. "But Mrs. Rochinni fancies herself a patron of the arts. She gives a couple hundred bucks a year to the NEA, you know? Now she wants a bigger and better art gallery, dedicated to Mr. and Mrs. Alfred Rochinni. Anyway, Dr. Boyle told Alfred that I'm a bit of an art enthusiast, so I'm sort of in charge of the expansion. Since I'm the grants director, it makes sense. Sort of. I'll be able to pull in some grant money."

I finished the ghastly pop and listened peaceably to Lydia's chatter. Here's a woman completely without guile. She's happily telling me all about her newest project, blissfully unaware of my pathetic eavesdropping.

"—art faculty are a little upset." She raised an eyebrow. "Do you know Ursula Faddle? She's in the art department."

"The weird jeans?"

"That's her."

Indeed...Ursula, whose clouded face and dilated eyes suggest chronic hallucinations, is a widely celebrated and widely cursed flake. With finger paints—she claims they arouse primal, vital energies—she decorates her frayed jeans with depictions of copulating men. And women. But not men and woman together.

"She wants authority over the expansion."

"Who is *she*?" I haughtily barked. "Can't operate a paint brush."

"Ursula even sent me a note. She demanded equal authority over the expansion."

"Pushy woman," I observed.

"Pushy!" she agreed loudly. Lydia was suddenly edgy: finger-drumming the table, eyes avoiding me. She offered a fake smile and gulped her diet pop. "Would you like another?" she asked, rising quickly.

I quietly declined. She stayed in the kitchen, pretending to busy herself with some mini-cacti on the window sill.

Clearly, my welcome was worn. And who could blame her? "Lydia?"

"Uh huh?"

I began to apologize. It was your standard from the heart apology, with humbly clasped hands and regretful voice. And I was speaking from the heart. My appalling taunts, my invasion of her neighbor's porch, my grating snore on her heretofore untainted couch—and my sudden, unthinking anger when that old prong Rochinni called. What a fool I am. Getting bent about an art gallery.

Lydia was crying.

"What's wrong?" I asked dumbly. The answer, of course, was me.

"You sound like my father."

Jesus.

She haltingly approached me, wiping at her eyes. "My father was a drunk, and he apologized. A lot. Apologies get cheap when they're over-used, you know?"

These heart-rending moments, they're too demanding for a shallow guy like me. I couldn't abide being the focus of Lydia's tangled emotions and weighty, red-eyed gaze. I suddenly realized that she really did care for me. She must. Any other chick would've demanded I drop dead.

Chewing my lower lip, I ached to say something both witty and assuring, a gentle bon mot that would warm and lift Lydia's spirit. But once again words failed me.

"Your drinking, it's not my fault. It's yours."

"Yes," I whispered.

"It's hard for me to say this. Do you understand?"

Not quite.

"I'm a passive person. It's hard for me to assert myself for a, in this kind of situation. Personal situation. A psychiatrist told me that I learned it from my father. I was afraid that if I got angry about my Dad's drinking, he wouldn't love me."

"Of course he would."

"It started when I was eight."

Eight.

"He drank all the time, and somehow I was the cause. My grades were low or my room was a mess. I was too mouthy. Or too quiet."

That's the beauty of a drunk's doublethink. It lets you keep drinking. Lydia's old man was indeed like me: the senseless temper, the self-serving guilt transfer. Of course, I hadn't been such a bastard as to blame Lydia for my drinking. I would never, even in my most self-righteous and vicious moods, blame her for drinking too much. Or would I?

Maybe once I got to know her better.

"What did your mother do about this? Or say?"

"She hid the bottles for a few years. Then she started drinking with him."

Her voice trailed off as a pained memory invaded her features. For several anxious moments, I feared that the dam would bust. But she gathered herself and held my gaze with composure, more or less.

"I'm not going to bore you with the details of my life. That's all history, and everybody's got problems, and—"

"That's okay," I assured her. "And you're right. I do drink too much."

Again seated at the kitchen table—her copper hair back lit by the dawdling sun—Lydia raised a quieting hand. "I just want to say, for my own sake and maybe for yours, that your drinking is a problem."

"I agree, and I know I should drink less." I began to say And I will drink less, but Lydia again raised her hand.

"Hey, I enjoy a drink as much as the next person." She paused to collect her thoughts. When she spoke again, her voice had changed: cooler, detached, resolute: "I like having a drink with you. But I don't drink with drunks. Or speak to them."

I sat motionless, accepting the ultimatum. Lydia's position made perfect sense of course; only a jerk or boozer could argue with her, and I dearly didn't want to disappoint her again.

"I don't know why I drink so much lately. I don't have a big booze history. Neither does my family, really." I related how Mum drank a kiddy cocktail on New Year's Eve, and occasionally sipped a backyard beer when the July temperature hit a sultry ninety. I added that Dad enjoyed a few drinks once in a while, but I tactfully eschewed his knack for getting drunk on a mere two beers.

Perhaps I take after Mum's brothers. They had an alchemist's mystical instinct for the right mix in the right glass at the right time. With the enthusiasm of cracked scientists—Uncle Don even kept typed and cross-referenced notes—they created original cocktails and shared them with my grateful Dad. Poor Dad, he just couldn't keep up. But he was a perfect drunk, affable and harmless. At family get togethers, he'd be snoring happily on the couch by eight o'clock, a hostile word never having crossed his lips.

Lydia had opened yet another pop; I'd been yakking for quite a while. I was in a confessing mood, which unsettled me. It's hard for me to go beyond the emotional barriers that we earthlings habitually and unfortunately erect. I mean, when we reveal ourselves, there's the chance that the other person won't like what's revealed. Yet it felt good and right: I was submitting to friendship's gravity. You know, heart-felt talk with no ulterior motive. I prattled on about Uncle Don and Uncle Dick, about Dad's distant third in drinking ability, about the pleasantly madcap summer weekends at Uncle Dick's lake front house.

Lydia laughed, her first spontaneous laugh of the afternoon. She was beautiful. Beautiful in her own way, not in the overwrought ways of makeup ads, brassiere promos, or glossy pornography. She's certainly not possessed of the body I'm obligated to whistle or grunt at. You know, willowy frame with big high tits and firm high butt. She's got the big tits all right, but her back is broad and her shoulders on the thick side. Big tush, and flatter than I—and probably she—would prefer. Her face is kind of big too, like a growing teenage boy's.

Her brown eyes are generous and quick to twinkle, her mouth small and cheerful.

Her best feature is that terrific hair. This afternoon, her workplace bun was down. The unseasonably humid weather had put in extra curl, too, and her coppery highlights were especially bright. I recalled the first time I spooled her: the curly copper hair, a few damp strands sticking to her neck or my face, her freckles prominent on her cheeks and chest.

This sappy musing upon a chick's hair...am I a romantic?

"Your father sounds very sweet," Lydia offered.

"Yeah, he was."

"—was?"

"He's passed on."

"I'm very sorry."

Yeah, Dad got killed in a car wreck seven years ago. A drunk driver crossed the centerline at eighty miles an hour, and Dad died on the spot. I didn't feel like revealing this fact, and Lydia didn't ask.

The late afternoon lazed into the evening. Our meandering talk was relaxed, nearly effortless. You know those occasional dead spots in conversations that can grow heavy? They weren't heavy at all. They were just silences, pleasant silences, with no anxiety.

Around nine I stood and offered my hand, which Lydia sportingly accepted. She walked me to the door and thanked me for the enjoyable company.

"The pleasure had to be all mine," I said, serious.

"It's nice, isn't it, to just talk and not worry about, oh, if your hair is right or—" She laughed. "Or your makeup is surviving."

"Or if you're keeping your stomach sucked in enough."

"Exactly."

I sucked in my gut, thanked her for her hospitality, and departed.

Chapter Thirteen: To: Steve Luken

Monday began breezily. I arrived at Boyle's suite of offices to learn that the first string meeting had been canceled. Rheena, Boyle's ever grandmotherly and protective secretary, told me that "Donny" was scoping out property for a second campus.

"That's been Donny's dream ever since he arrived," Rheena half-whispered. She fussed with her gold broach, a gift from her Donny. "He's very excited about some property just off the expressway."

"He'll come up with the best site possible," I assured her. I always praised Boyle in Rheena's company. Despite her blue hair and whimsically large bifocals, Rheena struck me as a spy. I imagined her running to Boyle if she overheard the smallest complaint about him. I suspected that Rheena, who always frowned at him, initiated former flunky Malvick's demise.

I wished Rheena a fine week and, with a light step, headed to the cafeteria. With the first string skull session canceled, the day was pretty much free.

Down in the cafeteria, I surveyed the entrees. Like almost everything else in the college, the cafeteria had been refurbished during Boyle's hectic tenure. Once a modest room of drab cement block walls and checkerboard tile floor, the cafeteria now boasted textured olive and cream wallpaper, a pebbled terrazzo floor, and discrete touches of genuine ivory trim. The local press, in fact, had pounced upon the ivory trim,; the use of ivory is, apparently, a heinous and unconscionable act of biological terrorism: you know, victimized elephants, the aggrieved ecosystem, the delicate balance of life, and all that. Boyle wriggled out of the press pinch by indignantly claiming that the ivory was recycled from a long-closed Chicago hotel. The retired hotel manager—thanks to some monetary persuasion—went along with the ruse, but briefly alarmed Boyle by loudly assuring the press that the rhinoceros was his very favorite animal. Fortunately, the codger was a well-known drunk, so his non sequitur was dismissed.

After a coffee and Danish, I meandered back toward my office. Cursing Christ, it's only 9:45 a.m. and I'm fatigued already. Once in my office, I'd bar the door and savor a snooze on the couch.

As I entered the Liberal Arts and Sciences suite, Barbara raised her fat pink hands. "Dr. Deyme, I told him not to dump them all in your office."

Uh?

"—told me not to worry about it. I told him not to, but he—"

I couldn't enter my office. Many, many boxes blocked the doorway: all identical, all ominously heavy looking, all bearing the huge black and red logo of Big Byte Computers.

"—were stacking them when I got here this morning. I knew this was a problem but he wouldn't listen, so—"

Barbara kept babbling. Babbling and loafing are what she does best. She's been bounced from one department to another by scores of infuriated bureaucrats. Her laziness is legendary. Some administrators even concede a grudging respect for her ability to do so little work.

"—could call him back and insist that they be moved out of here. I can barely maneuver around, and—"

"Please, slow down."

She did slow down. To catch her breath. Then she was babbling: "I said your office is where they have to go for now, and, but of course it's very hard for me to maneuver in here—"

I looked toward heaven in a gesture of surrender. I just wasn't up to one of Barbara's ten-minute dialogues, the subject of which is always that she is suffering, she needs an early break, she simply cannot get that report done for another week.

"Drock, he's still a jerk," I said after Barbara exhausted herself.

"Who's he?" Having made clear that she was terribly hampered by the boxes in my doorway, she studied her fire engine red lipstick in her hand mirror.

"You know, our new computer contractor. Some gratitude," I groused. "We save his financial rear and he dumps all these computers in my office. Why didn't shipping and receiving handle it until—"

"They were at shipping and receiving. But as I told you, he wanted them up here. As I explained."

"Drock?" I half-shouted.

"Mr. Derrickson."

"Derrickson?" I leaned over her desk, scowling. "Dwayne Derrickson brought these here?"

"Could you get out of my face?"

"So!" a booming voice accused. "All the whispers of a steamy affair are true."

Goddammit! Steve Luken stood behind me, getting a grand gander at my grand ass.

"Barbara," Luken continued, "I've always known you were a slut, but really! Couldn't you do better than John?"

Barbara cackled. "He was just, he was only—"

"Putting his tongue down your mouth!" Luken roared.

More merriment from Barbara.

I nonchalantly turned to face my tormentor. But nonchalance fails me when I really need it, and I bashed my knee against the corner of Barbara's desk. I crashed.

"Whatsa matter with our fine Associate Vice President now?" Luken mocked. "Somebody hurt themselves?"

"He's so clumsy!" Barbara bawled.

"Even in the sack?"

Barbara, that bag of fat, kept snorting and braying as I sat with my back against her desk and my throbbing knee in my hands. Luken prodded Barbara with more moronic quips, and Barbara dutifully reduced herself to wheezings, guffaws, and snorts.

After Barbara was all laughed out, Luken smirked at me. "On your feet, you overworked executive."

I refused Luken's extended hand and, using the lethal corner of Barbara's desk for support, I—I fell.

"What a loser," Luken laughed.

Oh, how I loathed Luken's cocky smirk and ceaseless insults. I vowed to get even with him. Getting him fired would be ideal but impossible. With his tenure and fifteen years of service, you'd have to catch him in his office playing nude Twister with a half dozen coeds. *Dead* nude coeds.

I finally gained my feet as Luken and Barbara bantered. Not knowing what else to do, I began moving the computers, one by one, away from my door.

"Wish I could help you," Luken said, "but I have class to teach. And hey, Barbara? Your little secret is safe with me."

Barbara gave a final idiotic giggle and waved to the departing Luken. Her offer to help me move the boxes was conspicuous in its absence.

After a half hour of grunting and sweating, I cleared an entrance to my office. There had to be at least fifty boxed computers now strewn about the room. Fifty...I scratched my sweaty scalp. How in the hell had that number been arrived at?

I sloppily pushed away the last boxes and, for rejuvenative purposes, administered several cigarettes, then called Dwayne's office.

"This is John Deyme. I wondered about—"

"The computers, yeah sure!" Dwayne breezed. "Well, the computers really had to be moved. As a business professor with a special interest in computer applications, I can tell that the college's shipping and receiving area—" Dwayne paused for a derisive chuckle.

"—suffice to say that, for the purposes of our discussion, the shipping and receiving area doesn't enjoy sufficient environmental safeguards."

My knee really hurt.

"You can't risk that expensive equipment in that damned drafty room. It's basically a dock with some flimsy walls and a roof that's ready to leak."

"This is my office, not a storage closet!"

"Take it up with Dr. Douglas. He suggested that your office was as good as any until, you know, we find room."

Dwayne, voice deepened by his new-found authority, kindly informed me that Dr. Douglas was keen on creating a new computer lab for the business department. The same department, of course, of which dear Dwayne was now chairman. The new lab would feature space-age pods with adjustable chairs, adjustable desks, stereo headphones, CD ROM drives, sound mixing boards, and next generation video capability. Systems were pretty much go, save for the small matter of space.

"Good thing you called," Dwayne remarked. "Dr. Douglas and I agreed that you should find space for the lab."

"Lovely."

"You'll probably have to convert some classroom space."

"Well that's just dumb. There's barely enough classrooms available now. The faculty will go nuts."

"I can't make that decision," Dwayne reminded me. I imagined his crooked smile as he pushed the dirty work off onto me. Anxiety formed a fat knot in my already unsettled stomach. "You're the chair of the computer committee. All that's holding us up is space. Hey, I hope fifty is enough."

"About that number. Who decided?"

"I did."

I hung up and wondered where in the hell I could scare up the equivalent of four classrooms for computers we didn't need. Oh yeah—! My amigo Steve Luken had an office that might fit the bill. It was at the end of a long hallway of classrooms. Luken's classes always met in those rooms adjacent to his office. Surely, the classroom walls could be quickly knocked down, and necessary power lines and computer network cables laid within a week or three. That clinched it! Here was a chance to lob some grenades back at wonderful Steve: I'd order the immediate conversion of those classrooms, along with his office for good measure. Luken, he'd go ballistic, but that was fine. It dovetailed wonderfully into Boyle's plan for me to become a big assed bull's eye.

Suddenly energetic, I visited the site of the future computer labs. Perfect. Luken would suffer major inconvenience, getting the heave-ho from both his office and classrooms. With any luck, his new office would be a musty closet in the ill-lighted and damp basement.

Luken was professing in a nearby classroom. What was this bullshit? Something about multilevel puns and "extraordinary evocation of alienation" in something called *Ulysses*. Or was it *Hercules*?

I edged closer. The classroom door was open, and I spied on Luken via his reflection in the door's glass. Wow, what a cultivated clothing choice: retrograde Hawaiian shirt and frayed denims that I wouldn't shovel dog shit in. His hair, too, could use a little work; it was both long and shaggy, perfect for a roadside bottle collector. He turned briefly to the chalk board and, like a wild-haired conductor, passionately scribbled more graffiti or Esperanto.

"It's Joyce's Irishness, the uncomfortable and self-conscious Irishness, that makes Joyce's contribution to England and entire Continent all the more interesting. And so—"

All the more interesting? Christ, how can you get excited over Joyce James? If she's so famous, why haven't I heard of her? I'll grant you that somebody like Luken, who has no skills worth peddling in the real world, might get excited about Joyce James. That's the thing. If Luken had any actual ability, he wouldn't be just teaching. At the very least he'd be a flunky like me, carrying Boyle's hatchet and cashing ever bigger paychecks. But not Luken, not him! He's an academic. He *knows* things.

"—an excellent question. What if we approached it from—"

Yeah, he knows things. That's probably why, I loathe to admit, that Lydia actually likes the jerk. Lydia knows stuff too, so it's natural she sees a kindred spirit in Luken. Lydia, she's just too nice. She tries to get along with everybody, even Luken. Even me.

"Let's take it from another perspective. Dr. Deyme?"

The call of my name didn't rouse me. I was deep in the valley of Luken loathing. Plus I was picking my nose. It's just a reflexive thing. Some people scratch their heads, some people drink, some people hum Beethoven's Ninth. Me? I pick my nose.

"Dr. Deyme? Ah, wonderful!" Luken stood in the door way. "Won't you come in?" Then he turned toward his students and encouraged them to welcome me. They applauded.

"Take center stage!" Arms waving, he led me to the lectern then tip-toed to the back, by the door.

The classroom was pretty small, but it seemed cavernous at the moment. As in a ghost or horror movie, the rear wall kept receding, inexplicably receding. The rows of desks stretched into infinity. And those goddamned students, they were laughing.

"Surely there must be some questions for Dr. Deyme?"

I fumbled through an apology for interrupting. I was simply waiting, I explained, for Professor Luken to dismiss his class because I wanted to speak with him: "So again I apologize. Please excuse me." My knees were wobbly, like those accordion elbows on kiddy straws. I began the long walk to the door, enduring stares and snickers. One pimply kid smirked at me, his baseball cap's visor obscuring his eyes. Little jerk! A chick in farm hand duds—blue overalls and plaid flannel shirt—stared at me, her eyes big behind the wire framed glasses.

Then I saw him: my teenage soul mate who occupies a parallel universe twenty years younger than my own. A chubby kid was sitting in the far corner. God, he looked bored. Probably thinking about a pizza. He yawned and rubbed his watery eyes. Then, for good measure, he picked his nose.

Now in the hallway, I faced Luken. He was no longer grinning and no longer sarcastic. Blunt anger had wiped all that away. "You want to speak to me, you see me after class. You moron." He turned on the squeaking heel of his tennis shoes, re-entered his classroom, and silently closed the door.

I stood there for a few minutes, reeling from it all: Luken's cruel grin as he invited questions, the students' laughs, and most of all that nap-prone dope, that Deyme dead ringer in the far corner. I felt a bittersweet solidarity with the kid. Like I had, he most probably was struggling through the simplest courses. He certainly looked flummoxed sitting here in Luken's class. And I thoroughly sympathized: all of Luken's highfalutin nonsense, all that exhausting triple-talk.

Like a big brother, I wanted to tell the kid not to worry. I'd say, "The world really holds a place for people like you, people who aren't bright or super-skilled. If you don't mind butt kissing and knife twisting, you'll maybe be okay."

And that's what it's all about, isn't it? Finding our way?

My fighting spirit was sapped, but I had to press on. So rather than tell Luken to his face that he was about to lose his office and four classrooms, I chose the administrator's more traditional medium: the memo, composed in impersonal and matter-of-fact bureaucratic syntax.

To: Steve Luken

From: Dr. James Deyme, Associate Vice President of Liberal Arts and Sciences

Re: Business Computer Laboratory

As you are a member of the college's computer committee, I am taking this opportunity to relate to you recent developments of interest. The business department is currently in the midst of developing a state of the art computer laboratory. To best facilitate this important and necessary project, the following classrooms will be converted to laboratory space: 4156, 4157, 4158, and 4159. Additionally, office 4155 will be implemented in the conversion. You might begin removing your books and materials immediately. Until we can locate new office space, you might keep your books and materials in packing boxes available in shipping and receiving.

Feel free to contact my secretary if I can be of further assistance.

Chapter Fourteen: A Male Perspective

For the next few days, I threw anxious glances over my shoulder. I imagined Luken storming into my office, firing insults and left hooks. But nothing happened. His silence unnerved me. Bastard! He was probably deep in revenge schemes.

Friday rolled around and, with the fifty Big Byte computers finally moved out of my office to who knows where, I decided to grab my paycheck and head out early—or, earlier. Boyle was off campus yet again, and I had no meetings scheduled. But halfway down the hallway, I saw Lydia approaching. I hadn't talked to her all week, and I suddenly felt terribly awkward.

I mean, where in hell did I stand with her? What was my status? Once and future suitor? Rejected sack mate turned unwanted "friend"? Cause for embarrassment? Hands clasped behind my back, I greeted her with a bland smile.

"Why aren't you swearing?"

Uh?

She waved a crumpled sheet of paper in my face. "After what he said about you."

"Who?"

She led me to her office and shut the door.

"You never know about people until you give them some power," she declared. She was agitated, aggressive. She ordered me to take a seat. Then she too sat, all business, behind her well-ordered desk.

"I thought he was sort of a wimp," she said.

"Again I ask: Who?"

"Dwayne Derrickson wrote a memo to the faculty." She thrust the now nearly mutilated sheet of paper at me.

"Dr. Deyme's counter-productive solutions," I read aloud, "are yet another example of why our union must remain vigilant."

"He's calling you a grade A idiot," she harrumphed. "And that makes us all look bad."

She said something more about the need for administrators to cease the back-stabbing and commence the team-building, but I was distracted by the spectacle of my name being gleefully ridiculed in print.

"An honest mistake is one thing; consistent and high-priced nonsense of the James Deyme brand is quite another, and we faculty must recognize that such incompetence works constantly and insidiously against our professional interests."

"Well?" Lydia demanded.

Well what? I thought. I couldn't take this personally. It was merely part of the First String strategy to secure little Dwayne the faculty presidency.

"His choice for the new computer lab reveals an appalling misunderstanding of both space allocation and computer applications."

What could I do? Dwayne was pitching and I was catching. From here on in, I was the carnival clown who sits in the polka dot wet-suit and goes ker-plunk in the water tank.

"As the business department chair and a member of the computer committee, I will soon with Dr. Boyle to resolve the situation. Be assured that I will share with Dr. Boyle my concerns about Dr. Deyme. In the meantime, I recommend that all faculty be extraordinarily wary in dealing with Dr. Deyme in any recommendations he makes regarding computer hardware, software, or utilization."

I fished a cigarette from my shirt pocket and, in a silent plea, held it before Lydia.

"Go ahead," she sighed.

I smoked in silence, avoiding her stern gaze and looking at the paintings in her office. More Monets, along with Renoirs. Even as I gazed at the soothing paintings, I felt Lydia's agitation. She was breathing loudly, snorting really, in a way that was both martial and erotic. When I rose to extinguish the cigarette's smoldering butt, she asked me what I was going to do.

"Cash my check."

"About the memo."

"Dwayne's just campaigning."

"But that statement about dealing with Boyle." She sadly shook her head at me.

"Big deal." But I understood her point. "Be assured that I will share with Dr. Boyle my concerns about Dr. Deyme." That little comment was the most cutting of all. In effect, Dwayne was saying, "Vote for me because I'm kicking Deyme's ass."

"He's treating you like you're nothing."

"That's my role."

Confusion clouded Lydia's face. I lighted another cigarette and, with my pride gone south, explained it all to her. Just as George Bush once needed Willie Horton, Dwayne Derrickson now needed me. By delivering a swift and dismissive kick to my rear, then promising to speak directly with Boyle, Dwayne was locking in the union presidency. By contrast, Sheryl Farella—Dwayne's opponent—looked like a loud-mouthed malcontent who couldn't get the time of day from Boyle, not to mention a private meeting.

"I'm appalled," Lydia finally said.

"I'm Dwayne's punching bag."

"It's wrong."

"I don't care."

And I didn't. With a swami's stoicism, I saw that money doesn't mix well with life's other necessities. Money is oil to dignity's water. If I stood expressionless beneath the various and sundry shit storms here at West Central, I would prosper. Sure, I'd be a horse's ass in the eyes of many. But so what? In such eyes, I'm already a horse's ass. At least I'll be very well compensated. Really, it's a terrific deal with no down side in sight.

Lydia was heavily silent. I couldn't tell if she felt sympathy or disdain for me. And I wasn't in the mood to find out. I rose and again mentioned that I was going to cash my check.

"Now don't go out and get potted."

What is it with people? I didn't want her hard-nosed advice. I wanted breezy encouragement to wallow in a long lunch and several guilt-free cocktails.

Regretting her blunt tone, she gently asked that I sit back down. I did.

"I was wondering if you might help me with something relating to the art gallery expansion."

I grunted, emitting twin-rails of cigarette smoke. "I'm not exactly cultured."

"I need a man's perspective," she claimed. "You know, I enjoyed our talk last weekend about the art gallery. I'd like your insights."

"Male nature," I mockingly professed, "demands promiscuity and alcohol. It is not in our nature to have, to, to be burdened by the romantic rose-colored glasses donned by the fairer sex. Pleasure makes life bearable, as that famous philosopher and First Brother Billy Carter said. Billy knew that life is short yet often filled with abject misery."

"What would the male viewpoint say about—"

I raised a silencing finger, not ready to step out of character. "Therefore, the male animal—and I do mean 'animal' in something more than the metaphoric sense—requests that the fairer sex get off our backs. And onto your backs."

"You're really good at that."

"I overheard Luken yapping the other day. He's got that hustle down cold." Actually, it was plenty of fun, playing the academic stuffed shirt. You are free—no, you are encouraged—to profess all kinds of bullshit, yet you sound profound if you throw in multi-syllabic tongue twisters and kept your nose arrogantly upturned.

"All right, Mr. Male Viewpoint." Lydia stepped around the desk and placed one of her over-sized art books on my lap. "Take a look."

Hmm. *The Erotic and Eroticized in Popular American Culture.* The cover featured a potently over-weight woman in leather underwear. Her leer wasn't inviting. "Artsy dirty pictures?"

Lydia nodded. "The college might purchase some of them for the new gallery's permanent collection." She gestured toward the book. "Help me out with your opinions, OK?"

I opened the book to a grainy black and white photograph of two chicks with limbs and tongues intertwined.

"What do you think?"

This was really quite awkward. To fully enjoy dirty pictures, I need privacy.

"C'mon, Mr. Male Viewpoint," Lydia prodded. "What's your gut reaction?"

I asked Lydia if she really wanted to bear witness to my gut reactions. She assured me she did, so I let her have it. "I'm grossed out because—"

"Because they're lesbians?"

"Don't interrupt. No, chicks together is good. But these women. Look. Their tits are small and their faces are just average. God, look at this one. She looks like a night-shift janitor. Her hair is stringy."

"So sex needs to be clean?"

"No, but it should smell good."

"Look at another."

Much better. A sultry blonde with deep-dish jugs reclined on a bed, her long fingers burrowing between her lithesome thighs.

"You'd fuck her?"

"Christ, Lydia."

"Would you?"

"Sure."

"How?"

"With my dick."

"No, I mean would you, would you fuck her hard, or gently? With you on top, or her maybe on her tummy?"

"Any way she'd let me."

Lydia had pulled a chair beside mine and sat inches from my heated face. I wondered—could this all be a ruse for her to get me in the sack? I doubted it. Lydia could get laid by me or plenty of other guys without the art gallery pretext.

"Look at another."

A big-boned Latina stood proudly before the camera. Her wet jet black hair was combed straight back, as if she'd just screwed and showered. She was understandably self-absorbed as she scrutinized her hefty hooters, one of each snug in her hands.

"That's a good one?"

As if she couldn't tell...my breathing had become embarrassingly hormonal, and my, my—

"Do you have an erection?"

Christ!

"You *do* have an erection," she confirmed. "Let me write down the page number."

It went on like this for another half hour, me gaping or smirking or grunting as Lydia asked questions and took notes. Some of the photos were standard glossy porno fare: young women with expensive make-overs, expensive tits, expensive air-brushing. Others were for narrow specialty markets: diesel lesbian couplings; lusty overweight broads manhandling frightened underweight men; some "narratives" of soaped and scented bum boys snapping towels at one another in the YMCA shower, followed by a spirited talcum powder fight. Oh and get this. A clumsy "political" shot of a chunky naked housewife rubbing against the handle of a vacuum sweeper; and—brace yourself—a harrowing photo of a naked elderly couple. Ughhh...

I recoiled from the semi-solid pile of thin hair and age spots. No wonder old rich guys dump their old wives for fresh young tits. I mean, to think you're wasting your last years gagging as your wrinkled wife ferrets out your shrinking prong. It's awfully depressing, don't you think? Well isn't it?

"Just one more," Lydia assured, her voice a little thick. She must have been getting a little worked up. All the bare-assed men.

I wrinkled my nose. A jowly, ruddy-faced fatso with a crooked blonde rug was on his hands and knees, ready to ride the bony, pony-tailed teenager beneath him. The guy's prong was alarming. But what the hell. When you've got an enormous gut, a footlong is probably necessary.

I slammed shut the book.

"You didn't like that last one?"

"That girl. What was she, fifteen? Where was her teddy bear?"

"I guess you didn't like it."

"What's the point of all this?"

"Like I said, I needed a male viewpoint." She returned to her desk, probably suspecting that I was hormonally overworked and ready to grab her. She was right. But could she be surprised? I mean, when a woman asks you to look at dozens of dirty pictures—and invites candid commentary—well, you can't help but imagine the sordid consequences.

"Why *my* male viewpoint?"

"We've slept together." She shrugged cheerily. "I figured you'd be honest."

I announced that I wanted to sleep with her again.

She dismissed my announcement with a friendly roll of the eyes.

Yeah, well I tried.

"I'm planning a special display of erotic art in the expanded gallery," Lydia explained. "It will use contrasting images—you know, standard images juxtaposed against sort of shocking stuff—to highlight how we've cheapened eroticism by putting it everywhere. Kind of like erotic inflation, if you know what I mean."

"Oh."

She was off and soaring, and I silently endured it all, doing my best not to frown and yawn. My worst suspicions were confirmed: Lydia wanted me as a friend, and only a friend. Therefore, I had little chance of getting her in the sack again.

Except...why can't we fuck our friends? I mean, imagine that I'm just friends with a chick. We gossip on the phone, exchange cheerful insults and solemn secrets, occasionally split a six pack and watch a movie. Then she lets me fuck her. Why not? We're friends.

But it never works. You just can't fuck your friends. Friendship can't endure sex's overwrought and conflicted emotions. Genuine friendship is too pure, too unscheming. Except if you're queer. Queers, as far as I can tell, fuck their friends all the time. It's actually a pretty good set up, don't you think?

Lydia continued to profess, and I continued to feign interest. She seemed as jargon-mad as Luken. Or Jo Ann Staulen! Neo expressionism tied to post-modern sexual attitudes? The ravisher fears the ravished, just as the psyche fears the Other?

"I shouldn't be keeping you like this." Ah, finally: actual English.

"It's interesting," I lied.

"Really?"

"Uh huh."

"Wonderful! Listen, why don't you come over—say 7:00? I have some more pictures to show you and maybe you can field some of my ideas."

"Sounds good." No it didn't, but who knows? I hoped there was still hope. I missed Lydia's innovative bed technique, her Jekyll and Hyde metamorphosis from responsible professional to slap and tickle pro.

Maybe Lydia would spool me tonight because...why? I have no idea. I can't figure women out. Nobody can, including women. Just when it makes no sense at all, they are touching you. They're on their back, gently raising their tushes as you crudely pull off the delicate panties. And they even kiss you with their mouths open, an achingly intimate act that requires far more affection than simple screwing. It must be that mysterious feminine sensitivity. You know, those gender-exclusive X-ray glasses that allow women to discern decency in anybody. Even in me.

Chapter Fifteen: Alfred Rochinni, Arts Patron

Those dirty pictures gave me a hormone buzz and lusty appetite. At Rossetti's, I ate with aggression, even perversion, like a sex freak or an evangelical Republican. Those daytime talk show shrinks say food can substitute for sex, so there you go. My pizza did look awfully sultry, what with its thick crust and heaps of Italian sausage.

I drove home with nude chicks flickering in the adult drive-in of my imagination. Man, I'd like to get laid...but in this dump? I've got to find a more upscale address. On my salary, this is beyond slumming.

Mrs. Kwang, peasant-like in a flowered, faded dress, was on her hands and knees weeding her vegetable garden in the back yard.

"You're home early today," she called, spade in gloved hand. "That's nice to have an early day."

"It's terrific," I agreed.

Mrs. Kwang, she'd pull weeds until dusk, pausing only for the hot green tea that she sips between the rows of ripening tomatoes and sprawling Swiss chard. And Mr. Kwang, he'd been busting his bony butt at his restaurant. Sometimes I notice him coming home at nine or ten in the evening, paint or plaster on his yellowed tee-shirt. Sometimes Kim is with him—on those nights they seem happy, chattering at eighty miles an hour. They seem so thrilled to work so hard. Immigrants, how do they do it? How do they work so goddamned hard? I'm relieved that my parents shouldered the immigrant obligation. Though Mum and Dad could navigate in American English pretty well, it still had to be hard. Imagine Kwang...coming over here not understanding a word, except maybe "money" or "work" or "opportunity." Me? I just wouldn't be up to it.

On my way to Lydia's, I paused at the Miles of Aisles Discount store to buy cologne. The choices were numerous: Slam Dunk, Booty, R.P.M., Hostile Takeover. Unfamiliar names, all. I'm stuck with a pretty unimaginative nose, so I buy whatever cologne is cheapest. But tonight, I needed every advantage just in the off chance that Lydia harbored amorous plans. I selected a tester bottle of Conquest and lightly sprayed my neck. Huh...smelled like, like...what? Like a mash of cherry tree bark and jockstrap sweat. And they charge twenty seven bucks for the stuff, even here! How about this stuff called Nude? Not much better: you'd get the same effect by spilling $3.00 champagne on your shirt. Impatient, I selected still another tester. This stuff was dubbed Missile. It was tolerable, your standard cool bracing scent. By now, the purchase of any cologne was an olfactoric redundancy. I hustled out of the store, leaving behind an odoriferous wake and enjoying a surge of optimism. Maybe Lydia would find me to be—well, I'd find out soon enough.

So I was all the more pissed by my pig-headed car. The damn thing wouldn't start! I turned the key several times and viciously stomped the accelerator. Soon enough, the battery was exhausted, the engine was flooded, and the pungent smell of petrol joined the scent riot in my car. I was reduced to back-fisting the dashboard.

Goddammit!

After slapping around the car a little longer, I got out and popped the hood. I figured I at least had to try. Manhood demanded it. But I didn't know what to look for. A melee of wires, little black boxes, hoses, the oil-caked valve covers. I'm ignorant about a lot of things, including cars. It again dawned on me that ignorance has practical and maddening consequences. I was about to slam shut the hood and call a garage when a pickup parked beside me.

A crag-faced guy with a black cowboy hat stepped out of the truck and approached.

"Car trouble, eh?" he inquired, toothpick in the corner of his mouth.

"Sure enough."

He shouldered past me and squinted at the engine for five seconds. "Well shit. Your posts'r croaded."

"What?"

"Your posts. They're corroded." He pointed at the battery. Crusty white crud suffocated one of the battery's posts.

"The battery, it can't charge with that shit on it," he instructed. "Got something to clean that off?" he asked.

"I—I'm afraid I don't."

He regarded me with sour amusement, then returned to his truck for a rag.

I felt suddenly effeminate in my professionally pressed white cotton shirt, black slacks, and bolero tie. As the cowpoke returned with a dirty red rag and two gallon gas can, his nostrils flared. Yeah, you guessed it. He'd caught wind of my riotous cologne mishmash.

He gruffly directed me to remove the battery cables, which I did with plenty of fumbling and apologetic grins. Then he wiped the terminals with the gas-soaked rag.

"Put them back on?" I said, my voice disgracefully high. "The cables?"

He nodded. When I'd finished—it seemed to take an hour under his stern gaze—he produced jumper cables.

"Here. Put the red cable on the positive post."

He instantly interrupted my work. "No, the red cable goes on that post. The red."

Christ, even I knew that, but the cowpoke was on a roll and not about to spare me humiliating supervision. I retreated to the driver's seat and turned the key. The car fired immediately. I was about to get out of the car to help him remove the cables, but he waved me off. "Don't get your hands dirty," he joked.

Jump-roping Jesus! I wasn't going to take this abuse.

I followed him to his truck and offered him money.

"Not necessary," he grunted.

"No, really," I insisted. "I owe you for your trouble." I pulled out my wallet and opened it so the cowpoke could see the thicket of fifties and hundreds.

He looked at the bills, then at me, then back at the money. He'd never seen such an amount in a wallet. Well maybe in the movies. But not in his wallet.

I casually pulled out a fifty.

He haltingly accepted the bill. "You really shouldn't."

"No, I really should. A tow truck would've cost at least forty just to jump me, and it'd taken longer."

"True," he admitted, looking at the fifty resting in his hand.

For good measure, I pulled out a very worn and limp ten—the thing's rag content was negligible—and placed it atop the fifty, and got into the Slug.

"You really know what you're doing," I called. "You should get a blue shirt with a name patch on the chest."

He stared at me, uncomprehending.

"You're welcome for the tip, boy," I laughed.

What a pick-me-up! That cowpoke no longer judged me an overweight pansy with too much cologne. No, he now understood I was his superior, and he was my flunky. For the first time in a long time, I enjoyed a long and spontaneous laugh. Granted, it wasn't a laugh born of innocent mirth and the wide-eyed joy of being alive. It was my Power Laugh, a laugh that erupts when I rub an inferior's nose in his own shit.

Oh? You don't approve? Then you're a hypocrite. If you had the money, you'd do it to. Yes you would.

I rapped quietly on Lydia's front door. No answer. I rapped not so quietly and heard her melodious call to please wait just a moment. I once more reviewed my strategy: I had to seem happy to see her, but not too happy. And I had to be reserved, but not too reserved. And I had to be— this was the hard one—I had to at least seem interested in her fine arts babble, her high culture kitsch.

"James! Please come in." She led me into her living room as I explained my vexing car problems.

"See, it was a broken fibulator, so I had to fix it in the parking lot and, and—"

"So good of you to join us," he said.

"Thank you. I'm glad to, pleased to see you." I glanced at Lydia. "Both of you."

"Lydia tells me you've been of enormous help to her with the art expansion project," Alfred Rochinni said. "I'm really pleased you're interested. Art is, it's opened up a whole new avenue of living for me." Alarmingly at home on Lydia's couch, Alfred Rochinni urged me to enjoy a glass of white wine.

Lydia, her hand discretely at my elbow, steered me to a chair then returned to her warm spot beside the Board Chairman.

"Alfred was just giving me some very good news," Lydia beamed.

Alfred cleared his oft-clotted throat and, with the first word, violently coughed. What with his drooping socks and disheveled hair, he looked a little drunk. Or maybe a lot drunk. Old guys just can't hold their liquor, especially when they're drinking with big-breasted women half their age.

Lydia patted Alfred's shoulder and, cooing like an ever-cheery nurse, asked if he was all right.

Christ, were his dentures slipping? That's nasty.

"Why don't you tell Mr. Nickel the good news?" he croaked.

"My pleasure. Well James, one of Alfred's long-time colleagues at Thunder Oil has decided to step in with a substantial amount of funding. Mr. George Prescott—"

"Old Prescott owes me plenty of goddamned favors," Rochinni loudly assured.

"Mr. Prescott said he would match the state's contribution. All in all, we could be looking at upwards of $350,000."

"What incredible good fortune," I offered, my eyebrows raised with fake enthusiasm.

"I just called in a few favors," Rochinni boasted. "It was an easy pitch."

"Well you did start off in sales," Lydia observed, "so you must still have those powers of persuasion."

"I was in sales when sales was, when it was sales. When things *sold*, dammit!"

"That's right—uh, dammit!" Lydia said worshipfully.

I rolled my eyes at her. She ignored me and attended to Rochinni. Her straight-faced adoration was masterful. She treated his bleats and brays with utter seriousness, often facing me to nod meaningfully. And I had to nod too, since Rochinni's demeanor demanded that I was absorbed by his ramblings of the good old days at Thunder Oil.

Goddammit, it was boring listening to his tales of the roaring 1950's and '60's, when Thunder Oil stock was better than gold. The oil shocks of the '70's were another matter. Rochinni didn't even talk about them; Bruce says that Rochinni had been severely demoted during those dark days. But not George Prescott. Like his classmate high school classmate Rochinni, Prescott started out as a sales hack and climbed the career rungs. Unlike Rochinni, he kept climbing and enjoyed steady bonuses, company cars, company condos, company chicks. Rochinni's despised Prescott ever since.

Rochinni's corporate free fall rendered him instantly neurotic, and he was seized by the desire to gain a seat on the college's Board. The power-starved jerk sunk ten times as much cash into the dinky race as anyone else, and he's been on ever since. He'd probably die if he couldn't make somebody kiss his ass.

"Your business experience," Lydia gushed, "has really helped West Central through the 'eighties and into the 'nineties."

"That's my greatest satisfaction, really. Education is our way out of those, the woods. The college has had some very difficult times. You remember that strike back in 1996!"

I'd not been at West Central during the strike, but I'd heard enough about the debacle. The strike lasted ten weeks and drew state-wide attention. Fortunately, it broke the back of the union rank and file. Unfortunately, it inflamed faculty zealots such as Luken, Pouris, and Farella, and their rage hasn't yet subsided.

"I really didn't savor those days," Rochinni lied. "The faculty just didn't understand the Board's dire financial situation. We simply had to fire all of them. I hired them back, of course, when they'd gained their senses. Hell, everybody but the troublemakers were grateful to get their jobs back with that fifteen percent pay cut."

"Do you know Jim Pouris or Sheryl Farella?" I ventured.

Lydia loudly cleared her throat.

"No."

"They're running for offices in the faculty union. They're quite the radicals."

"Oh them." Rochinni's laugh turned into a belch, which made him laugh even harder. At his age, even the basest body function is cause for joy. "Don told me about them. They're jokes. Besides, isn't there a more reasonable candidate running for president?"

"Dwayne Derrickson," I said. "I suppose he'll win, but still. Pouris and Farella are really disruptive to the, the educational process."

Lydia interrupted us with a chilled bottle of Chardonnay. Naturally, she poured Rochinni the first glass, leaning over to let him glimpse her cleavage.

"You're really marvelous," he told Lydia's tits.

"Without question!" I beamed humorlessly.

"Congratulations on your recent reelection, Alfred," Lydia said loudly.

"Yes," I said more loudly. "A job well done."

"It was nothing, really." Rochinni shrugged. "The campaign wasn't that rigorous."

No kidding. The old dick ran unopposed, thanks to me and my flair for deal-cutting. Yeah, me: a mid-level bureaucrat so obscure that Rochinni didn't know my name.

"That guy, that glorified computer salesman—"

"Patrick Drock?" I asked.

"That's him. Imagine a Republican thinking he could win a seat from me!"

"Listen, gentleman," Lydia interrupted. "Could I get your opinion on something?"

"Absolutely," Rochinni said. "I am at your service tonight. You know, may I say something?"

I wanted to bellow NO!

"As the Chairman of the Board, I want to say that I'm proud of the administrative team at West Central. It's people like you Lydia, that—and of course, you too, Nickel."

Don't mention it, fossil.

"That makes the difference. And now, I am at your command."

"Thank you for the good word," Lydia smiled, "and thank you for your interest in this project. Now, I have some artwork that I'd like you to examine. I'd like a male perspective on this."

Oh peeping Jesus. She placed *The Erotic and the Eroticized* on Rochinni's lap. What, was she trying to murder the geezer with a heart attack? With notebook and pencil, Lydia sat beside Rochinni and waited for his male perspective to arise.

After flipping through a few pages, Rochinni settled on a black and white shot. The pic was pretty tame: you know, the coy topless stuff that Hugh Heffner scandalized Middle America with in the 1950's. "She's beautiful," Rochinni finally said.

"How about the next one?'

He sucked at his dentures for a few minutes, then said, "She's beautiful."

It went on like this for twenty minutes, the monotony interrupted only by Rochinni's wistful groans and whinnies. Eventually he came across a blunt dyke shot that featured various sex toys: a vibrator, strings of pearls, a two-headed dildo. The ugly one—there's always an ugly one in the diesel setups—looked alarmed or anxious, her face turned half-away. Her eyes, though, spoke volumes about desire.

Rochinni coughed, then wiped at his nose. Hah, I thought, Lydia finally went overboard. The old guy's about to barf.

"I'm so moved," he finally said, voice husky with libido and phlegm. "What a lovely couple." Hand trembling, he managed to finish his glass of wine.

Lydia promptly served a refill.

"It's marvelous, isn't it?" he rasped. "Sex. Copulation. And women, they're so marvelous, aren't they?"

"So you like this one?"

"That's what makes it so sad."

"It's sad?"

"I shouldn't be saying this but—but my wife. She, she's repulsed by it. She won't let me touch her."

Lydia retired her pad and pencil and suggested that we take a break.

"Last month I accidentally touched her breasts. She kept slapping me."

Lydia's face was frozen, her eyes wide and unblinking.

"My marriage isn't, it's sexless, Lydia. Of course, you see why I can't be blamed for a few indiscretions from time to time. But it's been a damned long time since I've enjoyed those indiscretions." Rochinni's voice was little more than a whisper. "I guess that means my wife is correct about—" He shook his head, blinking back tears.

Nervous, Lydia stood and asked if we were ready to eat.

He stood and took a few pathetic steps, arms reaching toward his hostess.

"Mr. Rochinni!" Lydia haltingly put her arms around the lurching buzzard. She looked to me for help, but I laughed silently and pointed at him.

"She says I'm gross," Rochinni wheezed into her dress.

And he was. White and woolly eyebrows hooded his mean, smallish black eyes. And his mouth was just a lipless, crooked gash.

"You're not gross," Lydia assured while glaring at me.

He is gross, I mouthed at her.

"She swears I am," Rochinni blubbered.

Lydia eased him onto the couch. He almost fell off, and Lydia had to shove him back to a more secure repose. Then, tugging anxiously at her blouse, she led me to the entrance for a private exchange. Perhaps some light-hearted humor at the Chairman's expense?

"And you said I shouldn't drink," I snickered.

"Get out."

I held up my hands, nonplused.

She slapped my face.

"Goddammit!"

"Ssh!"

"He's asleep."

Yeah, Rochinni was asleep—or comatose. What a wreck: a yellow-white lock hanging over his crimped eyelids, his once-crisp shirt spotted with wine, and *The Erotic and the Eroticized* on his lap.

"You kept mocking me! And it's just not—" Lydia paused to gather her thoughts. "Jesus Christ! I invited you over here to, to help my standing just a bit. John Deyme, Boyle's new boy, spending an evening with the chairman and me. Goddammit John, Alfred might introduce me to Prescott himself."

"Will you do the peak-a-boo blouse routine with him too?

"It's called 'networking'. Isn't that the game all you men play?"

"Sure!" I pointed at Rochinni. "He didn't even know my name or what I did for him."

"He knows who you are. So he got drunk. Sorry."

"What, he can't even thank me? He can't even—"

"You once promised to help me," she abruptly reminded me, her eyes icy.

"—Yeah."

"Since you can't fuck me, you can't help me. Is that your ethic?"

Nah, it's just me being sour, I guess. I mean—okay. Yeah. It *is* my ethic. It's everybody else's too.

Chapter Sixteen: Best One for What?

I woke around 8:30 feeling pretty damned good. I'd accepted the fact that Lydia loathed me, and I took it in stride. At least Lydia confessed that Rochinni knew who I was. Damn straight. I saved his bacon from a bruising board election battle and kept the college's patronage treadmill rolling.

Yeah, a cigarette would go down very nicely. I torched one and sat, Buddha fashion, in the recliner.

A sudden banging on the front door startled me, and I dropped the cigarette onto my foot. They hurt, don't they? Cigarette burns? Swearing and hopping, I violently opened the door to face down the early morning intruder. Probably that kid who keeps trying to sell me a goddamned subscription to the Daily Trumpet. "Get dressed. Now."

Don Boyle stood on my creaking porch. Purring at the curbside was his stately black limo. "So you're not going to invite me in?" He glanced at his Rolex, reminding me that he was a man with little time to waste.

"Please come in," I blurted, wishing he would wait outside. Even by my lax bachelor slob standards, the duplex was a mess. Except for the kitchen, of course. The kitchen was freshly scrubbed and mopped and irradiated.

Boyle stepped in cautiously, as if a virulent virus awaited him. "You really need to move out of here." He disdainfully surveyed my quarters: the sour bed sheets on the couch, the pile of clothes in one corner, the dirty glasses and crumb-flecked plates stacked beside the TV.

"I've been looking at properties lately," I assured, oafishly stepping into my pants.

"Where?"

"Here in town."

He frowned.

"More upscale properties," I quickly added.

"Make it a lot more upscale."

"I'm ready," I announced, stuffing my wrinkled shirttail into my ever-tighter pants. I'd fallen from the diet wagon and vowed to cut back on those three-for-two cheese burger deals at Burger Stud.

"You're probably wondering where we're going."

I was of course wondering, but I hadn't dared to ask. See, the old Boyle persona—high octane, low patience—was back in force. Boyle detests questions. Or rather, he pretends to detest them. In fact, questions give him the prized opportunity to berate and belittle, to snort and stomp. Boyle treats questions as a boxer treats a weak jab. He instantly counter punches furiously, cornering you, pummeling you for daring to ask *such a goddamned stupid question!*

"It's funny what you just said about looking at some property," Boyle said. "Because that's what we're doing."

Once I settled into the limo, Dr. Douglas—weekend-casual in a blue wind breaker, cotton pants, and loafers—handed me a Bloody Mary.

"Rochinni called me this morning," Boyle smirked. "Claims he couldn't come along because he's got domestic problems."

"What hotel has he moved into this time?" Douglas laughed.

Boyle faced me. "The owner of the property knows Rochinni and—"

"Property for the proposed second campus," Douglas clarified.

"—and we're talking with him today. This could be perfect."

"Here are the details," Douglas told me. "Pay close attention."

It took me a little while to catch on. I was confounded by Douglas's talk of Net Operating Loss deductions ("They're called NOL's, John."), wholly-owned subsidiaries, governmental quasi-privatization, and unconventional investment strategies. But I tried awfully hard to pay attention, even postponing my second Bloody Mary. And then Douglas mentioned the property owner's name.

"Prescott? Of Thunder Oil?" I asked.

"How did you—"

"He's the guy who's helping with the art gallery."

"Exactly," Douglas nodded. "We could really be looking at an excellent relationship with him."

Boyle laughed viciously. "Rochinni is really jealous of Prescott, so he couldn't resist playing the big shot and, contact his, his—" Boyle puffed out his chest. "My old colleague at Thunder Oil," Boyle harrumphed, imitating Prescott's phlegmy baritone. "He and I, we go way back. We've seen it all together."

"What a pain in the ass ol' Alfred's been all these years," Douglas smiled.

"And with any luck, we don't need ol' Alfred anymore," Boyle remarked, more to himself than to us.

Douglas explained that George Prescott's land was ideally situated five minutes from the expressway, and it boasted plenty of land for long term expansion. The catch, however, was that a low-income housing complex occupied the site. Seems that George Prescott had bought the property from a state agency via a short lived and poorly planned government program to put low-income housing in the hands of local communities. The rationale was that state bureaucracies were too big, too inefficient, too stupid. The solution: quasi-privatization. Well, sly George Prescott—blinding the state with his dazzling business reputation and coveted political contributions—bullied and charmed the state into letting him buy the property. Why? Because, George claimed, he wanted to "give something back to the community."

In fact, George intended to raze the complex, then turn the surrounding seventy five acres into a high-priced condo and townhouse development. The development offered George prestige, profit, and a kaleidoscope of multi-year tax write offs. The scam would probably have worked had cruel fate not interceded: the state's Housing Secretary, a long time Prescott ally, died in the professional embrace of a hooker. The now-dead secretary's reputation was ruined. And with that wrecked reputation went Prescott's protection.

Even worse, a "reform" bureaucrat replaced the deceased secretary. Several local pols and real estate power brokers joined the fray. Eyes filled with crocodile tears, they told the new Secretary all about Prescott's nepotism and abuse. In actuality, the pols' motives were less altruistic: they simply didn't want displaced low-income riffraff to invade their precious neighborhoods. Prescott, of course, thumbed his nose at them and proceeded with plans. But the pols turned up the heat, brandishing all kinds of legal billy clubs: re-zoning, class action suits, fraud. Rather than risk a protracted and expensive legal row, Prescott caved in. He'd been licking his wounds ever since.

"That was six or seven years ago," Douglas observed. "Some of the locals opposed to Prescott died off or latched onto some other bullshit. Prescott's tried to develop the surrounding land, but no bank will touch it."

"Nobody wants to build a three hundred thousand dollar house next to welfare recipients," Boyle dryly noted.

"We're rolling the dice," Douglas said. "Try to follow me on this, James."

"I'm trying."

"Clown time is over, James," Boyle emphasized. "If this works out right, I'm going to make a lot of money. You'll have a cut if all goes well and you keep your end of the bargain."

What bargain?

"Well?" Douglas asked.

"What?"

"Will you keep your end of the bargain?"

"What is the, uh, type of bargain we're discussing?"

"Don't back out now," said Boyle solemnly. "You assured me you were a team player."

"You've got a lot to gain," Douglas reminded me.

"You've got a lot to lose," Boyle reminded me.

"Can we be more specific—?"

"Hey there it is." Boyle rapped on the passenger window. "Our second campus."

The driver turned onto a short gravel service road, then eased to a stop.

At first glance, the potential site of West Central's second campus wasn't inspiring. As we walked toward the apartment complex, I noted that most of the site was untended prairie. Plenty of weeds, plenty of prairie grasses, plenty of discarded junk food wrappings, Styrofoam cups, and broken beer bottles. An abandoned length of sidewalk was the only sign that this land had once been earmarked for high profile, big bucks development.

"Prescott wants to get the hell out from under this and get back to his condos in the Bahamas. This deal could be perfect for all of us."

"There's only one little catch," Douglas said.

"What?" I asked.

Boyle ignored my question. "Look at that roof—it's shot. The county inspectors have been on Prescott's back about code violations. But you can't blame him for putting off repairs."

We were soon on the edge of the complex's back yard. The yard was more yellow than green, and it was marred by a big patch of oily mud. In the middle of the yard was an empty sandbox and rusting swing set. All but one swing was missing. A half dozen kids danced to the accompaniment of a boom box.

"What a mess," Boyle observed. He pointed out the broken windows, splitting and absent soffits, and vibrant graffiti. "These kids don't have a family, not really. They'd be better off just out of here."

"Better off," Douglas murmured.

"If my father were alive to see this—" Boyle clasped his hands behind his back and recalled that America was built on hard work, horse sense, and education. "Americans still work hard, sure," he remarked. "But the nation has lost its horse sense. What will revitalize America?" Boyle asked rhetorically, looking toward the horizon.

"Education," Douglas answered. "There'll be a second campus here, and we'll be heroes."

"What is that, uh, the catch you mentioned?"

"Look over there, James." Douglas pointed to the farthest end of the field. A cluster of palsied trees was surrounded by remarkably ugly scrub brush. "That'll be the physical science lab."

"What about that one catch?" I persisted.

"Let's just hope we can persuade the state about the dental lab funding. And the CAD labs."

Boyle had turned and was walking across the field, followed by faithful Douglas. I stood watching Boyle: his hands were still clasped behind his back, and schemes orbited his head. Evidently, a fly was in the ointment of this land deal, and I was the greasy cloth that would dab away the fly. I just wished they would come out and tell me.

The autumn breeze kicked up, chilling my thinly clothed arms and legs. Greasy wrinkled fast food wrappers blew across the field like tumbleweeds. I felt a vague but abiding link with that garbage blowing across the blighted field.

By now Boyle and Douglas were near the car. I shooed away my musings and trotted to catch up. Boyle heard my heavy tromps and turned toward me with a half-smile or half-smirk. I joked about being short of breath after such a modest trot. Douglas confided that he too was out of shape; he suggested that we get together in the gym to run a few easy laps.

"Prescott will be really pleased," Douglas said to Boyle, though his gaze was on me.

George Prescott's face was tanned and pleasantly rugged. His eyes were a merry blue, just as you'd expect of a guy who owned three dozen condos in the Bahamas. His unlighted cigar seemed a fixture, like a luxury sedan's chrome ornament. His suit was appropriately top tab: dark blue, understated, wrinkle free.

As we took our places in the back of the restaurant, Prescott motioned for a waitress to bring additional menus. Boyle, however, impatiently waved her off and asked only for three coffees.

Prescott looked at me for an awkwardly long moment, then turned to Boyle.

"He's the best one?" Prescott asked.

"Certainly," Boyle assured.

Best one for what? Jesus, it's really aggravating being a flunky. The superiors talk about you, not to you, much less with you.

Prescott extended his hand. "You'll please pardon me. I'm not usually so rude. My name is George Prescott."

I shook his hand, doing my best to squeeze manfully, and crisply gave him my name, rank, and serial number.

"Has Don shared the details of our project? It's really very interesting." Prescott explained melodically that the proposed campus was a wonderful boon for both he and West Central College. "For several years, I mused I'd never rid myself of the property. And what a shame. It's prime real estate, but that low-income housing—vexing. Really vexing." He looked with long-simmering frustration at the ceiling. "At one time, I anticipated a minimum of three or four million dollars off the development."

Best one for what?

Boyle grinned as Prescott narrated the tale of the potential dollars lost as his land sat undeveloped. Prescott talked with winning bemusement of politicians, zoning boards, state bureaucrats, and even his spendthrift wife. "God knows I love Mrs. Prescott. But she has no head for money. Our BMW, the one I drove here today? She purchased it for $65,000 cash. That's at least eight grand too much, in my experience."

Boy, could Prescott talk. And talk. I'd finished a fourth cup of tepid coffee and made two subsequent strolls to the can before Boyle could utter more than a sentence without interruption. "Then I bumped into Alfred Rochinni at the grocery store, of all places. I made a remark about this land albatross 'round my neck, and the next week he calls me to talk over the land for your second campus." Prescott beamed at me. "Stupid Alfred wanted to negotiate the deal himself, complete with a broker's fee. I laughed out loud, hung up, and called your college President directly."

"And my offer remains the same," Boyle interjected. "$500,000. That's it."

Prescott offered a small, rehearsed laugh. "That's an absurdly low figure, especially given your cash flow potential. Donald. You'll have impressive seed money for your political ambitions after your contractors make their contributions."

"My contractors?" Boyle snapped. "You mean your contractors!"

Prescott raised his finger to correct Boyle. "My wife owns only half of the company."

"Who owns the other half?" Douglas cheerily prodded.

Prescott looked at me with mock guilt. "They've caught me, I'm afraid. My son-in-law owns the other half. He needs work, so he's starting with the art gallery expansion. Why not keep the money in the family?" he asked melodically.

As Boyle and Prescott traded cheerful barbs, my attention wandered to the usual subjects: Could I fuck Lydia again? Could I afford that hip townhouse on the shore of Lake Michigan? Why can't I lose weight? Could I fuck Lydia again? Did I run out of beer at home?

"—soil pipe is, John?"

Is that soft-porn movie on cable tonight? At the grocery store, I read that almost everything on that one skin starlet is refurbished. Even her feet.

"Do you know what a soil pipe is, John?" Boyle persisted.

Oh! I'm being spoken to.

"Oil pan?"

"Soil pipe," Boyle said slowly. "Starts with an 'S'."

Prescott laughed easily. "Don't be so impatient, Doctor Boyle. We've bored our friend, I fear, with all our talking."

Yeah, I knew what it was. "It's that heavy plumbing that hooks up to your sewer system."

"This is where you enter the plans," Douglas informed me. "Pay close attention."

I paid close attention. And I learned why I was the best one: Because I had a lot to gain. And lose.

Chapter Seventeen: Unsentimental Truth

I try not to delude myself. Take my appearance. I admit that I'm looking pretty overweight.

All right. I'm virtually fat. And if I put on another seven and one quarter pounds, I'll have to drop "virtually" from the previous sentence.

And take my personal life. I admit it. Lydia...I really blew that one, didn't I? No surprise, really. My marriage was an abject failure too, but then again marriages are supposed to fail. It's de rigueur, these days, for one's sacred state of matrimony to profanely flame out.

At least my career has prospered. I phoned Mum the other day and remarked that I'd be making seventy five K by next year. She burst into proud tears. Mum does that when she's pleased: she cries.

And when Mum finished crying, she told me how proud of me she was, and how Dad always knew that I'd make it. "That's why we came here," she told me for the ten thousandth time of my life. "For our child."

"Well it's really paid off," I agreed.

"And what do you do for that money?" she gushed.

"Leadership, Mum. Academic and professional leadership. Meetings, committees, working lunches, working drinks. The President, he sure keeps me busy."

"You should get a new car!"

"I'm looking at a new place to live, too. I found a nice townhouse."

"Such money that must cost."

"I'll have plenty of money after my next raise."

"You're in the professional class," Mum swooned.

"Uh huh. I can sabotage public housing with the best of them."

No, I didn't tell her that. I just continued yammering about my sparkling career.

John Deyme: real estate terrorist.

At one point—don't laugh!—I harbored tender daydreams about becoming President or Provost or at least Vice Usher of the new campus. Boyle had nothing so important in mind. He simply wanted me to pour ruinous amounts of acidic, industrial grade pipe cleaner down some selected plumbing at Garrison Apartments.

"It's an amazingly powerful substance," Prescott had whispered at the restaurant. His blue eyes twinkled with reverence for the miracles of industrial chemistry. "We use it in the oil fields to help blow out clogged pipes."

"It's easy, John," Douglas assured. "It's in crystal form. Pour it down the drain pipes in the laundry rooms of both buildings. Follow it up with a gallon of hot water."

Prescott breezily narrated the story of a Thunder Oil employee who'd stolen some of the stuff to invigorate his septic bed. While pouring the crystals down the toilet, a whiff of the stuff scorched his nostrils. Then the porcelain on the toilet cracked, and the bowl cleaved.

"His septic ruptured in three hours. He was walking around in the back yard with a towel to his bleeding nose and wondering why his back yard had to turned into a shit swamp." Prescott leaned back and enjoyed a full-throated laugh.

"Be careful with this stuff," Boyle urged. Even the Prez was uncomfortable with Prescott's cheerful narration of disaster.

"But it turned out all right," Prescott added.

"The guy's OK?"

"He's dead. Hepatitis. You know, from his soppy septic field. The ooze soaked through his shoes and—"

"My coffee's cold," Boyle complained to the passing waitress.

"—infected him. No, the guy stole it so we had no liability. The widow's suit was thrown out of court."

"Jesus Christ."

"Nobody will get hurt," Douglas whispered. "The county inspectors will be there on Monday morning, just a few hours after you. Everything's arranged."

"I still have some allies in the Health Department," Prescott purred. "When they see that the sewer lines are beyond repair—" His gaze wafted from me to his personal horizon of profit and pleasure; in his blue eyes, I saw private Bahaman beaches, a new beach house, and barely bikinied babes with deep dish tits and sag-free rears.

"You're just providing the last straw," Douglas gently insisted. "The sewer lines are already in bad shape."

I remembered that big muddy patch in the apartment's back yard: it was a failing septic field. No wonder hepatitis is making a comeback.

"The Public Health officials will have no choice but to declare the units unfit," Boyle said. He flashed his Victory smile: big, polished, remorseless. "And West Central will be there, check book in hand."

"At long last," Prescott said dreamily, "I shall be free."

Boyle dropped me at my duplex around one. Nearly hysterical, I cranked through a half pack of cigarettes, wheezing and hacking the whole way. Dammit, those low-tar, low-arsenic Third World cigarettes are terrible. Probably one hundred percent artificial ingredients. Hungry for authentic nicotine, I bolted out of the duplex—waving hastily at Kim, who was vacuuming her father's car—and sped to the convenience store to practice my unique form of stress management.

To conquer anxiety, you must bury your nervous system under

several inches of fast food, beer, and smokes. When you do it right, your gut bulges with so much high-calorie junk—burritos, cupcakes, beef jerky and beer—that you can barely breathe. All this activity has a soporific effect. Sure, you're nearly comatose. But you're not nervous. You want only to sleep.

And sleep I did, until five in the afternoon. The initial shock of my bush league Mission Impossible task had faded. In fact, I felt like a new man: ten pounds heavier but galvanized by quiet confidence. Hell, I could pull this thing off! And my income would finally be in the upper stratosphere of flunkydom. Feeling my oats, I had a quick shower, chatted with Mum, then ventured out for a few drinks.

I settled on Stadia, a drinkery locally famous for its high prices and big-haired waitresses. The crowd was okay, I guess. No hazardous riffraff or ungracefully aging bikers. Mostly upper middle-class boors: loudmouth lawyers, braying accountants, managerial blowhards.

The bar itself was terrific, abundantly stocked with bottles sporting exotic labels and romantic ports of call. Many rich unblended whiskeys and glimmering vodkas, plus a bustling caravan of cheerful liqueurs. The bar's rear wall was basically one long mirror, so you could drink and eyeball the babes and ogres that came sashaying and hiccupping into the place.

I held up a crisply folded twenty. The strapping Greek barmaid, hemmed up in a starched white blouse and red vest, promptly delivered my third carafe of white wine. This stuff, it's not cheap. I mean, I should be getting drunk. See, I'd doggedly stuck to my White Wine Only pledge, the pledge I made for Lydia. Sure, I'd blown it with her, but I resolved to keep my pledge, if only for myself. Already, my memory of Lydia was distant, even unreal. I'd idealized her image—her butt was smaller and higher, for instance—the way you idealize chicks you can't have again.

But now, sitting here in Stadia, my vow was pointless. What the hell. I'm an adult. I'm not stuck with some nagging mate cum parole officer who keeps an unsmiling count of my intake.

"Bring me something different," I asked the barkeep.

"What would you like?"

"Surprise me."

She returned with a thick mocha colored concoction that smelled like herbs or high priced hair conditioner.

The stuff was on the fruity side, but after two quick swigs I fell victim to its Old World charms. The warm mud of alcoholic stupor oozed over my limbs, and I grew befuddled by the details of lighting my cigarettes and keeping the toilet bowl in the cross hairs of my urine stream.

The bar was filling with Saturday night's hustlers, dimwits, loudmouths, and weak sisters. A cross-eyed divorcee sat beside me. I figured she was interested in me. My suspicions were confirmed when she asked for a light, so I asked her what she was drinking. She insisted that she wanted only a light. But her coy act didn't trick me, not even when she retreated to a booth. I started to follow her but tripped on my shoelace. Thankfully, nobody noticed except the dozen or so patrons just in my immediate vicinity.

I returned to my barstool and nonchalantly ordered a drink to replace the one that had inexplicably crashed to the floor.

"Easy does it," a quiet voice advised.

I waved away the voice, interested only in the barmaid's boobs, which were becoming, well, so well defined and invigorating and beautiful under her vest.

"Your mother's annoyed here," the barmaid said.

"You're drunk," I accused. "My mother doesn't even live in this state."

"Your money's no good here," she repeated.

Now the quiet voice offered a steadying hand. The hand was connected to a pudgy face and balding pate. "My turn to buy," beamed Bruce Herrig.

"Bruce ol' pal!" Man, it was good to see him. "Thanks for the drinks. Sit down, buddy."

"I'm over at a booth with a date."

I whirled around with show-stopping panache and fell from my stool. "Women!" I barked as Bruce pulled me to my feet. "You brought one for me, I hope?"

"C'mon, she's waiting."

I plunged into the crowd, following the back of Bruce's sport coat. But I got lost and found myself in the clutches of a seasoned party chick with a dozen shades of blonde. Her offended date grabbed my lapels and suggested we discuss matters in the parking lot.

"Parking lot's all right by me!"

The oaf's nostrils flared.

"I like being the man!"

The party chick was laughing or gagging, and Bruce dragged me through the crowd to safety.

"You're an idiot," Bruce scolded good-naturedly.

"I'm your superior, buddy," I scolded not so good-naturedly.

Bruce guided me into the booth, then sat opposite me with his date.

"John Deyme," Bruce announced, "I'd like you to meet Jo Ann Staulen, Dean of Academic Diversity. Jo Ann, this is Dr. Deyme."

Jo Ann Staulen extended her tiny pale hand.

Bruce? Dating Jo Ann Staulen, crusading critic of every patriarchal pig in the Western Hemisphere? Poor Bruce must be desperate. I mean, he was one step from going queer. But given my luck with Lydia, so am I. What the hell—maybe Bruce and I will trip the light fantastic.

"We've not met in an informal context," Jo Ann observed. "Not surprising. West Central's social structures are still defined by a hierarchy of masculine power relations."

"Jo Ann's been having a, a really interesting time at West Central," Bruce said.

"Not really." Mirthless Jo Ann reflexively tugged at the collar of her mirthless white blouse, as if my company made her uneasy.

"Hey, how about a carafe of red?" I suggested.

Jo Ann was silent, which gave Bruce permission to agree.

For the next half hour, Jo Ann analyzed West Central's ills. West Central, it turned out, was painfully phallocentric, unabashedly patriarchal, naively logocentric, and shamefully apolitical.

"But we are political," I objected. "That big greenhouse, the one you spoke in a while ago. Boyle wheeled and dealed the Republicans to get that built!"

"That's gutter politics, the marginal that so distracts those who lack the enlightenment of theory. I'm assessing the truly Political. The episteme."

"Huh?"

"The ideological, John. The political assumptions by which the power relations are played out yet hemmed in. Certainly, you'd agree that the phallocentric structure of power relations has, materially, made moot the ideal of democratizing West Central's discursive practices." She paused for a long pull on the wine. After her taxing oration, she'd certainly earned a respite. As she lingered over the drink, she looked back and forth from me to Bruce. Her face momentarily softened and had a delicacy at odds with her grim personality.

Jo Ann's rhetorical pyrotechnics dumbfounded Bruce, and he asked about a certain word.

"Discursive?" Jo Ann queried, glass still poised at her mouth. "Phallocentric?"

"—No."

"Logocentric? Episteme?"

"Episteme," Bruce repeated. He turned to me. "Isn't that a good word?"

"Let me look in my thesaurus first," I sighed. Christ, Jo Ann wore me out. She just keeps coming at you, her mouth never stopping. Huh...maybe she was a real marathon performer, sack-wise.

"That really disgusts me," Jo Ann proclaimed, again dour. She glared at me, then at Bruce, who obediently bowed his head.

"Christ, I'm sorry if I don't what episteme means," I laughed. "I'm just here for a drink."

But Jo Ann was not disgusted by my ignorance. At least, not at the moment. Rather, she'd aimed her professional indignation toward customers at an adjacent table. Two women barely out of their teens preened and giggled as two hopeful studs performed their pick-up pitch. One guy, attired in a thread-bare designer tee shirt, recalled his latest fist fight. He illustrated his narrative with gestures: a left jab to the nose, a right cross to the chin, a sneer as he passed a palm across his extravagantly greased hair. His buddy nodded excitedly and loudly vouched for the narrative's veracity. The scene was pretty charming, and I recalled—or maybe just imagined—the thrill of a young woman marveling at my sharp wit, hip clothes, flat belly.

"It makes me absolutely sick," Jo Ann snorted.

"It's called flirting," I explained.

"It's rape. Violation."

"Another drink?" Bruce asked sportingly.

"Fill mine up," I told Bruce. "And hers." I pointed at Jo Ann's glass.

"I don't need any," she protested, hand covering the glass.

"Yes you do. You need to lighten up."

"The rapist speaks."

"C'mon. Take it easy, you two," Bruce whined.

"You *two*?" I snorted. "I'm not making indictments!"

"All men are rapists, if not in practice then in theory—"

"You're a cartoon," I sneered.

We went at it for a few more minutes, the argument growing awkwardly loud. This small woman, drab black hair pulled into a drab bun, had a snotty attitude that I especially despise. You may call me stupid and shallow, you may dub me greedy and gullible. At least I'm not a snob. Maybe it's my parents' immigrant history: you know, English society's systemic snubs and relentless reminders that you'll never measure up. And snobbery was what little Jo Ann was all about: she was forever pointing out the failings of everyone. Everyone but her; she, predictably, was without fault.

In the middle of an endless sentence, she shot a condescending smirk at the adjacent table. The males had approached the bar for more pitchers, so the chicks were inspecting their faces with compact mirrors. I momentarily blocked out Jo Ann's ranting to admire one of the women: a hormonally blessed blonde, her big tits showcased in a black tee. The blonde tresses on the black shoulders made for compelling contrast. She glanced at our table, and I waved cheerily.

Flunky

"—just submitting to degradation, to subjugation," Jo Ann was rattling.

"You were born in the wrong century," I laughed.

"—valuable only to the extent they can be dominated by men, by fashion, by rape ritual."

"The Puritans would have let you toss the first torch on the stake. And by the way," I advised. "Get a perm and makeover. You'll feel a lot better."

"Pathetic! The old saw that feminists are bitter ugly women!"

"You're sick!" I insisted. "You don't see pretty girls on a date, laughing and gossiping and getting horny."

"Subjugation!"

"You hate flesh."

"Rapists love flesh."

"You hate beauty."

"What beauty?" she blinked.

"Them." I gestured toward the chicks, who were clucking excitedly as their dates returned with pitchers of beer. "They're gorgeous. And you hate it."

I turned my heavy furrowed brow to Herrig. "So, Bruce. When are you taking Jo Ann home to meet the parents?"

Poor Bruce, he didn't like this scene. As Jo Ann and I had bickered, Bruce had anxiously smiled and fiddled with his thinning hair.

"The nuclear family!" Jo Ann blustered. "Capitalist subsidized rape."

The carafe was empty, so I grabbed Jo Ann's glass, drained it in one gulp, and thanked her and Bruce for the wonderful time. Pie-eyed Christ. The bar was packed with big boobs, short skirts, happy drinkers, soaring hormones.

"Glad to see you're back," the barmaid smiled.

"Really?"

"Sure I am." She gave me a free drink.

"How about a free drink for me?" Bruce Herrig settled in beside me.

"Where's little Mary Sunshine?"

"She called me a rapist."

"You told her to fuck herself, right?"

"No. She called me a rapist and walked out."

I ordered a double scotch for Bruce. We sat silently for a while, alone with our drinks and thoughts. The bar's festive racket made for a rather poignant backdrop to Bruce's love life ineptitude. He looked like a kicked dog, wet-nosed and sad-eyed.

"When we got here," Bruce finally said, "I was in a good mood."

I ordered Bruce another double, then clinked my glass against his.

"Here's to a better mood."

The booze loosened Bruce's tongue considerably. And by now, of course, my tongue was beyond loose. We hadn't talked for a few weeks, so we caught up on campus politics, bitched about the jackass faculty, and hoped for big raises.

Abruptly, he told me that he was sorry about Lydia. "You two were the hot gossip for a few weeks," he said wistfully. Emboldened by the booze, Bruce confessed that he'd always wanted to spool Lydia.

"Go for it," I declared cavalierly.

"Just like you to, to—" He belched loudly, even painfully, like a gaseous water buffalo. Man, he was potted. His mouth was open, a slight trail of liquor or saliva glistening on his chin, and he stared with unabashed fascination at our barmaid.

"What, fuck off then. You want Lydia?" I asked rhetorically. "You can have her now."

"You're just pissed that she's fucking the old geezer. Goddammit I spilled my drink."

"What geezer?"

"I just bought these pants."

I grabbed Bruce's arm. I was poised to demand he tell me who Lydia was fucking. Then, in an act of psychological self-defense, I told myself that I'd simply misunderstood Bruce. He's drunk, I'm drunk. If I remained calm on my comfy barstool, the awful news would evaporate. Lydia, it would transpire, was fucking nobody.

"You're just pissed she's fucking Rochinni." With an indignant yank, he freed his arm from my grip.

"Liar." I raised my hand as if to strike him.

"Don't spill the, don't kill the messenger."

His claim was absurd, yet somehow it had the hurtful ring of truth. Lydia Fairview, arts supporter, and Alfred Rochinni, henpecked big shot. Obviously, Lydia had certainly not filled her lonely hours by knitting afghans and completing cross word puzzles.

"Well I'm not completely sure, but it's the rumor, and he does call her a lot at work, so I just thought that—"

"Would you just drop it?"

Bruce muttered something more, but I didn't hear him. Learning that an ex is fucking somebody else, it's always dreadfully painful. Really, you should be sober for the bad news. Then you can go out and get drunk. But to be drunk when the news hits...you can't escape.

I flattened a twenty onto the damp bar for the barmaid. With stinging eyes and addled gait, I shouldered past the plunging necklines, sport jackets and perms. From the corner of my eye, I saw Bruce pick up the twenty and order another drink.

Lydia and that enfeebled relic...? No way. Bruce must be trying to get back at me, what with my career dwarfing his.

Lydia and...? Fuck. I'll just go ahead and call her. I spent a couple bucks in change on wrong numbers—right, it's six oh four followed by a nine, not an eight!—before getting it right.

"Lydia, it's John. Listen, I'm juss down here with Bruce and the, that woman. That woman who's his date, and we were thinking—"

Lydia remarked that I sounded awfully drunk. Not wanting to be pushed around, I informed her that my drink was my business.

She hung up.

It took me several tries to get her to pick up again, but finally I managed to invite her to join Bruce and me at Stadia. She declined, then cursorily asked what I'd been up to.

"This and that," I fumbled. "You know. The regular." Stuff like vandalizing property. No, I certainly couldn't get into that. Not that I didn't want to. When your heart teems with ache and your blood teems with alcohol, you want to confess everything.

She gave me some polite chat about her art gallery business, deftly parrying my inquiries into her private life. When I demanded more details, she hung up.

I stared hurtfully at the receiver.

"What'd you expect?" a fellow reveler demanded. "You was talking, telling her she can't fuck the old guy and all."

"I said that?"

"Yeah. Now lemme call my wife."

I stumbled across the street to the brimming parking lot. A couple frisky kids were standing beside their car, blowing a joint and bellowing to the fiercely amplified "songs" of Six Jamming Dicks or Foam or whatever metal band was momentarily popular. Christ, don't kids listen to jazz? Ever? Hell, Sonny Rollins and Art Pepper could play loud, if loud is what kids want...Where was my car? After a couple false starts and swearing fits, I leaned against it and rested. O hobbling Jesus...better take a leak before the drive home. I stumbled to the Slug's rear and relieved myself on its rear tire.

"You fuck!"

A muscle-faced youth suddenly stood beside me. Behind him, a scandalized young woman—hey, the hot blonde in the black tee!—covered her gaping mouth with both hands.

"You're a pervert!" muscle face yelled at me, blue eyes bright and hard in a pair of passing headlights.

"Fuck off, it's my car."

"It's my car!"

And so it was. This Slug was a two door. A red two door.

"He's the creep who was staring at me!" accused the blonde.

"Christ I'm sorry." I sloppily zipped up.

The aspiring stud—this sinewy tough guy who was about to take home the blonde for the pasting of her life—he wouldn't accept my apologies. In fact, the stud could imagine no more erotic foreplay than punching me out.

So he punched me out. With a triumphant war cry, he shoved the cheering blonde into the car and drove away, leaving me with a snout full of exhaust.

Sitting in my car—yeah, I finally found the damn thing—at three in the morning, I was a sight to make eyes sore. Purple nose, red eyes, yellow teeth. But my reflection in the rear view mirror galvanized me with the simple and unsentimental truth, which supposedly shall set us free. So what if I'm everybody's choice as horse's ass and nobody's choice as sack mate? And so what if, in the next twenty-four hours, I'd earn my keep by depriving women and children of their homes? These were the cards I'd been dealt. There was no other game in town at the moment, so I'd play my hand without complaint.

Chapter Eighteen: A Wing In My Name

Around 2:30 on Sunday morning, I parked next to a rusting, boat sized Buick on the far south end of Garrison apartments. Feeling ridiculous in denim overalls and work gloves, I stepped out of the car and surveyed the parking lot. Nobody in sight. Douglas had assured me that Sunday nights at Garrison apartments were quiet. Garrison's working poor—mostly women with rug rats—were in bed early, bracing for the demoralization of another low pay work week. And Garrison's career socialites, whose lifestyles left little time for employment or family, were out searching for more exciting nightlife.

I placed the four one-gallon plastic jugs of acidic crystals onto a dolly. The crumbling and crab-grassed sidewalk led me to a battered steel door. My key, supplied by Douglas, fit with frictionless ease into the lock. The building's interior was what I'd expected: institutional fluorescent lighting, a drab green tile floor, and scuffed walls sporting the occasional hole or stain.

The laundry room was at the far end of the corridor. The six ancient washing machines were a sentence to move: I had to drag them a few feet from the wall to get at the cast iron drain pipe. With muted swearing, I freed one of the washing machines' drain hose from the drain pipe. Then I dropped my plastic funnel into the pipe and opened the first jug.

Stalled by a momentary failure of nerve, I stared at the jug. Was this episode for real? A part of me—the Chicken Little part—feared that once these crystals went down the proverbial drain, the sky would fall. On me.

Beyond the din of my immediate fears, I heard Boyle: "You have a lot to gain," he was quietly noting. "And lose."

Gain? Lose? Who knows? But if I chickened out, I'd lose for sure.

Sod it.

I double-checked my safety glasses, plastic face shield, and canvas gloves, then gingerly poured the crystals down the pipe. The crystals were caustic, all right. They smelled like radioactive lye, and my eyes watered despite the facial protection. At one point, I readjusted my squatting stance, and a few crystals fell upon my exposed wrist. Then, as luck would have it, a few of the crystals got lodged between my wristwatch and sweating skin. It burned. By the time I yanked off the watch—breaking the wristband in the process—my wrist had several simmering red marks. I pulled up my gloves and resumed pouring, all the while expecting to come mask to face with a frightened, pistol toting tenant.

Working just on the productive edge of panic, I got two gallons down the drain and administered the hot water chaser. Within thirty seconds, blistering fumes rose from pipe, and I labored to force the suddenly recalcitrant hose back on. My eyes stung and my nose ran as I belly-bumped the washers back against the wall. An ominous fizzing now joined the fumes, and I hustled down the hallway and out the door to the shelter of my Slug. I half-expected the goddamned sewer system to explode, showering me with white-hot sewer shit.

After a few anxious minutes, I had a cigarette for medicinal purposes. Then another.

Huh...no explosions. No yelling. Everything would be all right.

A giddy determination took hold. This was actually pretty fun. You know, it's satisfying to just not give a damn, to trespass and wreak havoc. Sure, it's unethical and illegal. But so what? The movers and shakers aren't slowed a step by the hurdles of "ethics." They just run roughshod and keep attorneys on retainer.

Douglas, in fact, had reminded me of this earlier in the evening when he called to deliver a last minute pep talk. He spoke of Donald Segretti. The name rang a vague bell and I would've asked for clarification, but Douglas talked so fast.

"This is just another kind of rat fucking," Douglas insisted when I voiced half-hearted reservations. "Realpolitik. Hardball. James, somebody's going to get that land when the apartments are condemned. Why shouldn't it be a college? Our college?"

"These people are, they're losing their homes."

"They'll get better places now," he snapped.

"Yeah sure."

"They will! The state'll pick up the tab. What, that place is wonderful?"

"—No."

"That place is a goner anyway. When that septic system finally fails—it's archaic, it would cost way too much to repair. This way, everybody profits."

"—Yeah."

"The building is going to be condemned. Period!"

"But I'm the guy with my neck out."

"Period! If you don't do it, somebody else will, and they'll enjoy the profits. You don't want that, do you?"

"Not really."

"You can't stand on the sidelines with your thumb up your ass. Boyle is staking the future of the new campus on this. On you."

"Maybe Boyle'd name a wing of the new campus after me," I joked.

"You've got it."

"Huh?"

"Your own wing."

My own wing, indeed. Mum would be ecstatic.

I quickly made my way to the second building, hidden in the shadows of the moonless night. Things went quickly. I was really proud. I've never been handy with wrenches and hoses and widgets, but I sprinted through the job with ballsy precision.

Back at my car, I stepped out of my overalls, then removed my goggles and gloves. The heavy-duty janitor duds were Douglas's idea. Pretty clever, really.

Douglas says he got the idea from the JFK thing; seems the shooters wore uniforms. When I asked what kind, he stated that he was not at liberty to say.

Christ I was excited! I'd gotten through this job with surprising swiftness. I'd arrived at 2:30, and it was now—what?

My watch was gone.

I patted at my pockets, then searched the car. Then I remembered: I'd removed it earlier, when the crystals burned my wrist. My Chicken Little voices clucked and squawked. Here I was sitting in my car, marvelling at the effortless brio of my rat fucking technique—and I'd left behind my watch.

No way around it. I had to retrieve that watch for two reasons: first, it was a gift from Mum. Second, it just happened to bear my first name in ornate, engraved script: To dearest James, from Mum. Such indiscretions are the stuff of criminal charges or Boyle vengeance, neither of which my career would survive. I again put on my disguise and went in.

Halfway down the hall, I knew there was trouble. Two women—one young, one old, both hysterical—stood before the laundry room jabbering at a thousand miles a minute. I hid in a janitor's closet and listened. Seems that one of the women had left some clothes in a washer. Upon opening the washer, she got a nose full of chemical fire and brimstone and an eyeful of disintegrating clothes. Some crystals had backed right up the pipe into a washing machine.

If these two women saw me lurking about, they'd high tail it to the nearest phone and punch 911. Just last week, a tenant had lost her purse and front teeth to a thug, so anxiety was high.

The older woman trudged down the hallway past me. If she'd decided to search the janitor's closet for some rags or a bucket...well, I'd pull my overalls over my face and bolt screaming from the closet. With any luck, she'd faint.

But she kept going, leaving the younger woman by herself. With no other options, I waited. And waited. My feet and legs were sore, my nerves overextended. The woman was just standing there, smoking and muttering. Finally she opened the laundry room door. I heard some cursing—really energetic, considering the hour—then banging and stomping. She emerged with a laundry basket of ruined clothes. As she passed my foxhole, I got a glimpse of her. She'd been crying.

Her ruined clothing was probably pretty new and cost her more than she could afford. And everybody needs luxuries once in a while, especially those without luxuries. This woman had lost more than a blouse or skirt; she'd lost the pleasure of owning something for its own sake.

After another two minutes, I padded down the hallway to the laundry room. I almost heaved. The air was electric with chemical snap and crackle. Down on my hands and knees, I immediately saw the tell-tale gold glimmer of my watch beneath a washing machine. I grabbed a wire hanger, straightened it, and began poking at the watch. Given my smudged safety glasses and the poor air quality, my aim was lousy. Several times, I thought I had it, but I just couldn't snag the damn thing. Finally, with my lungs boiling, I did a line backer number on the washing machine, banging into it repeatedly until I'd pushed it a few feet to the left. This time, I hooked the watch, reeled it in, and ran out of the room—

Whoa!—I collided with a skinny guy in baggy jeans and white undershirt. Behind him stood the red-eyed woman who'd passed with her tattered clothing in tow.

"County health department," I boomed, voice vibrato through the mask. "This laundry facility is, is, is, it's completely not up to our code."

"What the fuck!" they shouted in unison.

"Should've gotten here sooner," I blustered, "and I would've if the supervisor had kept me on the first shift. Who's the manager here?"

"She asleep," the woman said, voice hard and skeptical. "So I brought down Billy to look."

Now, I'm not especially quick on my feet, but I do understand the value of volume and confusion. That is, if you can boom and bark well enough, you buy yourself just enough time to escape.

"So you're the proxy manager?" I rasped at the skinny guy.

"No. Like Tonya said, the manager's asleep." An anxious smile played across his face; he was almost certain that I was bullshitting. Almost. He folded his arms cockily across his wrinkled undershirt and began shifting his weight from foot to foot, as if expecting a brawl.

"Let's not stand here," I said. "Let's wake her up and get her down here."

"We not going to wake her up," Tonya argued. "If you from the health department or whatever, then you take care of it yourself."

I took another two or three steps until I was in a passage made dark by poor lighting. I turned to the couple and explained with convincing weariness that county policy requires a complex manager be informed of damages before a private contractor could be hired to submit an estimate for repairs.

"Typical of this motherfuckin' place," Tonya complained. "None of this shit ever get fixed."

Billy held up a silencing hand. "Why are you here? At this hour?"

"I told you."

"No you didn't."

"I'm callin' the police," Tonya told Billy. She disappeared around the corner.

Billy pulled something from his pocket. Maybe it was a freshly oiled handgun. Maybe a knife with shark-like serrated teeth. Maybe a cupcake.

"What's the problem here?" I barked.

"You can answer that. You might be the motherfucker who robbed Martha Robinson last week."

"I'm James. Mr. James, and here. I'll show you my I.D."

"So what? Don't mean you can't be a robbin' scum besides a county worker."

Tonya returned, jabbering that the pay phone around the corner was broken.

The guy shook his head and instructed her to use her apartment phone.

"I've got a phone in my car," I said. "Use mine."

"I think this motherfucker robbed Martha last week," Billy announced.

"It wasn't a white guy," Tonya said.

"The fuckin' papers always say it's a black," Billy complained, his voice growing higher. "It's that conspiracy that I was telling you about!"

"You're trippin'!"

"It is!"

"You're crazy."

"Come with me," I insisted. "You can call the police from my car phone." I stepped forward, still talking. "Or my supervisor. Call the police then my supervisor."

Now I could see what Billy had taken from his pocket: a palm sized leather sap. What a nice touch. You can smash skulls in near silence.

"Take it easy," I insisted with mock offence. I stepped toward Billy. "I'm here to fix the problem and you're reading me the riot act."

The guy's shoulders tensed as I took another step, but before he could raise the sap, I grabbed his neck and head-butted his face.

He flailed once with the sap, but his timing was lousy. I shoved him against the wall.

"Billy run!" Tonya shrieked.

Billy pawed at his bleeding nose, then crouched to grab his dropped sap.

My kick landed squarely on his shin. It hurt. My toe, that is. But the guy's shin hurt a lot more, and he collapsed into a submissive heap.

Tonya stood motionless, hands covering her face. This shell-shocked veteran of low rent housing and low hope living had figured that the easiest and safest way from this mess was to just give up. Her covered face was the gambit of a victim with no negotiating power: Just go away and I can't report you because I don't know what you look like.

My survival switch had lurched from fight to flight. My limbs were suddenly weak and soggy. I galumphed down the hall and out the door. There waited my Slug, my wonderful adoring Slug. I backed out recklessly, nearly sideswiping the car parked beside me, then burned authentic rubber toward the exit. I felt like a desperate astronaut in one of those science fiction flicks. I'd been ejected from the mothership in my little space pod: ten seconds and counting before the mother ship explodes. Will I make it?

I made it!

True, the ride was inexplicably rough, but what with my nerves, I was shifting raggedly. The car jerked and hopped all the way down the driveway and onto the road. One minute later, the car belching and rattling, I pulled onto the expressway and sighed with relief and resentment.

I was relieved because I'd escaped Garrison without a scratch. But at the same time, I resented Boyle's machinations. He lured me onto the first string, dazzled me with big checks and big talk—then put me in a corner with this pathetic second campus dirty work. What a horse's ass I felt like, speeding down the expressway in sweaty overalls.

But as I caught my breath, another emotion shouldered its way to the fore: greed! I'd done it! Boyle and Douglas had promised a payoff. What degree of payoff, I didn't know. No sum was mentioned. But it had to be big money, right?

A sudden metallic howl startled me, and giant orange and white sparks pin-wheeled out from beneath the Slug. I was losing power fast, and I barely made it to the shoulder as a semi thundered past with its air horn in full throttle. I scrambled out and examined the Slug's underbelly with my faltering flashlight. The exhaust system had collapsed. Everything. Tailpipe, muffler, exhaust pipe.

Then I saw that somebody had taken a goddamned hack saw to my exhaust pipe, just below the manifold. Huh...While I'd been in Garrison apartments, an auto parts entrepreneur must've been scrambling for some capital. A spreading puddle of petrol indicated that an errant swipe of the hacksaw had slashed the fuel line, hence the loss of power.

I didn't feel like sticking around for a highway patrol cop. I crawled up the highway embankment and huffed toward 111th, where an all night service station had a tow truck. The teenage grease monkey was agreeable enough, though the extravagant ninety-five dollar fee surprised me.

"Sure, it's a lot of money," he grinned. "But if you chance leaving your car out there, it'll be stripped."

"Whatever. I make a lot of money." I handed him a hundred dollar bill.

An hour later, the tow truck dumped me and the Slug in my driveway. Besides the amputated exhaust and snipped fuel line, the Slug had lost its hubcaps, its license plate, and radio antennae. The Slug, she just wasn't up to these nights out anymore.

Inside the duplex, I stepped out of my janitor duds and enjoyed a soothing final cigarette. Goddamn...what a night! Outside my dirty front window, the sun ascended over the frosted horizon. Reflexively, I glanced at my watch. Then I swore.

I'd lost my watch again.

The phone woke me at 6:45.

"Deyme!"

"—Yes."

"Did all go well?"

"Dr. Douglas?"

"I told you I'd call early." His normally burnished, tactful timbre was ratcheted up several pitches. "No problems?"

I lighted a cigarette, but it burned cockeyed. I paused to relight.

"James?"

"What kind of problems?"

"Any kind you might want to mention. Better me than Don."

"Nothing serious, really."

"There was a 911 there last night."

911? Better he than Boyle, indeed.

I told him everything: the hellish chemical, the irate tenants, the hallway rumble, the mugged Slug. As my narrative unfolded, Douglas's anxiety gauge redlined. A couple times, he interrupted like a breathless child. But I calmed him—"No, they didn't see my face"—and proceeded. As the tale neared conclusion, I felt heroic. Admittedly, property damage is not admirable, but surviving the night's adventure was, I thought, pretty impressive.

I imagined Douglas shaking his barely-haired dome in disbelief. He'd sussed me as a no brains, all thumbs jerk, but my limited talents were an ironic spur. With my back against the wall, I'd rolled the dice and won big.

"There're only a few potential trouble points," I conceded, explaining that my watch and license plate were MIA.

"That's nothing," Douglas assured.

"My name is on the back of the watch. Just my first name, but it's from my Mum, and her name is on it too."

"Just her first name?"

"No, I mean, her name isn't—"

"So it isn't? Her name?"

"Just the word. Mum. You know, the British spelling."

"—Spelling of what?"

It took me a few minutes to explain. It's not that complicated, is it? I supposed that Douglas was just jumpy. Only natural, I admit, what with his fate tethered to last night's intrigues. Once we had clarified the matter of my watch and the British spelling of Mum, Douglas again relaxed: "There's nothing incriminating about a lost watch. No way to trace it, as long as you've never been fingerprinted—Christ, why did you even bother?"

"Just to be on the safe side," I said, a bit peevish. "It's my watch left behind, not yours."

"Sorry," Douglas chuckled. "You had to be pretty nervous. No harm done. And as for your plate? Just report it lost in a week or so. If you get pulled over, just play dumb."

"So you're sure there's no problem?"

"Absolutely," Douglas soothed. "Our people are already at the site. And residents are already being herded into new digs. Prescott's brother has a moving company. The county hired him to move out furniture, the elderly, and so on." A satisfied pause. "Nice touch."

"I'm buying a new car," I found myself boasting. "Today. I mean, Boyle won't mind if I take the day off will he?"

"You've earned a day off," Douglas breezed.

Douglas, he's pretty cool.

"Don's presenting a paper in Tucson and won't be back until Thursday." Douglas made an oblique reference to Boyle's strategic campus absences—"Like Clay Shaw was on the West Coast when Kennedy got hit"—then urged me to treat myself to that fine new automobile.

In my kitchen, I enjoyed a cup of freshly ground coffee. My mood, my entire being, was free of my normal nagging thoughts of trouble and failure. I felt great, like I'd hit the lottery and lost fifty pounds.

I stopped in at Big Fella for a three-egg scramble and half pound of bacon. The eggs were wonderful, and the bacon's crisp happy crunch was a metaphor for my terrific mood.

"You're looking chipper today," the waitress noted.

"Chipper?"

She lightly placed my check on the table. "You must have the day off."

"Indeed I do. And here." I returned the check, along with a fifty dollar bill. "Keep the change."

Her eyes widened. "Is this right—?"

"Yes."

She tucked the fifty into the pouch of her white apron and did a cowpoke dance step, little fists on her hips and a twangy melody on her lips. "Thank you so much."

"My pleasure. You've served me many times over the years and, what the hey, you deserve a big tip for putting up with me."

"I just started here last week."

"Like you said. I'm chipper today."

Some days are just made for buying a car, you know? The sun's good cheer, the sky's lustrous blue, the waxed cars preening in the showrooms. I browsed through several dealerships, the salesmen and saleswomen keeping a respectful distance. They sensed that I was a savvy buyer, not easily bulldozed or sweet-talked.

One shrewd dealership employed several lovely sales babes. The cars were pedestrian, but my sales gal was worth a careful look. Long neck, longer legs, sharp black jacket and skirt. I even hopped into one of the showroom's cars just to prolong my study of her tits, cupped in an inspiring black bra beneath her gossamer white blouse. It occurred to me that some spoilsports, such as my colleague Jo Ann Staulen, would condemn the use of sales chicks as exploitive. Or maybe she'd just call it rape. But the auto industry is determined to recover, and sales chicks help.

Hormones still aflutter, I stopped next at a dealer on the north side of town. A new copper Sail caught my fancy; its neo-fins and flaring rear fenders promised high-tech torque and silent highway cruising. As at the previous dealership, a female member of the sales team greeted me. She was a dish, with dewy skin and a sleeveless red blouse and knee-high red skirt. She played it cool and professional as I scoped the Sail but got hot under the collar as I opened the door and eased into the leather bucket seat. The Sail's console seemed stolen from a Venusian space pod, with rows of gauges, buttons, lights, dials, levers, digital read-outs, and soothing recorded voices.

"Try the electronic seat adjuster and heater," the sales babe suggested. She reached inside the car—her milky and fragrant arm brushing my gut—and turned on the ignition. "See these buttons?" She pointed at a panel on the arm rest. "They control the height and angle of the front seats. These buttons control the heat."

"The heat?"

"All the seats are heated. For those cold mornings." She smiled, and her slender nose wrinkled winningly.

"They thought of everything."

"Just this morning, we got a fax from the front office. The Sail is going to be named Auto Flash's Car of the Year."

"I'm impressed." And I really was. Just sitting in this car was pleasurable. I remarked that I was certainly interested in a new car purchase but demanded a car of the highest quality.

"Car of the year," she smilingly repeated. "And an eight year bumper to bumper warranty."

Man, this woman was an eyeful. Her narrow waist and big bust rendered my dirty thoughts unusually graphic. Equally impressive, her face had that natural healthy hue that puts any makeup job to shame. For a few long few moments, I nodded at her sales pitch, not hearing a word, as I imagined her in my bed (the sheets miraculously fresh and crumb free), wearing only that shoulder length blonde hair. Natural blonde hair too, not a tinny dye job.

Typically, when I am face to face with an authentic babe, I get a little, you know, a little anxious. My gut feels fatter and rounder, my ass feels fatter and flatter, and I suffer the gnawing suspicion that my sack performance would be an unfortunate episode of flaccidity, flatulence, and hasty departure.

But today was different. My confidence was soaring. I casually leaned toward her and offered a dazzling smile. "Did you say bumper to bumper?"

"Seven years."

"I really do like it." I gripped the steering wheel and imagined driving it home. Today.

"Do you have a trade in?"

"I'm keeping my Slug as a backup. But not to worry. I have a big wallet."

I sat in the car a little longer, making small talk about my European-bred passion for quality engineering.

"You wouldn't be disappointed."

I regarded her for a long moment. "I'm sure I wouldn't. You've got really nice, a very nice car here."

Surrounded by fake ferns, we sat at a desk in a corner of the showroom. She explained several financing options. I was just going to put ten grand down, which would pretty much clean out my checking account. But so what? Big money was on its way.

"I'll put ten grand down. Is a check all right?"

"We haven't talked about price."

"Huh. Well, what's the sticker price?"

"Thirty seven thousand five hundred and seventy three dollars. And no cents."

"Make it thirty four and no cents, and you've got a sale." What the hell—you've gotta knock down the price a bit, just on principle.

"Wonderful," she beamed. And she was beaming at me. She excused herself to talk over my offer with her boss—as if he'd say no—and returned with cheeks flush and hand extended.

What a lovely hand.

"When can I pick it up?"

"Is three o'clock convenient?"

"Will you be here at three?"

"With the keys."

"Then it's convenient."

Flunky

I walked with authentic verve out of the showroom and to my sad-eyed Slug. The Slug and I, we'd been through a lot together. But now she seemed beneath me, a relic of my underwhelming past. In fact, a small but potent loathing of that car welled in me, and I took a brutish pleasure in racing her tired engine and jamming her bruised gears.

As I pulled into Annie's Dump for a bite and drink, it struck me that the relationship between car and owner is like that between spouse and spouse, or friend and friend. These relationships can be laugh-filled and supportive for several years, but then something happens. You know, one grows beyond the other. Your wife is dumpy and nagging, your friend is dull and grasping, or your car is a drag on your ascending lifestyle. And so it was with the Slug and me.

Annie's Dump found me to be an invigorating breath of fresh air.

The place seemed dim and dispirited after my glorious morning of power shopping, so I bought a pitcher for every patron. True, this required only three pitchers. And one of the patrons, a surly and ungracious oaf, expressed his gratitude by telling me to fuck off.

But I didn't care on little bit. "Certainly it's high time to cut that gentleman off," I announced with mock arrogance to Annie, the beer-sipping proprietor/bartender.

The other two patrons, however, held gratifyingly high opinions of me. They abandoned their booth and joined me at the bar.

"It's just something I've always wanted to do," I explained. "Buy everyone in the house a beer."

"And I've always wanted to get a free beer," laughed one of my new friends. Filterless cigarette dangling from his mouth, he introduced himself as Gill. His friend George, wearing a fatigued blue leisure suit, extended a callused hand.

"We ain't seen you in here before," Gill remarked.

"I'm a regular," I assured him. "I like the burger baskets."

"They really are good," George concurred. He gazed at me, then at his beer, then back at me.

"So be it," I smiled. "Annie?"

Annie nodded curtly at my request for three burger baskets.

"With fries!" George called.

"With fries!" I agreed.

We broke bread and chatted amiably. George and Gill, it turned out, had retired last month after thirty years of work.

"Where're you retire from?"

"From all the bullshit!" George explained.

"From U.S. Steel," Gill added. "Thirty years there, and most of them on the pickle line. Management, they always tried to keep you down, keep you in your place." Gill's narrow face hardened. "I'm bitter? You bet I'm bitter."

"Shut up," George instructed. "Where do you work, my friend?"

"West Central College. I'm Associate Vice President of Educational Services and Auxiliary Academic Systems."

"Sounds like you're management," Gill said warily.

"—in a way, I—"

"Shut up," George repeated. "He's at a college, not at the mill." He wiped a foam mustache from his whisker-thick upper lip. "And he bought you a beer!"

Gill held up an apologizing hand. "No offense, my friend."

"No harm, no foul," I assured. At George's prodding, I talked more about my work at West Central. For laughs, I tossed around some multi-syllabic bullshit—diversity orientation, proactive dialogues, goal-oriented directives, commitment renewal—and these two duffers nodded politely, even pretended to be nearly interested. But I didn't want to bore my new buddies, so I abruptly changed the subject by remarking that I'd bought a new car.

Gill brightened at my announcement. He asked what kind of car I'd chosen.

"A Sail. It's a real beauty."

"An American car," Gill noted over the vibrato of a long wet belch. "Made with American steel."

"It's a beauty. I'm picking it up today."

"Another pitcher over here," George called to Annie. Annie, her blast-from-the-past beehive tipped to the left, delivered the brew. When she held out a hand to George for payment, he pointed at me.

But I didn't care...I was getting good and lubed, and these two amusing old gents made for good drinking company. True, they were cheap. But they were honestly cheap and offered not even a half-hearted attempt to pay their freight.

Quarrelsome Gill revealed himself to be thoroughly likable, a product of that bygone era when men's lives were well defined. He regaled me with some fairly hair-raising tales of life with Lilly, his first and last wife. "I was young and stupid, and liked Lilly 'cause she liked to drink. And had big tits." Illustratively, he held his cupped hands a yard from his chest. "But she wouldn't fuck when she was drunk and, but, she liked to drink. So she wouldn't. Fuck."

Young Gill took to chasing tail in bars and even invited other free spirits to his house for some rough and ready, whiskey stained spooling. On July 4th of '66, an enraged husband followed his AWOL wife and Gill to Gill's house. Emotions were running high: taunts, slurs, and dares were lobbed freely as fireworks exploded outside. Gill and the husband took their disagreement to the front lawn and sparred a couple rounds for the cheering neighbors.

"I socked this bastard right in the chops," Gill exulted, reliving the decisive one-two. "This broad. She came stark naked right onto the lawn. I laid her right in front of the husband."

"Great story," George marveled.

"She was more turned on than any woman I ever was, that I ever laid," Gill told me. His tone was now pedagogic, his palm slapping the bar for emphasis. "See, women want to submit."

I glanced at George, who shrugged.

"It's the truth. They want to be chased and fought over and, you know, conquered." He leered at Annie. "Isn't that right?" he called to her passing backside.

"You're an idiot," she called cheerlessly, disappearing into the kitchen.

Gill playfully punched my arm. "I still get laid."

George laughed.

"Because I *know*. Woman, they want you to just take charge."

"I've got a date this afternoon," I told Gill. "The sales gal who sold me the car."

"Let's drink to the fairer sex," George suggested.

We did, then drank some more. Time was flying, as it does when drink is factored into the time-space equation. This beer or ale or whatever we were sloshing had a potent kick. To be on the safe side, I ordered another burger basket, explaining that I didn't want to be grossly
lit when I picked up my lovely date.

"What's her name?" George inquired.

"—I don't know." I shrugged happily, confident that all would go well.

After a sobering discount cigarette, bummed from George, I bid my friends farewell and strode out the door whistling "Spring Is Here."

I pulled into the Sail dealership at three o'clock sharp. Sure enough, my sales gal was waiting with keys in hand. Before she could say a word, I asked for her name.

"Lauren," she smiled, holding out the keys.

"Lauren," I repeated. I took the keys from her, then gave them back to her. Her eyes widened. "You haven't changed your mind?"

Not at all, I assured her. I explained my logistical problem of having two cars to drive home: the Slug and the Sail.

She shook her head, grinning. "I should really have one of the mechanics do it."

"That's unacceptable." With my buddy Gill's advice in my head, I put a hand on the padded shoulder of Lauren's blouse. "I need you to make delivery."

She hemmed and hawed a bit, trying to beg off. But I could see she was pleased by the invitation, so I insisted.

"I'll make it easy for you," I said. "My address is 572 Norris. Bring it over when you're off work."

She broke into a big grin and asked that I wait for a moment. She walked to the rear of the showroom and disappeared into the manager's cubicle. Presently she returned with her coat over her arm. "I'm off work now."

"Follow me!" Rendered daft by my madly rising fortunes, I flipped on my emergency lights and honked the horn. In my rearview mirror, I saw Lauren and the Sail emerge from the lot. The drive home took ten minutes, but I tried to soak in the totality of this milestone event with a Buddhist's concentration. Yeah, nirvana: a bonny babe following me home in my new sports car. The Sail and Lauren were a consummate match: both bright and wrinkle-free, both of prepossessing shape and tone, both high performance models. Certainly, this was a snapshot for my life's picture album.

And here we were. I pulled into my driveway and hopped with impressive ease from my car. Lauren was just up the street, tooling with panache toward my driveway where I now stood, hands on hips.

"Hi John!" Kim called. Kim skipped down the porch steps, cola bottle in hand. "What's—" She glanced from me to the approaching Sail, which was now reflecting the afternoon sun with a brilliance usually reserved for full color brochures. "What a beautiful car!"

"A dream," I agreed. "We'll all go for a spin when—"

"Ohmygod!"

The sickening crunch of metal filled the crisp air.

"*Ohmygod!*" she repeated, eyes half-closed. Then she raced past me toward the car, which had collided with the Slug's sagging and rusted rear.

Lauren was already out of the Sail. "The clutch pedal," she panted, "I swore it was the brake." Her teary eyes and snotty nose were right in my face. "I'm so sorry." She glanced over her shoulder at the Sail, then back at me. Then she grabbed me and bawled, swearing she would pay for all repairs.

"Are you all right?" I tried to pry her face from my chest, but she held tight.

"What a shame!" I heard Mr. Kwang yelping. "Shame!" Eager to help, Mr. Kwang clutched me from behind. At that moment, Lauren nearly collapsed and I struggled to hold her up. This human crush of grief and squawking, it was damned awkward. I tripped over somebody's foot and fell gracelessly onto the edge of the driveway.

Mr. Kwang tried to help me up, but I quietly refused. "I'll just lie here a minute," I sighed. "I'm trying to keep a positive attitude."

And so I did. I stared up at Kim, Mr. Kwang, and Lauren, and they stared down at me. After a minute of this soul-baring stare-down, Lauren turned her attention to the wounded Sail. Then Kim and Mr. Kwang, wondering how to talk to a man who insists upon lying on the ground, joined her.

Chapter Twenty: Twenty Five Percent Artificial

By six p.m., I'd fetched Lauren her hundredth tissue. Her five-alarm bawling eventually drove Mr. Kwang to the front door, where he tactfully reminded Kim that there was work to be done.

"Just one night off from the restaurant?" Kim asked, pointing a brilliantly lacquered fingernail at the dark circles beneath her eyes.

"You'll be in the way," Mr. Kwang suggested.

"It's okay," I assured. "Kim can help me cheer up Lauren."

Mr. Kwang nodded reluctantly and departed.

"I'm such a jerk," Lauren sniffled.

You sure are, I thought. Or rather, I tried to think. My new positive attitude was dented but resilient. With an admirably forgiving tone, I observed that accidents are unavoidable.

Kim asked me the Sail's cost.

"About thirty eight."

"Thousand?" Kim asked, dazzled.

"—Uh huh."

And Lauren was at it again, bleating apologies and wiping her raw nose.

"You need a little glass of wine for your nerves," I told Lauren.

"Me too," Kim said, hands trembling with impressive theatricality. "My nerves are just *so* shot."

"Your father wouldn't—"

"Oh he won't be back until midnight. I'll just have a glass. C'mon."

"You're under age."

"By a measly three years. Besides, I have a little wine with dinner at home. Didn't you know that wine prevents heart disease and high blood pressure?"

I sighed. Just a hint of Kim's teen persistence wore me out. I retreated to the kitchen, happy to let Lauren cry on Kim's shoulder. Standing at the pantry, enjoying a sly slug of Chablis, I found myself surprised by my patience and good will. I mean, my Sail was really damaged: the space age nose cone cum grill was splintered, the turn signal housing was crunched, and the front left fender suffered a deep crease that nearly reached the door.

"Where's that wine?" Kim called.

I returned to my guests, three filled wine glasses on an ersatz silver platter. "Just three?" Kim noted. "What will you guys drink?"

"Quiet, or you'll get Kool Aid."

"Cigarette anyone?" Kim offered.

"Thanks," Lauren said, weary.

Teens sure take over, don't they? Kim commandeered the bottle and kept our glasses happily filled. She had deep pockets for cigarettes, too, and she kept our lungs stimulated with menthol poison as she yakked about her boring classes.

"Slow up a little," I directed as Kim refilled her glass for the—the what? I thought it was only the third, but it had to be more. The Chablis bottle was dry, and a new bottle of sticky sweet Vouvray had reported for duty.

"This is so good. Cheers." Finally smiling, Lauren held out her glass. We clicked glasses, then Kim resumed her narrative of teen angst.

"—but the history class is so boring. Mr. Wilson, I can't stand him. He's the basketball coach and all the basketball team is in there and they all get A's. And most of them are brain dead. My nail clipper is smarter."

"Don't be too critical of your school," Lauren cautioned. "Our host is an educator himself."

Kim giggled. "He hates teachers too. Don't you."

"Most of them are okay really. Most of them—Yeah, most of them are horse's asses."

"Who's the one you hate the most?" Kim needled.

"Huh?"

"Luken?"

"How did you know that?"

"I've heard you and Dad talk."

"Who's this?" Lauren asked, getting in on the act. "Luken?"

Luken...With minimal prodding, I aired my complaints about Luken: his unflagging arrogance, his ceaseless and sour ribbing, his jargon-choked lectures.

"He's a complete jerk," Kim judged.

I had a full head of steam now, and paused only to refill my glass of Vouvray...no, check that. We're into the bubbly already?

"And he wears the dumbest clothes," I continued. "I'm no fashion plate, but I wouldn't wear—" I faced Lauren. "Would you wear Hawaiian shirts and teach a college class?"

Lauren forbade the thought.

Then I faced Kim. "Would you wear mismatching socks and dirty gym shoes?"

Kim forbade the thought.

"How anyone can stand his company, I don't know." How could Lydia, for instance? I still hadn't come to terms with Lydia's tolerance of Luken. I pulled savagely on my cigarette, and twin rails of smoke barreled from my flaring nostrils.

"Must be a real pain, all right," Lauren fumbled, unsettled by the hostility that rolled off me like heat off a hot car hood.

Jesus, I ordered myself, get over her. Get over Lydia. I snubbed out my cigarette and did my best to laugh. It sounded like a bark. Then I suffered a lung-ripping coughing jag, with the accompanying gut ache and snot expulsion.

Lauren was out of her chair immediately for a glass of water as Kim pounded my back.

"I'm fine," I assured between gravel gasps. "Went downa wrong pipe."

That Luken. That damned Luken. That damned Lydia!

The coughing took some steam out of me, and I calmed myself with only slight aftershocks of hacking and gagging.

Lauren sat down opposite me on the couch. "It's really me."

Man, what a hormonal shot in the arm this babe is. She leaned forward, fully revealing the spherity of those choice boobs. Plus her skirt had inched up her thighs to a revelatory height. It occurred to me that if I couldn't get laid tonight—what with a tipsy babe on my couch practically begging forgiveness—well, I'd just resign myself to a subscription to *Peek* and hand jobs.

Lauren, oozing sincerity, leaned closer and breathily apologized. "You're angry at me, not Luken or whatever his name is."

Just a few more inches, I asked her skirt. Ah, that's it.

"I'll pay for the repairs." I could smell the clashing but pleasing blend of fine spirits and crass cigarettes on her breath. "I'll take out a loan and—"

Cleverly, I slid from my chair and sat on the floor. Wow...a great view.

"Silly," Lauren teased.

Thar she blows! A glimpse of her white—or faintly pink?—bikini brief. No, it's white. Classic white. It looked like a triangle, with the triangle's tip cozy between her thighs.

"—Are you all right?"

"Uh huh."

The little white triangle vanished as she yanked down her skirt.

I tried to straighten up, but—ugh, my gut.

"Are you all right?" Lauren repeated.

"It's my back," I grunted. See, I'd bent over so far that my heavy gut became an anchor upon my back. "Kim? Help me up."

Kim, just returning from the rest room, loudly laughed. "You're on the floor."

"It's his back," Lauren explained.

"C'mon, I'll get you up."

Lauren rose to help, and they carefully lifted me to a sitting position. All the grunting and clutching was terrific fun, what with the wine and four female hands clutching and massaging me.

"That's why I got a little edgy. My damned back."

"More wine will help," suggested Kim.

"No more, please." I looked at Kim; her eyes were remarkably clear, considering. She's obviously spending her senior year in a drinking apprenticeship to prepare her for a robust American life.

I gingerly returned to my chair. "When it goes out like that—" I grimaced, indicating that the pain was very great indeed.

"All the stress," Lauren observed.

Peeping Christ, what was I thinking? Sliding onto the floor to look up Lauren's skirt? I suppressed a chuckle. It was a lot of fun. If Kim weren't in the way, I'd have my head up Lauren's skirt, my snout savoring that classic white triangle, and the, the—

"It's all my fault," Lauren offered meekly. She patted my knee.

"I've worn out my welcome, I see," Kim said matter-of-factly.

"You don't have to run off," I insisted. "Just switch from wine to cola. I don't want your Dad to think I'm corrupting you."

"Father thinks you're the perfect neighbor and the perfect gentleman."

"Just wait 'til he gets to know me." Wonderful Mr. Kwang. He's got that gift of making you feel good about yourself.

"And you are." Kim bent over me and gave me a peck on the cheek, offered her condolences to all concerned, and departed.

"What a nice girl," Lauren noted. She refilled my glass, then hers. We drank quietly for a few minutes, enjoying the absence of teen-talk. The silence wasn't burdensome—after this afternoon's noise and grief, it was a relief.

Lauren, after finishing a whimsical mix of champagne and lemon-lime soda, suddenly asked: "Do you know what I like to do when, when I'm a little tipsy?"

"How many guesses do I have?"

"One."

That's easy, I told her. You like to perform fellatio. Nude fellatio, of course, followed by a champagne mouthwash, then some banned-in-Alabama fornication. And—

No, I didn't say that.

"I like to shop."

Uh?

"Go to the mall and crank up those credit cards!"

I protested mildly that the hour was late for shopping, but she noted it was only 6:30. So it was. Drinking and time: I never quite grasp their relationship.

"I'll buy you something," Lauren promised, pulling on my arm.

Once I was up on my feet, the idea was attractive. I declared that I would drive, but Lauren insisted that the least she could do was play chauffeur.

"You're a fine one to talk," I joked.

She smiled sheepishly but refused to let me drive. "I'm just a little buzzed, but you're pretty drunk. Take this tissue, you've got a little dribble on your face."

We took the Sail. I was adamant about taking the Slug, but Lauren argued with cracked yet persuasive logic that the odds favored the Sail. Lauren had crashed the Sail once already; certainly, odds were extremely remote that she'd crash it again.

She drove with reassuring caution toward the highway, all slow turns and complete stops. Once on the expansive expressway, however, Lauren stomped the accelerator and impatiently dusted a herd of semis. Soon we hit eighty-five. I mumbled a few cautions about attracting the cops. Lauren mocked my feeble protests by downshifting into fourth, making the RPM's rise, then slamming back into fifth. The rhythm of her upshifting and downshifting—the alternate roaring and purring of the engine—was exciting. The link between sport car and sport sex became palpable. During one especially loud downshift, I grabbed her thigh and squeezed. She cackled and downshifted into third—the engine seemed ready to explode—then worked through fourth and fifth.

"This car is *such* a stud," she enthused.

Too soon, Lauren pulled into the mall parking lot. She was immediately out of the car and hoofing toward the entrance.

She walked fast, her stride filled with a professional shopper's purpose and passion. No silly complaints from me, though. Lauren's rear view was as entertaining as her front. She'd really lucked out in the chassis department, and our long walk through the parking lot let me relish her buttocks, pumping potently beneath her skirt.

In the mall, she dragged me from store to store in search of "bargains": eighty-dollar swimsuits, hundred fifty dollar blouse and skirt combos, two hundred dollar jackets. The stores became a blur, what with all those chrome clothing racks, sales babes, and Lauren's peer group of shopping black belts.

My feet were bitching and moaning pretty quickly, but Lauren showed no mercy. And she put her charge cards where her mouth was. She directed a spending attack that captured a chiffon blouse, a green boater, a black bodice, nylons, and a one-piece tomato red swimsuit. Finally, she declared a reprieve. We sat on a cement bench beneath fake palm trees in the mall's central courtyard. As she studied her mall booty, I mugged a few quick ciggies and indulged in people watching. Lots of resolute female shoppers passed. Like Lauren, they aggressively surveyed the mall for the next store to plunder. Several of the women were followed by huffing and hobbling men.

Most striking, however, were the roaming teen tribes. The boys stuck pretty much with the boys, the girls with the girls, though a few tribes were coeducational. They dressed expensively and preposterously. The girls—many only fourteen and fifteen—arrogantly displayed their flesh. Some of them, I swear, had tit jobs and face lifts already. The boys, dressed as ragamuffins or basketball stars, swaggered and leered as the girls passed.

For a moment, I envied the kids' youth. To be young again, with your twenties still ahead of you—what a blessing! But being young again would mean being stupid again. They say youth is wasted on the young. I agree. And wisdom is wasted on the old.

On the way back, we visited a Burger Stud drive-through.

"Now admit it. You had a good time."

"I confess." I unwrapped my second Stud Burger and offered her more fries.

"I shouldn't. They ruin my figure."

"Your figure could stand a little ruining."

"That's very nice of you, but it's been an absolute ordeal to get in shape." She enjoyed a few French fries but refused my further proddings. "An ordeal," she repeated quietly, more to herself than to me.

Once in my driveway, Lauren revved the Sail's engine a few times, then let her long-fingered hand momentarily rest on the ignition key before killing the engine. She turned, faced me squarely. I shrunk back a tad, still feeling incompetent in her beauty's glamour and glare.

"Did you see what I bought you at the mall?"

"A bodice?"

She reached into her purse and pulled out a box of King Tut condoms.

"Color me flattered," I grinned.

She showed me the cute little over-night kit that she'd purchased: hand soaps, creams, oils. "Color me fragrant."

We were in the house and up the stairs so quickly that I had no time for nerves. I started to pull down the shades, but she insisted that the shades remain raised. She also told me to turn on the dresser light. She disrobed with care free esprit, tossing her skirt at my feet and her blouse over her shoulder. The brassiere and bikini briefs were gone just as quickly.

Christ! She really was built like that. Earlier, I'd had fleeting suspicions that her bust was kept at attention by some concealed engineering trick.

She chugged one of the beers we'd fetched from the fridge. "It's the best to start screwing just as your buzz hits."

After draining my own bottle in record time, I discarded my shirt in record time. My disrobing technique was pretty damned impressive, though the last button was stubborn. After a few failed attempts at freeing it from the buttonhole, I crudely yanked and the button hit the floor. My slacks hit the floor next. Lauren assertively stepped forward and, doing a little belly-to-belly shimmy, pulled down my boxer shorts.

"You were funny looking up my dress tonight," she said, lips brushing my shoulder.

"Funny ha-ha? Or funny weird?"

"My husband, he tries to be filthy like that."

Uh?

"But I won't let him treat me like that. Dirty like that." She pushed me toward the bed. I obligingly fell atop of it, clenching my gut and butt to prevent jiggling.

She rolled the King Tut onto my swelling prong. "He's such a pig."

For a moment, I thought she'd called my prong a pig.

"He's always wanting me to do degrading things, but I can't. With him."

Ahhh...she lowered herself onto me, and it was...what? It was sumptuous and scrumptious. I anticipated that rarest of sack episodes, one that leaves you feeling both romantic and debauched. Heaven and earth, yin and yang, tender French kiss and randy rim job.

"Squeeze my tits."

I did.

"How do they feel?"

"Very nice."

I grew so absorbed that I forgot to keep my butt bouncing, and she gave me a good natured slap. After progressively more exotic positions—including one in which I assumed an agonizing wrestler's bridge—she rolled off and welcomed me into the missionary position.

The missionary, despite its fuddy-duddy reputation, is my favorite. I can rest on my elbows and really put some heft and bulk into the performance. I started out slow and easy, no sweat, like a marathoner putting in the first few laps. Then I stepped up the pace, deepening my stride till we reached a gallop. And she liked it, I'm obliged to inform you. Her smooth forehead developed little lines of pleasure and concentration—or maybe my gut was just making it hard for her to breathe.

Without warning, I developed a crippling case of runner's side pains. I didn't let that stop me, though. I wasn't going to wave the yellow flag for a simple side ache.

"Put your hands on my ass."

This demanded that I dismount. I was secretly grateful for the break, what with my wheezings and side aches and threats of a back blow-out.

Her buttocks were truly lovely, with that rare high and full curve. And they weren't marred by the overly aerobicized, muscled look that's far too common today. No, she possessed the subtle and necessary layer of lushness.

"Keep stroking," she murmured. She turned to gaze into the large mirror atop my dresser.

The mirror afforded a striking, full-length reflection of Lauren. The mirror also afforded, unfortunately, an uncensored view of me. The contrast of our bodies was perverse. I looked like a really masculine, really ugly woman. A really masculine and ugly pregnant woman. Judging by my belly, I was about seven months along. No wonder I've been craving chocolate mint ice cream.

Lauren kept talking, but my dismaying reflection distracted me.

She said something about cosmetic surgery, and I laughed mirthlessly. "Liposuction's my only hope," I muttered. Why was she doing this? Does she get off on cruelty?

"No, silly. I mean me."

"What?"

She rolled from her side onto her back. "You can't tell?"

"Tell what?"

"I'm at least 25 percent synthetic."

"What is?"

She was. Her boobs and buttocks, her nose and lips. Synthetic.

"He thinks he owns me."

"Who does?"

"My husband."

Her husband, she explained, is a plastic surgeon.

"His name's even Stein, can you believe it? I call him Frankenstein, and I'm his monster."

Well, here we go. She's talking. She's going to share fiercely guarded secrets, the secrets that bed-sharing strangers force upon one another. I was suddenly very tired.

Ignoring my yawn, Lauren explained that she'd met Dr. Stein in his office. She'd come in for a boob job because her bust was "only 34 C." Rather than assure her that 34 C was well-nigh perfection, the good doctor eagerly offered his services. The boob job became grounds for romance; Lauren was thrilled when he proposed marriage three months after the surgery. Marriage to a plastic surgeon! And she happily agreed to a few more surgeries to hoist the butt or bolster the bust or refine the nose. Judging by his handiwork, Dr. Stein must've used girlie mags as a template for his bride's new bod.

"I don't care what some of those woman say," Lauren declared, a tad defensive. "They want to look good. They want to look hot. Besides it was all free. I'd still be with him, probably, except he wanted to do something really sick."

"If you'd rather not talk about it—"

"He wanted to put in a new hymen."

"Uh, I'd really rather not—"

"A new one every year, so I'd always be a virgin on our anniversary. Did you know it's pretty common in Japan? So the brides will be virgins? I told him he was a sick creep, but he really insisted." It was at this point, Lauren explained, that she helped herself to a large chunk of his savings, moved out, and got the job at the Sail dealership.

"I try to screw every guy I a sell a car to."

A select group, I guessed.

"Well, every guy I sell a new car to. Used doesn't count. Usually I call up the customer to ask how the car is, how it handles, you know. Then I invite them to stop by to see me, and pretty soon we're screwing. With you though," she laughed, "it was record time, with me wrecking your car and all."

"Lucky me."

"Anyway, I'm really driving that creep crazy. Especially since he turned fifty this year and he's neurotic."

She got off the bed, hopped lightly down the stairs, and returned with a couple more beers. She never shut up. She was yammering about her plans to open her own dealership—her eventual divorce settlement, she figured, would be a jack pot—when I fell asleep. The sleep was welcome, too, because I was depressed. Well, perhaps discouraged is the better word. While Lauren was an unqualified babe, she was also an unqualified head case. And that's the thing about head cases.

They're head cases. Their motives are flaky, their thoughts are disjointed, and their lives are disasters.

I missed Lydia.

Barbara had taken the day off. Again. She's collected lots of sick days in her many years of laggard service, and she freely admits that she's just using them up. "The sick days can't be converted to cash," she complains as if it's my fault.

I killed time thumbing through the newspaper, smoking, and playing Chinese checkers on my Big Byte computer. The computer usually wins. Ah, the Big Byte computers. A dozen of them, still boxed, gathered dust in a corner. My inspired plan to convert Luken's office and classrooms to a computer lab was scuttled by Dwayne Derrickson. Dwayne had sure made a big deal of putting me in my place in an orchestrated show of institutional brawn. The faculty union elections are right around the corner, and Dwayne's a shoe in, thanks largely to me.

Being Dwayne's big-assed bull's-eye, it isn't that fun. But at least I'd squeezed out a moral victory: I couldn't have the classrooms, yet Douglas quietly okayed my plunder of Luken's office, which enjoys new life as a janitor's closet. Luken's stuck in a windowless cubicle in the basement. A small victory, but still sweet!

I was wasting time at a quick rate, moving right along, but Barbara's shrill phone kept interrupting me. No, I told Gert and Liz and Japholinniea, she's not in today. These secretaries, all they do is jabber on the phone.

Around eleven, I abandoned my post to harass Bruce Herrig. He's a dependable ad hoc punching bag for my petty complaints and smug insults. But he wasn't in.

"What is it about Mondays?" I quipped to his secretary. "Nobody's around."

"Today's Tuesday."

Uh?

"Mr. Herrig is participating in the Gender Studies workshop."

"Huh?"

"I said, 'Mr. Herrig is participating in the Gender Studies workshop." She regarded me with disdain. "Jo Ann Staulen's outreach program," she continued archly, "for local businesses and government agencies. They're quite popular."

"Sounds fun as the cancer ward."

With a little huff, she resumed typing. The click of lacquered nails on keys told me to leave. Well, I wasn't going to surrender this easily, not to a goddamned secretary. I cleared my throat a few times.

"Shall I leave Mr. Herrig a message?" she finally asked, making a great show of not looking at me.

"Tell him he's worthless," I harrumphed.

Jo Ann was holding forth in one of the college's suddenly constructed conference rooms, all of which were made possible by generous support from Thunder Oil. On one of the walls hung a large black and white portrait of Mr. Prescott; the benevolent power broker had a twinkle in his eye, as though pleased that all who enter must genuflect before him.

I had to give the old prong his due. The conference rooms were top drawer: deep pile carpeting, textured cream wallpaper with ennobling pale blue trim, ergonomic swivel chairs, recessed track lighting, and computer controlled multimedia with Dolby stereo and 70 millimeter movie projection. Bruce told me the other day that the tasteful decorating was provided by Panache, Inc., a company owned by Mrs. Prescott's sister.

Jo Ann's so-called outreach programs were a raging success. Businesses, government agencies, hospitals, schools and other repositories of societal power structures, as Jo Ann deftly dubs them, happily bus out their employees to West Central. Jo Ann's program facilitates heightened sensitivities toward modern Western culture's historically extreme patriarchal practices. At two hundred bucks a participant, Jo Ann's program is an astute investment in one's work force. Jo Ann offers her hodgepodge of jaw-breaking jargon, paranoid pleasures, and—always a showstopper—masturbatory insights. Jo Ann's big on whacking off. Whacking off frees chicks from putting up with dicks. Wanking is not merely fun, Jo Ann asserts; it's also a brave political act.

Weirdly, some of Jo Ann's most fervent disciples are men. Yeah, men, especially white males, those cunning heartless plundering bastards. During her sessions, Jo Ann knocks the men from pillar to post about America's sweaty hatred of women, I mean womyn. Sorry. I mean *wemyn*. Jo Ann's especially interested in degradation, which is how men control women. The more humiliated chicks are the better because they're more easily subjugated and marginalized and fucked over. One of Jo Ann's ironical ideological therapies is to stick a guy under a spotlight in the middle of the room, then urge the women to belittle his thin hair or fat torso. This bashing sensitizes men to the semiotic rape of lookism, which American women suffer in historic proportions.

I discretely took a chair right beside the door. Uh oh—rosy-cheeked and dewy-eyed Bruce had just "volunteered" to occupy the hot seat. Bruce looked pretty hapless, squintily facing the thirty or so women and half dozen men. He was perspiring already.

Jo Ann, decked out in an eye-catching feedbag *cum* pantsuit, started out gently enough. Standing beside her lamb, Jo Ann explained that Bruce was a long time employee of West Central College. His experience as public relations director, she noted, gave him numerous opportunities to experience, and to be experienced by, the capitalist—and therefore necessarily phallocentric—episteme that subjugated education to the narrowest imperatives of white male moneyed interests.

"Is my analysis correct?" Jo Ann asked rhetorically.

"Sounds about right," he anxiously agreed.

"Haven't you profited by the phallocentric episteme, that same episteme that makes vagocentric ideology virtually unthinkable—?"

"If you say so." He winced like an oft-kicked puppy.

"Don't interrupt!"

"Sorry."

"As I was saying, have you benefited by this episteme even without necessarily trying, even if for example you consciously tried not to benefit by it?"

"By what?"

"The episteme."

"I—"

"Of course you have," Jo Ann instructed him. She faced her audience. "In a sexist and racist society, a beneficiary of the sexism and racism cannot disentangle himself from the benefits, which destroys the simple minded argument that the rugged individualist is rewarded solely on merit." She returned to Bruce. "You wouldn't try to deny your hegemonic world view, would you?"

"No."

"Then quit your job!" shouted a woman in front of me.

Bruce wiped his forehead.

"Quit your job," the woman repeated. "Renounce your sexism."

The woman's hoarse demand was sweet reason to several other women, who'd been whipped into quite a vagocentric lather.

I couldn't resist. "Quit your job!" I bellowed through cupped hands. My quick wit got a roar of approval from the audience, though the woman in front of me turned and cursed me as a hypocrite.

My jest, however, quickly left a sour aftertaste. One woman complained with startling bitterness that my remark merely illustrated male condescension. Jo Ann agreed. Several audience members lobbed feminist jargon and pig Latin at me. I took it all in stride—iron-clad smirk and eye-rolling incredulity—though I was secretly rattled by one woman's challenge to live on 1200 calories a day.

I found myself bullied into confessing that I'd really like to lose some weight. "But what's this got to do with anything?" I belatedly complained.

Derisive laughter and hateful hoots. I glared at Bruce, who, hare-like, was motionless in his seat. Fortunately, Jo Ann suggested that we return to the issue of Bruce quitting his job as a means of protesting white male privilege. Quitting one's job, Jo Ann conceded, was perhaps asking too much. Perhaps a more modest but still valuable step in Bruce's ideological therapy would be to abdicate the male's hegemony in gender-driven relations.

Nobody understood what Jo Ann said, but everybody agreed.

"Simply put," Jo Ann explained, "men should give their sexual partners a vibrator."

The overheated audience erupted into snorts, hoots, savage applause.

"Minus their penis, men must confront their own sadomasochism, their culturally encouraged urge to violate."

Like all polished grifters, Jo Ann knew exactly when to shift gears in her con. She pushed a button on a control panel behind her, and a projection screen descended from the ceiling. The room darkened.

"What you are about to see," Jo Ann advised, "is explicit. But I believe it offers a concrete step towards dispensing with the phallus, which is necessary in breaking the Western episteme. In psycholinguistic-political terms," she helpfully added, "it's about acknowledging the divide between signifier and signified, and so the division of penis from phallus."

—What the hell! A naked woman was on the screen. Belinda Bellweather, Ph.D. in Radical Feminist Studies, no less. Belinda talked to us quite breezily about masturbation, about clitoricentric eroticism, about controverting the phallus. And I know what you're wondering at this point, so I'll tell. Basically, Belinda Bellweather wasn't much to look at. Plain round face with the obligatory drab hair pulled straight back in a frayed ponytail. Her tits, for a fortysomething feminist, they weren't bad. But not good either. They were just there, you know? But anyway. After a bit more of her exotic argot, Belinda held up an orange plastic prong. She flipped on the power switch. She used it.

Normally, I would've enjoyed this chaste bit of porn. But with all these women around me, I couldn't really relax. The woman in front of me, however, seemed fully engaged: she rocked back and forth in her chair, her tiny fists clenched atop the arm rests.

Meanwhile, Belinda Bellweather broke a sweat and really started manhandling her dildo. Yet she continued professing in her carefully modulated tone.

"An orgasm untainted by testosteronic tyranny," she explained, "is the goal of our project." Then, clamping shut her eyes, she averted her face to enjoy a fully feminist orgasm.

The lights came up and the audience applauded. The woman in front of me kept rocking back and forth, cursing under her breath.

Jo Ann loudly asked for attention. "I have here a very important document." She held overhead a bright red loose-leaf binder. "This contains the names of female political prisoners. Of female prisoners of conscience. Jailed for the crime of dismemberment, but in actuality—"

Bleeding Christ! Chicks who slice off dicks!

"—and an especially despicable miscarriage of justice is Michelle Dulvel's. She has been sentenced without hope of parole."

Oh yeah...her. She was sentenced just last year, I think. Remember? Michelle Dulvel performed radical feminist surgery on a guy she didn't even know. "So it could hardly be an act of crude revenge," Jo Ann proclaimed. "It was purely political! If we tolerate the cynical manipulation of—"

Bruce was gone, so I left to find him. I expected him to be pretty pissed off. I mean, Jo Ann ordered him to surrender his dick for a battery-powered prong. He'd never raise it again. I found him around the corner, loitering by a coffee vending machine.

"How can you date that woman when she, after she beats up on you like that?" I demanded.

"I'm learning to, um, interrogate cultural gender matrixes in the hopes of, you know, of opposing those false Western binaries of sexual personae."

"Bullshit," I snorted. "You're just trying to get laid."

"That too," he confessed, sheepish.

"You're depressing me." Bruce must be unspeakably desperate, I figured, to chase Jo Ann's bony ass. "By the way," I barked. "Fire your secretary."

"But she's marginalized by our episteme."

"Goddammit, you're really letting me down falling for all that drivel." I playfully punched his arm. "C'mon. Let's have some fun. Let's tie one on at Boyle's house tonight."

"That's right!" Bruce brightened. "It's tonight."

"Just don't bring Jo Ann."

"Just don't bring Lydia," he retorted.

"Fuck off," I smiled. But as I turned away, I was smarting. Maybe Lydia would show up at the Boyle bash. With Rochinni.

In the mood for a big lunch and big cocktail, I hurried to my office for my jacket and car keys. Passing the classrooms, I heard gibberish about the electron's wave properties, about carbon dating, about Galileo's house arrest by the church. All this bullshit. I mean, these do-nothing faculty go to great lengths to avoid real work. In one classroom, Jim Pouris concluded a lecture about...about what? I don't know. Something about irrational numbers. Irrational numbers? That doesn't make sense; Pouris must've made it up. Somebody should report him.

Pouris's students hurried past me, then Pouris emerged from the classroom, clutching notes in one hand and ancient coffee cup in the other. He looked surprised to see me.

"How are you today?" he inquired politely if warily.

"Fine. You?"

He studied me for a moment. "I was going to call you later on in the day, after my classes. But if you have a minute now—"

"Only a minute," I said, glancing at my watch.

"You may know that I'm the faculty's grievance officer."

How could I not? The zealot was always filing grievances.

"Mr. Luken has filed a grievance against you, and we may as well have a preliminary meeting about it."

"About what?"

"About the grievance."

"No, I mean what's the grievance for?"

"The faculty contract states that all faculty shall be provided an office with a desk, chair, three bookcases, phone—" Pouris couldn't resist a quick smile.

"What?" I demanded.

"You've converted Mr. Luken's office into a janitor's closet."

"I got him an office in the basement. Luken, he's always complaining about things, so—"

Pouris raised a patient hand. "The office you've provided has no bookcases, and the desk is missing a leg."

"He'll get his stuff. The physical plant guys are just a little slow."

"There's also no ventilation in the room you stuck him in, and—"

"The contract doesn't require ventilation," I smirked.

"Yes, but the state department of health does."

Uh?

"Mr. Luken has contacted the state, claiming that the poor ventilation is ruining his health. Today he's practically bedridden. He has allergies that require—"

And on it went. Pouris, brandishing his photographic memory, recited various state regulations regarding air quality in public places, including enclosed office spaces. I got the whole spiel, from soup to nuts. Pouris concluded his recitation by noting that Luken might file suit.

"For what?" An unfortunate whine invaded my voice.

"He's seen his physician several times for his allergies, which are aggravated by that basement office. He wants punitive damages."

"Huh?"

Pouris's posture grew fully professorial, replete with illustrative gestures and a slightly cocked head. "Mind you, Mr. Luken would not sue you personally, but he would sue the college pursuant to your actions. You would be named in the suit as the agent of the college whose actions harmed Mr. Luken's health."

Whoa...Luken, he's vicious. These lawsuit shenanigans could mightily piss off Boyle. "I'll get him an office by the end of the week," I assured.

"His allergies won't wait until—"

"Goddammit, I can't satisfy his every whim."

"He wants your office."

The day's remains were spent in the red tint of rage, with occasional blue streaks of melancholy. I just couldn't hide from pain. Luken, he's a real pain, a radar-guided missile with an unerring lock on my rear. Luken wants my office? Bullocks!

And Lydia. More pain. The thought of losing her to Rochinni, who likely needs reminding of where his old prong is located, and of how it works—that thought, that's a big pain. It just can't be true. Bruce's scoops have never been wholly trustworthy, though what can you expect from a P.R. hack? He's a salaried bullshit artist.

What a mess I am. What happened to my new positive attitude, my gleaming armor of optimism? I can't even take solace in giving the high hard one to Lauren. I should be pleased, I should be ecstatic, I should be boiling with testosteronic pride. But it doesn't matter. Dammit, I really love Lydia. For a few brief days, Lydia Fairview saw the good in me, and it felt wonderful.

On the drive home, I realized that I'd been tiptoeing around my true nature for far too long. I've been walking on the most delicate of psychological eggshells. Face up to it, I told myself: Sobriety—crude, simple-minded, humorless sobriety—isn't the answer. Granted, one shouldn't push matters too far. As with all of the vices that make life enjoyable, moderation is the key. Or more precisely, rhythm is the key. Yes, the accomplished drinker's life is based upon rhythm: a tipple at noon for a candy-coated lift, a few slugs after work just too relax, and the periodic Dionysian drunk, laughing at or yelling at or fucking someone at two in the morning. Drinker's rhythm protects you from life's crushing hay makers, just like a boxer's rhythmic bob and weave.

Tonight was the perfect time to regain that rhythm, to recapture that galvanizing gaiety of spirit and joyous slur of speech. Why not? After all, I am one large cause of Boyle's party tonight. Yeah, the Prez is hosting a soiree to hail the immanent second campus construction. And since I contributed mightily, I will tonight enjoy my just desserts. With a few wisely chosen cocktails in me, Lydia won't lay a glove on my tender psyche.

Lydia thinks she's too good for me. She's right. Still, her snooty dismissal makes me remember my lowly English roots, my family's second-tier status. Sod it. I'll turn the tables on Lydia and be rip-roaring, rip-snorting new money American with a monstrous salary and a trophy on my arm: yeah, *Lauren* on my arm.

As I pulled into Boyle's runway sized driveway, Lauren made a last minute appraisal of her surgically endowed lips in the rearview mirror. Before entering, we clicked glasses and enjoyed some very nice Champagne that Lauren had pilfered from her ex's wine cellar.

Robobabe was endearingly excited. When I asked her on three hour's notice to be my date, she instantly agreed. Ironically, she gets few date requests. Lots of blunt and drunken fuck requests, but few courteous date requests, especially post-fuck requests. Lauren observes that once guys screw you a couple times, few continue to offer the perks that, in the chivalric past, would accompany fucks. You know, a nice dinner or pretty dress or thorough car wash.

"You surprise me sometimes," she remarked on the phone. "You can be pretty sweet."

"—Thank you. Very much." Ah...kind words. We all need more of them.

Bruce Herrig answered my rap on the massive oak door. He ushered us inside with a long sweep of his arm.

"This is my buddy Bruce," I told Lauren. "And Bruce, this is my buddy Lauren."

"Wow." My buddy Bruce was instantly muggy with a hormone buzz. "That's a dress."

Indeed. Lauren's dazzling white sheath dress was a smashing accompaniment to her triumph-of-modern-science bod.

"Damn glad to meet you," Lauren said, vigorously shaking his moist hand. "Let's join the fray," I suggested.

We moved from the foyer to the kitchen. Huh. Those rumors of contractor kickbacks, I figured, must be true. Even on Boyle's Herculean salary, a kitchen like this? Dozens of hand crafted oak cabinets, recessed track lighting, triple oven, stove with eight sealed burners, marble floor with curlicue etchings, and a floor-to-ceiling wine rack.

"I love this kitchen," I declared.

Lauren giggled, accepted a drink from goggle-eyed Bruce. "That's so sweet."

"Don't mention it," Bruce squeaked.

"No," Lauren told Bruce. "Though you're sweet. I mean you, John, so in rapture by a kitchen."

"A kitchen is the most important part of a house," I said, reverent. "And this is a world class kitchen. Check out this island. Three tiers!"

"Hey!" Don Boyle roared. "It's really great to see you!" Boyle heartily shook my hand. "Really glad you're here!" He must've meant it, too, because he kept pumping my hand and grinning madly. His face and breath were aflame from a fresh belt of unblended whiskey, and fresh freckles rose on his face. He looked ready to burst into "Danny Boy."

"It's a pleasure to be here," I assured, amused by Boyle's interminable handshake. Finally, when he released my sweaty hand, I introduced him to Lauren.

"It is a genuine pleasure to meet you, Laura."

"Lauren," she corrected.

Damn. The first faux pass of the evening, and a potentially costly one. Correcting Don Boyle.

"My apologies, Lauren." He offered a quick little bow. "Help yourself to anything at all. Anything. Now if you'll excuse me, I'll talk to you a little later." With a big smile for all of us, Boyle gracefully moved on to greet arriving guests.

"He's a very nice man," Lauren said.

"Tonight he's Dr. Jeckyl," Bruce mused. He then shared some late-breaking gossip: Boyle had shipped his latest wife—bride number four, Bruce thought—to her mother's for the week. Boyle liked his parties to have kind of a stag feel. You know, no frowning or clinging wives. Dates? Absolutely. But wives, Boyle had learned through hard experience, were a wet blanket on party spirits.

"I'm hungry," I announced. We headed to the living room, which featured a professionally catered buffet. Tonight's food theme was Mediterranean: aromatic stuffed grape leaves, perfectly boiled pasta shells, fresh breads and rolls, shellfish, and plenty of sauce, fragrant with freshly ground spice and extra virgin olive oil.

We sat on a wrap-around couch beneath high priced prints of Renaissance paintings and happily stuffed ourselves. By eight, the house was bulging with guests. Boyle sure opens his house up during a party. Even some faculty coming in.

"Look who's here," Bruce whispered.

Jim Pouris entered the room, tentatively looking about for a place to sit. What a loser. Here he was in Boyle's palace, and he wears the same old flannel shirt and jeans. What is it with intellectuals? Why can't they dress properly?

As he surveyed the room, Pouris spotted me. He waved in a nearly friendly fashion.

"Oh no," Bruce whispered without moving his lips. "He's going to sit with us."

But he didn't. Instead, he disappeared into the kitchen.

Reminding myself to be a good date, I sportingly fetched more food for Lauren. Yeah, and for sad ol' Bruce too. I figured I should stop beating up on him all the time. It's classier, I concluded, to abuse him only during business hours.

"How nice of you," Lauren said, accepting the fresh food.

"Very thoughtful," Bruce agreed.

Bruce and Lauren were chatting happily, which pleased me. Bruce had looked uncomfortable, frequently and unwittingly touching at his remaining tuft of hair. He probably felt like a third wheel. I'd seen him discreetly look about the room for his ball stomping womyn. Christ. His plaintive eyes revealed him to be a love-struck sap. Talking with Lauren, I figured, might inspire Bruce to find a mate who was at least recognizably feminine.

Presently, Bruce was downright festive, laughing and gossiping and eating and drinking. See? I'm not a complete bastard. I'm letting—nay, I'm encouraging—Bruce to chat with my trophy.

Food and wine: they're civilizing, aren't they? They bring out the best in people. What a joy to feast on fresh pasta and salad and—what do we have here?—a Chablis. Very winning Chardonnay, to be exact. Yeah, I switched to the white stuff. Got to maintain my drinker's rhythm.

With Lauren and Bruce chatting away, I wandered off to mingle. Boyle, a shot glass in each hand, was holding court in the living room about local politics. The guy lives for politics, and the rumors grow more emphatic that he's an object of both Republican and Democratic lust.

"Howz my man!" Boyle hailed me.

I raised a glass in a salute.

"Please join us, James."

Boyle introduced me as the College's "renowned" Associate Vice President of Academic Affairs, and a "driving force" behind the second campus.

I nodded deferentially at the power brokers' approving smiles and backslaps. Boyle then introduced his friends. One old dick was a highly placed church administrator and long-time family friend. The rest were well-connected business guys, I guess. Their names? I forgot. Huh...the Chardonnay had put a vapor lock on my short-term memory, which isn't sharp to begin with.

"What about the zoning?" one guy asked.

Boyle twisted his face in mock exasperation. "You worry even after it's been handled."

The guy wasn't satisfied. I wouldn't be either. I mean, I wouldn't be satisfied with his hair surgery. Tiny but numerous little holes or scabs marred his pate. This guy must've been really impoverished, follicle-wise, to let his head become a surgeon's pin cushion.

"Yeah Richie. You worry too much," another guy griped.

Richie, he of the painful scalp, conceded the point under the weight of his colleagues' jeers.

"Besides, Reilly's been a big contributor to Russell," a third guy explained, his mouth crowded with pistachio nuts. "Russell won't let us down. He's a stand up guy."

A fat guy lightly elbowed fretting Richie. "I told you Don's got everything figured out."

The pow-wow broke up, and Boyle moved off to greet another wave of guests, none of whom I recognized. I turned to find Lauren and Bruce when a thick handed slap on the shoulder made me spill my drink.

It was Richie. The nearness of his face rendered his features bulbous and sweaty, as if viewed through a fish eye camera lens.

"Sorry I spilt your drink."

"Not at all," I assured, resisting the urge to look down my front and survey the damage.

He put an arm around me. "So you're the chemist?"

Uh?

Richie snickered. "No, it's all right."

He kept grinning at me, our noses nearly touching.

"That's a good touch, with the disguise."

I glanced around for someone to rescue me.

Richie's eyes narrowed, and he laughed. The laugh became a bellow. His breath wasn't that bad, though. Irish Crème.

"Didja ever think," Richie demanded, "that you'd ever go to college all those years and do that for your promotion? Fuckin' A, huh?"

"Fuckin' A," I agreed.

"See, I never went to college but I'm still gonna be lucrative." He again slapped my back, and he spilled his own drink. On my jacket.

Boyle was suddenly at my side, offering me a sport jacket. He took my soiled attire and assured me he would have it dry-cleaned. I feebly protested, but he patiently insisted. Then, for a few seconds, anger hardened his voice. But he was not pissed at me. He was pissed at Richie. "Get out there and watch the front door for a while."

Merriment drained from Richie's face. Patting at the scabs on his head—somehow, several had started to bleed a bit—he again apologized and departed.

"That's Richie Prescott," Boyle revealed. "The old man's nephew. He's a building contractor and he's going to be doing lots of work for the college on the second campus. That is, if he submits the lowest bid." Boyle winked. "Hey, go get a drink for yourself."

It made me a little nervous, I guess, knowing that Richie Prescott, familial hanger-on and loose-lipped moron, knew the inside second campus scheme. Calling me a chemist, raucously announcing that I'd made him a rich man...Christ, at this party, in front of all these people with the booze flowing and the tongues wagging. To relax, I grabbed a mega-cocktail. It was getting crowded. Lots of shoes and legs and elbows to negotiate with, plenty of boobs to brush past. Just go with the flow, right? I stopped to chat with several people, none of whom I knew but all of whom I impressed. One aging party tart in a leopard skin print dress and young punk date heard me say I worked at the college.

"You're at a college?" the punk sniffed.

"Don't be offended," leopard lady breezily laughed. "Poor Roger graduated from Rutgers and can't find a job."

"Please shut up," Roger the punk sighed.

"Roger's very bright." She paused to put down her drink in one gulp. "He studied anthropological criticism."

"Cultural criticism," Roger smugly corrected.

"We've got one of those at the college," I said. "Jo Ann Staulen. Heard of her?".

No, they'd not heard of her.

"Me neither. But she's in that, that field of yours, Roger. She just came on this semester, and she holds these seminars about centrifugal ideas."

"You mean phallocentric ideology?" Roger smirked.

"Whatever," I laughed loudly, suddenly and completely relaxed as the booze put some brain cells into a deep and final sleep.

Roger looked at me, then at leopard lady, and faded into the crowd like a dissolving lozenge.

"He's a pain in the ass," I announced.

"He's an old fling, and I needed a quick date tonight," she explained, the slightest smile on her sun-fried face. "And yes, he's a pain in the ass."

We talked for a while about what a hemorrhoid Roger was, then talked about money. Making it and spending it. That last mega-cocktail had really loosened my tongue, and I found myself boasting about my beefy five-figure income. Leopard lady didn't know professors made that much, but I explained with a playfully thrust index finger on her chest that I was a Vice President, not some parasite teacher.

I flagged down a mini skirted chick who carried a tray crowded with wine-filled flutes. I offered my new friend some refreshment. Boy, I was cracking her up with my briskly paced jokes and incisive critiques of the balding guys and sagging gals.

"You're such an asshole," she chortled. "Just like me." Then her face thickened into an oval of angry wrinkles. "So fuck you, asshole!" She tossed her drink into my face.

Man, some people just should not drink. She tottered away on her high heals, bumping heavily into amused or annoyed guests. Where's Lauren? After one more refreshing pause in a hallway corner, I pressed forward. Halfway through a fern and lithograph infested hallway, I tripped and found myself face first against some guy's shoulder blade, which saved me from hitting the deck. But the hallway was so crowded that I had trouble getting my mug off the guy's back, and he started slapping at me. Fucker! I was about to start swinging when someone behind me slipped their hands beneath my armpits and righted me.

I turned to thank the hands.

"You're welcome," Steve Luken grinned. "For Christ's sake, you should slow down."

Uh?

"You're drunk."

"The hallway's crowded."

"I want your office," he goaded. I leaned forward and wetly laughed into his face.

"I'll have your office," he promised.

"You'll have a janitor's closet."

"Hey, how about a truce?" Luken suggested, looking about the room. Several guests looked on, eager for a pissing contest. "I mean, here we are, guests in the President's beautiful home."

"Fair enough," I conceded.

"Cheers." Luken handed me a glass and joined his buddy Pouris.

Huh. I was holding Luken's empty glass. Empty, that is, save for a cigarette butt.

I found Lauren where I left her, sitting with Bruce on the couch. They were sitting rather closely together, her bare thigh touching his dweeb-blue slacks.

"Moving in on my woman, eh?" I teased.

"Where've you been?" Bruce teased back. "I've had to keep your date's paws off of me."

"Bruce is sad." Lauren said.

"Jo Ann's here," Bruce said glumly. "But she's not talking to me."

"She doesn't seem your type," Lauren offered.

"I'm surprised she's here," I huffed. "I mean, all these men and women together, talking and laughing and drinking, and maybe even fucking." I winked at Lauren, and bless her heart, she winked back.

"Jo Ann's not a people person," Bruce allowed.

I separated Bruce from my date by standing over him with my big ass inches from his face. He retreated quickly, and I plopped recklessly onto the couch.

"You look really lit," Lauren said.

"I am."

"So am I." She pointed at two empty wine bottles in the corner.

I wiped at my hot face. "I just got jerked around by that creep."

"Steve Luken?" Bruce asked.

I nodded, and Bruce offered Lauren his own hateful description of Luken. At key points, I offered detail and anecdote. But mostly I kept drinking. I'd lost control of the drinker's rhythm and stumbled into an stumbling stupor. Fortunately, Bruce and Lauren had too. In fact, as far as I could tell, just about everybody was getting good and potted, with raucous laughter booming through the house. At one point, Luken walked past us, and Bruce pointed and laughed. Lauren did too. I wanted to join suit, but my finger was caught in my nose.

Luken paused, smiled, and repeated his claim that he would one day occupy my office.

Fighting words! Our ancestors invaded the enemy's caves and castles. Today, we invade the enemy's offices.

I rocked back and forth on the couch several times, gathering momentum to stand. Lauren, laughing freely, helped by pushing me up and at Luken. Luken looked every bit the hostile wretch he really is, despite his academic pretensions. I was face to face with him, and dimly aware of a gathering crowd. What a party: drinks, chicks, fist fights. Fleshlust and bloodlust, the way it used to be. I recalled the machismo of my ol' retired pal Gill, who'd battered his chick's husband on the front lawn.

I stomped the floor and bellowed a war cry. The crowd noise rose steadily, then a woman was shouting. Hey who tripped me?

Suddenly I was lying on the floor, and Luken's eyes were wide and distant. They kept floating skyward and finally stopped at the ceiling. Did he punch me? Did I just fall? I thought about it for a moment, but the floor was pretty comfortable. I'll suss this out later, I figured.

I woke on the couch. Lauren was gone, maybe in the kitchen—hold on. I was in a softly lighted den. Classical music occupied the background, and a portrait of Cardinal McGowan studied my besotted profile.

"Told you he'd wake up," someone said.

Don Boyle sat across from me in a throne-sized recliner, a tightly rolled hundred dollar bill hanging from his moist nostril. A mirrored tray lay across his lap.

"Let him have some," Dr. Douglas suggested. "It'll sober him up."

Boyle handed a vial to Douglas, who passed it on to me. Boy, this evening...it's endless. Boyle's and Douglas's eyes converged upon me, and I felt that old gnawing need to impress them, to show them that I belonged in their elevated company. I tapped out three thick rails upon the table beside me and snorted them with authority.

What a lift! Already, my heart was jumping and my head clearing.

Feeling my oats, I crisply prepared and consumed a fourth line.

"Wonderful stuff, isn't it?" Boyle queried. "Courtesy of George Prescott."

"Thank Christ for the war on drugs," Douglas opined, an elegantly constructed joint in hand. For comic effect, he wore mirror sunglasses the size of welder's goggles. "It keeps the best shit away from the street trash."

My pre-blackout memory returned. "Did Luken cold-cock me?"

Boyle's bark-like laugh made the tray on his lap dance.

"I'm sorry," I said plaintively to Boyle. "You invite me here and I—"

"It's nothing," Boyle breezed. "Hey, your date got all the attention when she kicked Luken's shin."

I strained to see the digital clock on some far shelves. 12:40 a.m.

Boyle snorted another line, wiped his nose, and congratulated me on my good chick taste. "She's a big hit. Bring her back anytime."

"Did she leave?"

"No," Douglas assured. "She's downstairs with a few other folks, having a nightcap. We'll join them in a moment. But first—" He glanced at Boyle.

"John, you've been just an enormous help to the college and to me personally, and I don't forget that." Boyle removed the tray from his lap, stood, and assumed an oratorical pose. "This is a big moment for me. In seventy-two hours, I will sign a new contract. It will be the best contract for any college president in the state. Period." Now he strode slowly to the end of the room, then returned, hands animated and voice booming. He seemed to address not Douglas and posterity, but me. "And I deserve that contract. I've increased the operating fund at this college by three—"

"Four," Douglas quickly corrected.

"—by four fold! Four! And next year, it might hit five. And soon we'll have that second campus. Much thanks goes to you, my friends." Boyle's eyes moistened. He motioned that Douglas and I should rise. Boyle hugged me, his face pressed against my chest. "Thanks for your contribution," he huskily assured. "You'll be taken care of."

Then he faced Dr. Douglas. Douglas removed his sunglasses and flung them across the room. They stood looking at one another, bottom lips trembling and eyes welling. Suddenly, Douglas raced toward Boyle and nearly toppled him in a passionate embrace. Embarrassed, I turned to give them privacy. To my relief, they were soon laughing and joking, manfully ribbing one another about the "puny salary" Boyle had coming his way.

After a final bracing nose powder, we skipped down the lushly carpeted stairs to join the remaining revelers.

Ah, there was my Robobabe, her dress alluringly damp under the arms. She gave me a very sweet and dirty smile, the tip of her tongue stroking her oft-polished teeth. I joined her on the couch, then patted bleary-eyed Bruce on the shoulder.

"What a great party," Lauren whispered, hand resting on my thigh.

"What a great party," a woman said, entering the room.

"Marvelous," hobbling Alfred Rochinni croaked, following Lydia Fairview.

So...it was true. Lydia and the chairman an item? Actually, it was hard to tell. As soon as the old prong sat, Lydia took a chair two away from him.

"Here's to all the wonderful people," Don Boyle announced, "who've helped me realize my vision." He removed a bottle of Dom from an ice bucket. "We must begin with our greatest patron, Mr. George Prescott."

Rochinni snorted.

"Mr. Prescott couldn't be here tonight," Boyle stated, "because he's somewhere else."

"Scotland," Dr. Douglas explained. "He's buying a town that's on top of an untapped oil field."

"He can buy all the backwater burgs in Scotland he wants," Rochinni harrumphed.

"And then some," Boyle smiled. "Anyway, thanks to Prescott. And thanks to—" He shrugged. "You know who you are. And aren't."

More mutterings from Rochinni, who made no effort to hide his foul mood. He looked pathetic, really, sitting in an oversized chair in his wrinkled suit, a glass of wine unsteady in his bony hand. He occasionally glanced toward Lydia, but Lydia paid him only fleeting attention.

Lydia, she looked so very desirable. Not just physically desirable. What was desirable was she. All of her, the aggregate affect of her body and her smile and eyes. And her hair. That lovely red hair, now gathered into a graceful braid.

And her voice.

Her voice, a few pitches lower than average, is an instrument that soothes and warms. It rises from her chest and its modulation is tailor-made for this kind of intimate after-hours nightcap. She spoke of her art gallery project, of the gallery's early acquisitions and long term plans, and we listened. We didn't listen to the subject matter—I mean, nobody but her cared about art. No, we listened to her voice, a voice that charmed us with its music.

"—even feature some Dionysian themes," Lydia noted.

Jo Ann Staulen entered the room, armed with a giant bag of chips.

"Dionysus wasn't all male," she asserted. "He was androgynous. Mostly feminine, actually."

"Not that much femininity," Lydia softly corrected.

"No, you're entirely wrong," Jo Ann gracelessly insisted. Yeah, she's great company, isn't she? "Besides, it's our duty to shatter dominant male archetypes. The man who makes a woman submit."

"So what's wrong with submitting?" Lauren loudly asked. "I'm not turned on by pussy men."

Boyle popped another bottle of bubbly and, in a gesture freighted with institutional power, filled Rochinni's glass dead last. "A toast to George Prescott," he urged.

"I'm sick of hearing about Prescott," Rochinni whined, voice clotted with phlegm and bile.

"He's done plenty for us," Boyle noted.

"So have I!"

Rochinni launched into a stultifying recitation of his days at Thunder Oil. We listened for about a minute. Then, one by one and two by two, we turned our attention from Rochinni to one another.

I stealthily moved beside Lydia.

"Hello John." Her smile was courteous and emotionless.

"I'm glad to hear the gallery work is coming along so—"

"I'm leaving!" Rochinni shouted.

Lydia coolly wished the Chairman a good evening, rose, and sat beside Bruce.

"Please Lydia, if we could talk," Rochinni insisted.

"Leave her alone," Robobabe demanded. "You're too old to be acting like this."

A snicker—half delight, half disbelief—escaped Lydia's nose.

Rochinni stood dumbly, caught in the crossfire of our disapproving stares.

"I shouldn't try to talk business at such a gala affair," he finally said. "Better be getting home. Mrs. Rochinni, she'll be worried that the old fellow is working too hard." He retreated to the hallway and fumbled with his coat.

"Yeah, don't make her worry about you," Boyle jeered.

"A good evening to you all, my friends," Rochinni called.

Nobody returned his departing words, and he left with sagging shoulders and sagging ego.

"That old fucker is really drunk," Lauren cheerfully observed.

Everybody laughed.

"Well stated," Douglas said to Lauren.

"That old bastard," Boyle laughed. "He's been a pain in the ass as long as I've been here. Maybe I shouldn't be saying this, but—" He paused to refill his glass. "But I'll say it because we're all friends here. We're the new guard."

"Finally," Douglas sighed.

"When Rochinni learned how much Prescott would make from our second campus deal, he tried to get the other trustees to vote against it. To stop it." Boyle rolled his eyes skyward, momentarily reliving nearly unbearable frustration.

"Nobody stands between Prescott and half a million," Douglas dryly observed.

As the group chattered, Douglas quietly shared the inside dope. "We had to make absolutely sure Rochinni got elected again, you see. Don's future is with the Democrats. Prescott's a Democrat. It would've been a terrible mess, any money going toward Drock's Republican friends. We just couldn't take any chances. Prescott would've been—well, 'angry' doesn't begin to cover it." He laughed wearily. "Everything was finally in place, and then Rochinni gets a hair up his ass about all the money the deal would bring Prescott. We had to persuade him to be more reasonable." He looked at me meaningfully.

"—How?"

He lowered his voice to a whisper. "Mrs. Rochinni is, you might say, very jealous, and over the years Don's provided discrete companionship for the Chairman."

"You blackmailed him?"

"Of course not. We gave him a choice, that's all. Put the college's interests first, as a trustee should. Or—" Douglas winked. "Try to explain away hours of some very awkward videocassettes."

"You think of everything, don't you?"

Douglas nodded and raised his glass, saluting his own peculiar talents.

Boyle was now calling for a toast. "Thanks to my friends, it's all blue skies."

"Here's to blue skies," Douglas agreed.

"To blue skies!" we all sang.

"To future U.S. Senator Donald Boyle!" someone called, and we all cheered.

As I assembled a late night sandwich in the kitchen, Bruce appeared. "What a night!" he enthused. "Rochinni, he's history."

"And Lydia really dusted Rochinni, huh?" I teased. "So much for your rumor about Lydia and old Alfred."

"Maybe their fucking is past-tense," he argued. "Maybe they broke up."

"Bullshit!'" I cheerfully declared.

The party was winding down and the revelers taking their leave.

I grasped Robobabe's willowy arm and offered Boyle and Douglas a good evening.

"Hope to see you again," Boyle called to Lauren. Then he gave me a vigorous thumbs up gesture. "My man! My *mule!*" He whispered something to Douglas, who was again wearing those ridiculous sunglasses. Douglas guffawed, and Boyle's laughter rose like a siren as Lauren and I stepped into the starry winter night.

"Your mule?" Lauren asked, puzzled.

"They're just loaded."

"There goes that nice woman," Lauren observed.

Lydia Fairview was getting into the passenger side of a red compact. I'd seen that car before, I thought, as it pulled away from the curb and turned the snow-flecked corner. Goddammit, who's she screwing?

"Who's she screwing?" Lauren asked.

"I don't know."

"—Is she screwing you?"

"No. You are."

"I sold a Sail today," she revealed, "but know what? I was faithful to you." She put her hand in mine. "You've really been sweet to me."

Chapter Twenty Three: How Far the Mighty Do Fall

I woke at 6:30 a.m. to find Lauren standing before the dresser mirror, searching for the slightest imperfection. I feigned sleep and enjoyed Lauren's absorption in her teenage-thin waist, her loud and proud tits. Go ahead. Jeer those vain women who submit to vein collapses, to nips and tucks, to butt shrinks and boob boosts. It's gotta be gratifying to look that good in the morning. Imagine: no need to suck in your tummy as you shimmy into those jeans. Your tummy's already sucked in, automatically.

As her inspection ended, Lauren's back surrendered its tension, and she disappeared into the bathroom. Soon I heard the shower and her tuneless humming. Lauren departed without a word, and I couldn't fall back asleep. I rose, scratched, and showered. Mmm. The bathroom really smelled nice, what with Lauren's rich creams and luxurious oils lingering in the moist warm air. These enchanting feminine scents, along with the hot pulsing shower, acted as a balm on my cracker jack hangover.

After a quick breakfast—three bagels and a half jar of peanut butter—I was out the door. My disfigured Sail cowered in the driveway. Damn it, Lauren had better pay for repairs. But at least I had the Slug. With a sentimental lump in my throat, I treated my ol' faithful Slug gently on the drive in. The Slug must've been grateful, for she never once stalled, and she even passed a belligerent semi like a coltish youngster.

Once at work, I wondered what to do. That's the educational bureaucrat's burden, killing time until the coffee break. I tossed that pile of vapid surveys that cluttered a desk corner. Then I opened a desk drawer. More junk: notes from pointless committee meetings; various and sundry communiqués between myself and various and sundry fellow flunkies; a meaty stash of skin rags. Everything but the skin rags went into the wastebasket. I just couldn't bring myself to dump them. True, the glossies no longer thrilled me—I mean, how many times can you cop a hormone buzz from the same pic, no matter how endowed or brazen the chick? But I just couldn't part with them. See, my relationship with these skin rags has matured, has grown from rough lust to tender friendship.

Hey! Coffee break!

Thank wheezing Christ I brought some cigarettes to chase down the coffee.

The cafeteria had a java special, and I bought a thermos sized cup of plum and ginger protoplasm for a buck. I nodded at the many secretaries in the staff lounge, then bellied up to an empty table at the room's rear. I was halfway through my coffee—my pulse already goosed by the coffee—when Dr. Douglas and Dr. Olsen entered the lounge. Olsen was agitated, her hands and mouth even busier than usual. They were nearly out the door when Douglas stopped and slowly turned to face me.

"It *is* you." Douglas pointed histrionically.

"Uh?"

"You're here so early...on time, in other words," he ribbed.

I was trying to think up a witty reply as Olsen approached my table. Her blue eyes were bugging. "What a break you're here early. Dr. Douglas was going to call you when we got upstairs."

I hurriedly stuffed the remains of a donut in my mouth.

"Don's called a first string meeting." Her face was hard with anxiety. "He sounded so angry."

"Let's not overreact," Douglas counseled. "That's how rumors get started." He paused to glance about the room. The secretaries, who'd been straining to hear our conversation, returned to their coffee and cigarettes, to their commiseration about lousy bosses and lousy diets.

On the way to Boyle's conference room, we passed those faculty firebrands, Karen Farella and Jim Pouris. The caped crusaders were waist deep in their failing campaign for President and Vice President of the faculty union. Wonder wimp Dwayne Derrickson's campaign, covertly directed by Douglas, was wildly successful. Phase one of the campaign had been to make me look like a horse's ass. Phase two was to have Dwayne resolve the many "problems" I'd created and simultaneously foster "a spirit of cooperation" with Boyle. Phase three, currently in effect, was to smear Farella and Pouris as malcontents who lived solely to belittle Don Boyle. The election was in a week, and Farella and Pouris were desperate.

Douglas slyly stopped to chat with them. His easygoing tone and friendly posture—hands in pockets, attentive nods—disarmed them. It would never dawn on these two arm-waving loudmouths that Douglas had worked so hard to ruin them. The tag team was especially strident today, complaining about campaign sabotage. Farella, hand over her eyes in disgust, complained bitterly about dirty pool.

"What's she talking about now?" I whispered to Olsen.

Olsen raised a mischievous eyebrow.

Douglas's mellifluous tone calmed Farella, and she lowered her voice to just below shouting as Pouris stared into space, lost in private musings. Douglas eventually excused himself and rejoined Olsen and me.

"I actually like them," Douglas smiled as we resumed our walk to the conference room.

"They look absolutely lost," Olsen noted.

"They're really pretty interesting," Douglas claimed. "They act on principle, though the principles are naive and self-defeating. They don't understand realpolitik."

Olsen dismissed them as jerks.

"Even Boyle likes them."

"That's absurd."

"Yeah it is," Douglas cheerfully conceded. "He curses the day they were hired."

Inside the conference room, Douglas continued. "The campaign has gone beautifully. Word is that Derrickson and his running mate—that dim-wit sociology instructor, Mary Green—are going to win big."

Olsen cleared her throat. "Well, thank you for giving credit where credit is due."

"You're right," Douglas agreed. "Your rat fucking scheme was brilliant."

"The concept was yours," Olsen deferred to Douglas with rare modesty. "I just crossed the t's and dotted the i's, really."

Olsen explained that she'd spent Saturday evening in the faculty union office, where she created campaign literature in the names of Farella and Pouris. Olsen imitated Farella's writing style with remarkable fidelity: the hysterical tone, the hard-nosed, no-compromise stance, the occasional bursts of martyrdom, and—most crucially—the relish in attacking Boyle.

Flush with triumph, Olsen placed a copy of her torpedo before me.

"Read it," she urged.

I began to read.

"Read it aloud."

It was an authentic white knuckler all right, a fiery missive that would terrify and outrage West Central's numerous weak sisters. They'd scurry as far as they could from Farella and Pouris, squeaking and trembling, to embrace Dwayne Derrickson.

One section was especially slanderous: "Since his arrival five years ago, Don Boyle has most certainly been the agent of change he claims to be. The change, however, is disastrous. With the aid of Board Chairman and all-around idiot Alfred Rochinni, Boyle has transformed West Central from a run of the mill college to a foul pit, where obscenely paid administrators, lackeys, toadies and flunkies multiply with the rapidity of bacteria in your septic tank.

Unlike the bacteria, the toadies and flunkies serve no purpose. Like the bacteria, they stink."

Douglas was crippled by a long snorting laugh. I had to crank up the volume to be heard over the merriment.

"First-rate rat fucking," Douglas finally offered, wiping away tears.

I agreed. The document even boasted a union letterhead. Even better, it had been reproduced on the union copying machine, which always left a faint but tell-tale smudge of toner on the bottom left hand corner of documents. With all these damning details in place, Farella and Pouris were finished. Nobody would believe they didn't write the document; they'd be dismissed by everyone as maniacs.

"So this is what you were jawing with them about," I said to Douglas.

"They don't know what hit them," Olsen crowed.

Olsen and Douglas continued this self-congratulatory shtick. What the hell—they'd pulled of a coup, just as Boyle had wanted. Still, their glee was a little forced. Olsen was plainly nervous, blaring more loudly than usual. Douglas kept glancing at the door, apparently bracing for a violent entrance by the Prez.

And here he was. Hair disheveled, Boyle took his place at the table. He looked like terrible, as if he'd lost a lot of money or his Mum had died. "Good morning, Don," Olsen peeped.

"What makes this so—Christ!" Boyle's mouth did an amazing turn, expressing simultaneous grief, rage, and exhaustion. For a moment, he looked like a portrait by Bacon, that English guy whose grotesque paintings seem produced by meat cleavers and blood rather than brushes and paint.

Boyle cupped his face in his hands. Was he laughing or crying?

"Do the want to good blues first?" he honked through his fingers.

Douglas calmed the anxious Olsen with a pat on the hand. "What—can you repeat that, Dr. Boyle?"

Boyle removed his hands from his face. "Good news or bad news first?"

"Good news," Douglas suggested.

"The good news is that Alfred Rochinni, that rat, has officially resigned from the board."

"Wonderful," Olsen ventured.

"The bad news is that an hour ago, I received a call from Acting Board Chairman Leon Carmichael. He said I'm fired!"

Uh?

"The Board's not going to renew my contract!"

A tiny yelp escaped Olsen's mouth.

"It's over!" Boyle jumped up, kicked a chair from his path and fled, loose shirttail flapping behind him.

Olsen's voice trailed off and her eyes squeezed out tears.

"Fired?" Douglas whispered to himself.

We sat tingling in our overstuffed chairs, silent and bewildered. It was like just waking from a vivid dream. Now, fumbling for a cigarette, I shook my head to gather my wits.

"It's a conspiracy," Douglas whispered.

"What is?" I asked.

"All of it." Douglas's eyes lost focus as he imagined a serpentine plot to bring down Boyle. "It began, I think, in 1987 when—"

Boyle loudly re-entered. His pants were around his ankles, and his shirt, freshly and violently shorn of buttons, was open to the waist. "It's my destiny to be fucked over," he bawled.

Olsen covered her eyes, Douglas's jaw tightened. Me? I wanted to duck under the table.

"And I did everything for you! For you, my first string!" Boyle hammer fisted the table top, and Olsen began weeping.

"You're not crying for me!" Boyle bellowed into Olsen's purple face. "You're crying for yourself. For you, for you, for you!" With each knotted cry of "for you," Boyle struck the table.

"Please stop!" Olsen pleaded.

"Slut!"

Now he faced Douglas. "You're a traitor!"

"You're wrong."

"Take my shorts," Boyle demanded.

"Please calm yourself."

"Fuck yourself!" Hopping about one leg, then the other, Boyle yanked off his boxer shorts and whipped them at Douglas. Douglas, spookily self-possessed, deftly moved his head. The shorts arced past him to land on the floor.

Now Boyle tore his shirt off. "I'm naked!"

Boyle turned toward me, and I figured now was a good time to duck under the table. He scrambled after me.

"I saved you!" he bellowed. "You were absolutely nothing."

"Let go of my leg!"

"You *are* nothing!"

I turned on my haunches and scurried on hands and knees the length of the table.

"You turned on me!"

"Shut up, you maniac! Ow!" My skull collided with the leg of a chair. But I was nearly at the table's end, and before me were the blue slacks and black shoes of the campus police.

I gained my feet, aided by a cop.

Boyle was right behind me, and the cops grabbed him. He resisted for a moment, cursing and wailing about betrayal. I glanced at Douglas—could he have done it? Was there a grain of truth in Boyle's mad rants?

"A twist on the patsy concept!" Boyle accused with pointing finger. "You set me up, didn't you Deyme? You're so good at playing dumb!"

The cops tried to soothe Boyle, talking in hushed and respectful tones. One cop draped his jacket across Boyle's shoulders, while the second led him to the door.

"It's Prescott!" Boyle screeched. "He paid you off to ruin me!" Boyle insisted. "That's it, isn't it!" After some struggle, the cops led the jabbering Boyle out.

Douglas's nerves were finally betraying him, and he lighted a cigarette with trembling hands. "What an ingrate," he hissed. "I waited on him hand and foot. Bastard." He smoked violently, smoke rolling from flaring nostrils.

I surveyed the room. "Where's Dr. Olsen?"

Douglas looked about, shrugged. "I guess Michelle ran out. Who can blame her? Boyle's been balling her for years, and then he turns around and blames her."

"Balling her?" I marveled aloud. Bruce had been right all along. Fleetingly, I imagined Boyle pinning Olsen on his cluttered desk. It wasn't difficult, after all: I'd just seen Boyle in his birthday suit, and my imagination, refined by years of porno, filled in the details.

Douglas smiled faintly, as if he could see my musings floating comic book fashion above my head. "Nice fringe benefit, yes?"

After another smoke, Douglas suggested we retreat to his office. On the way, we passed several reporters who roamed, vulture-like, about the campus in search of a scoop.

One guy blocked our way. Douglas politely sidestepped him, shaking his head at the guy's yammering. The guy turned to me. "Can you confirm the report that Don Boyle was having sexual relations with several top female administrators?"

Another reporter—a pimply faced youngster for whom the term "cub" was invented—asked shrilly about Boyle's sexual orientation.

I couldn't suppress a laugh.

"Is that a 'yes'?"

"What?"

"Don Boyle was having relations with Alfred Rochinni?"

"He what?"

"Dr. Boyle was taken from the building nude," the cub rattled at me, "and Alfred Rochinni was watching from his car."

"Was he naked too?" I joked.

"So you confirm the report that—"

Now I imagined Boyle pinning Rochinni on his desk.

Douglas rescued me from the cub and my own incredulity. "We have no comment to make on any of these matters."

The reporters now descended upon Jean Bowler, a Trustee. Rumor had it that Jean, a grade school teacher, was literate in only the narrowest sense of the word. Because she could be easily manipulated, and because she received money under the table to support Alfred Rochinni, she'd been prized by Rochinni and Boyle alike. Now, as the reporters salted and peppered her, confusion and excitement enlivened her face, a face that normally betrayed few signs of cognition. She played nervously with her fake red leather purse and faced the reporters.

"Well he didn't seem queer," Jean ventured. "But you can't always tell, can you?"

"No you can't," the cub encouraged.

"Well—there you go," Jean nodded meaningfully. "He acted queer to me sometimes. Just my opinion."

We hurried away, leaving daft Jean to create sensational headlines. Once in his office, Douglas was greatly amused by my barrage of questions: Was Boyle boffing every broad in the college? What in Hell's name was going on around here? Did Boyle swing both ways? Or Rochinni?

Douglas revealed that Don Boyle always had a bustling harem of career babes on the side.

"Why he keeps getting married, I don't know."

"In any event," Douglas observed, "Rochinni is certainly not Boyle's type."

Uh?

"You're probably more his type," Douglas continued. "Big shoulders, big hands. Big everything, I imagine." Then he laughed loudly—a laugh colored by equal parts whimsy and confusion—and offered me a cigarette. I accepted. Douglas was really OK, I thought. He liked me enough to joke around, engage in some mock locker room banter to help me relax.

"The rumors are really going to fly around here," Douglas warned. "Keep your head down. If you look up for even a second, the shit'll go splat, right in your face." For emphasis, he wiped at his eyes with his fingertips, like a silent movie comedian wiping pie from his face.

"If we're lucky," he offered, "we might survive the fallout. Then again..." His gaze drifted skyward. "We could be sacrificial fodder. The real power brokers might make us the patsy." He looked at me seriously. "It's happened before. Many times."

Douglas's concern for our jobs was, in its own way, quite appealing. And his weakness for conspiracy theories now made a little sense: West Central's political machinations naturally gave rise to dark suspicions. It was hard to tell who was pushing whose buttons, and for what reasons.

"I wonder if Marina Oswald's baby sister was one of Boyle's chicks,"

I teased. "It would explain a lot, don't you think?"

"I'll call Jim Garrison immediately."

"He's dead, isn't he?"

Douglas hoisted his eyebrows with mock skepticism.

Around noon, I suggested we grab lunch. "My treat," I offered.

"May I join you?" asked someone—a female? Olsen?—just outside Douglas's door.

"Please join us, Michelle," Douglas called.

The woman stepped in. "Thank you," said Lydia Fairview.

Chapter Twenty Four: *She loves me, she loves me not*

Douglas, Lydia, and I assembled in a dimly lighted corner booth at Ralph's. As Douglas and I gabbed over drinks and complimentary batter fried mushrooms or tadpoles, Lydia was quiet. What's the deal? I wondered. I mean, she's a chick, right? They might deny it, but chicks love to gossip.

"Maybe Olsen blew the whistle on Boyle," I offered. "What do you think, Lydia?"

"It's plausible."

Douglas and I exchanged glances.

"But I doubt it," she concluded.

Douglas frowned. "What do you know, Lydia, that we don't?"

"A few things," she teased.

"Well come on," Douglas urged. "Tell us."

"After we eat."

"No," I insisted. "Now."

"After we eat."

So we ate. I've always been devoted to Ralph's corned beef sandwich, and this one really hit the spot. Strangled Christ I was famished! The events of the last sixteen or so hours—Boyle's party, the spiraling institutional intrigue—it'd caught up with me. I needed time to rethink, to regroup, to overeat.

Douglas tried to pry details from Lydia. "I actually don't have that much news," she protested cheerfully. "Just a couple little nuggets, really." She illustrated just how little those nuggets were by holding her thumb millimeters from her forefinger.

The waitress returned with fresh cocktails, and I took the opportunity to order a second corned beef sandwich.

Douglas glanced at me with vague disapproval.

"So I'm hungry," I said, a tad defensive.

"Go on," Lydia encouraged. "Have another."

Hmm...was she mocking my relentless appetite?

"Besides, it's on my expense account," Lydia revealed. "My treat."

Douglas struck the table in mock anger. "I thought only the first string had an expense account."

"Did have," Lydia corrected.

Did?

"That's it, Lydia," Douglas demanded. "Come on with it."

"What?" she grinned.

"The first string is losing its expense account?"

"The members of the first string," Lydia revealed, "are losing more than an expense account."

"Even our pagers?" I blurted.

"Everything. In fact, the first string doesn't exist anymore."

Douglas was suddenly restless. "How do you know this?" he urged, his hand on Lydia's.

"Alfred Rochinni told me. This morning."

Douglas was puzzled, but I understood immediately: "You've been fucking him."

"Who?" Douglas and Lydia asked in unison.

"Rochinni."

"--I knew it!" Douglas belatedly claimed.

"I knew it weeks ago," I harrumphed.

"You're both so full of absolute nonsense," she laughed.

"So you're not fucking him," I sneered.

"You poor men are so wrong," she remarked, arrogance coloring her voice. "In fact, Mr. Rochinni is resigning from the board as of January first, but so is Don Boyle. They're both history."

"That's absurd," Douglas said, his tone growing bitter. "You're fucking Rochinni, and you believe all his sour grapes. We locked him out of everything."

"There's no other explanation," I insisted. "You know way too much."

"There certainly is another explanation," she retorted.

And after Douglas and I pleaded sufficiently, she finally explained.

I didn't want to believe it, her explanation. Several times, I interrupted her with a guffaw or a grunt or an incredulous thwop on my big forehead. Still, the more I listened, the more I grudgingly believed.

Seems a tight-assed busybody, maybe a disgruntled citizen with a tax hangover, had gotten wind of the second campus shenanigans. Then the over aged Cub Scout complained loudly to several state bureaucrats, and even phoned the governor's chief-of-staff.

"The second campus is a dead duck," Lydia announced. "So are Boyle and Rochinni. And Prescott's stuck with some high priced repairs."

"I thought we kept the scheme airtight," Douglas complained. "But with a job that big—" He studied me with accusing eyes. "—Well, even some of the Kennedy conspirators talked. Before they expired."

"Where was the leak?" I asked.

"Nobody knows," Lydia said evenly. "But whoever it was kept shouting until somebody paid attention."

My stomach did a double-axle reverse flip: My watch, left at the scene. Fleetingly, I imagined myself in prison attire.

I belched. It was like a sick fart, damp and sour.

Douglas's eyes were hard. I saw the wheels racing in his head: Is Deyme the leak? But I was the last guy who should talk—I did the dirty work!

I returned Douglas's stare. "Just fuck off, why don't you?" I blurted.

"Christ John," Douglas snapped.

"Christ yourself," I shouted. Several diners glanced at me.

"This isn't the time to go wobbly," Lydia advised, her hand lightly touching mine.

"Uh?"

"You're getting hysterical."

"We all are," Douglas added, apparently reconsidering my culpability. It had to dawn on him that I'd be a full-fledged moron to talk. "Have a drink. We're in this together."

Douglas apologized, bought me a cocktail, and apologized again. "All this topsy turvy shit," he explained, "it's clouded my thinking."

"Be a sport, James," Lydia encouraged.

I grunted and tossed back the cocktail. As if to show some solidarity, Lydia too tossed back her drink. Huh...she must be pretty stressed out, just like Douglas and me. We gossiped and speculated a while longer, though Lydia insisted she didn't know the leak. Douglas, sick of coaxing and pleading, suddenly stood to leave.

But he first bent over to whisper in my ear. "We can't turn on each other. I'll—"

"Oh, a *secret*," Lydia teased.

"—establish plausible denial for both of us."

"What did you say?" asked in a theatrical whisper.

"I said, 'Lydia's got the expense account. Order anything you want.'" Then, with a curt nod toward Lydia, Douglas was gone.

Suddenly alone with me, Lydia was caught off guard. She picked up her purse as if to leave, and I gently clasped her hand. "Please stay. Just for a moment. Please?" She smiled patiently and agreed, though refused my offers for another drink.

"You still drink too much," she noted as I looked lustily at my empty cocktail glass.

"You're holding out on me," I insisted.

"You're wrong."

"I'm right. We made a pact, a bedroom pact." Yeah, I'm pretty low: I'll shamelessly appeal to bedroom memories.

"It's different now," Lydia said colorlessly. "You turned out to be—" She paused, as if measuring her words.

I waited, nonchalant. What could she possibly say to hurt me now?

"—to be an asshole."

Ouch. When a woman calls you an asshole, it really hurts. Men, we call each other assholes all the time, yes? It's practically a term of endearment for us, we awkward clods who are embarrassed to show affection for fear of being suspected a faggot. Hey, asshole. Good to see you. But when that foul term is shot from a woman's sweet lips, it hurts.

"Don't change the subject. I still say you were doing Rochinni."

Lydia took a long breath. "You're enough to drive me into the office of Jo Ann Staulen. To say that I slept my way into some position of power."

"What position of power?" I probed.

"After the housecleaning, I'll still be around. My hands aren't dirty." She looked pointedly at my hands.

We sat silently there, looking at one another for several weighty moments. I'd be damned if I was going to confess anything.

"There's nothing left to talk about," Lydia finally said, standing to leave.

"There's plenty." I grabbed for her hand, but the booze had ruined my hand-eye coordination, and my hand rather ungracefully brushed her thigh. "Please excuse me," I assured. "Really."

She studied me. Oh, screaming Jesus. Here it comes: I'm a drunk, I'm a loser, etc.

"I said I was sorry," I protested, uncomfortable under her stare.

"I know." She lightly touched my shoulder. "Once in a while you're a lovely man."

I began to stand, but Lydia, hand still on my shoulder, kept me in my chair. "You're a fool, James," she half-whispered. "I really cared a lot about you."

"Maybe you still do."

"No I don't." She took a twenty from her purse, placed it on the table, and hurried away.

She still loves me! I thought. *Yes!* She'd looked at me with that half-smile and those narrowed eyes, as when I first took her out for drinks and ended up at her condo.

I jumped up to follow her out.

The sky was already dark at 4:30 p.m., and it took me a minute to realize that Lydia's car was already gone. I stood in the parking lot, gazing at the rollicking red and blue Christmas lights around the lot's perimeter. A car passed, its radio blaring "White Christmas." It's really a magical time, isn't it? Despite the dirty snow and muddy street corners and chronic head colds, the holiday season really thaws your heart. Even Lydia's!

A silly romantic image coalesced in my head: the sherry, the flowers and the chocolate. I was rapping on Lydia's front door, and she was opening it, the caution draining from her face. I murmur that I'm sorry—

and damn it, I really am!—and she presses her lips to mine.

Finding the sherry was easy. I stopped at the local Booze Barn and grabbed a bottle that sported a cheery little green ribbon around its narrow neck. I grabbed some cigarettes, too. Lydia likes a smoke after...oops. Can't be too presumptuous. Full of holiday cheer, I smiled broadly at the sullen Pakistani behind the cash register.

"Happy holidays," I grinned.

He frowned.

"I said, 'Happy Holidays.'"

"I know what you said," he snapped in his reedy accent. "You want me to kiss your behind because you patronize my store?"

Huh?

"I'm most surprised you have the nerve to come in here again."

"How's that?" I waited for an explanation, though even at this moment I recalled that a few weeks ago...

"Phone still isn't fixed!" With an angry jerk of his head, he motioned toward the pay phone near the entrance; the hand set was missing.

"—I did that?"

"You were drunk." He reached beneath the checkout counter and produced the amputated hand set.

Yes, now I remembered something about coming in here, upset about Lydia and her rumored dalliance with that old prong Rochinni. If memory served me, I'd called her. Or rather, I tried. But she hung up.

"I can't thank you enough for not calling the authorities." I dug into my deep pocket and pulled out a wrinkled fifty. "Please take this for the, for your inconvenience. And your customers."

"—I shouldn't."

I pushed it into his shirt pocket, and he couldn't fight off a grin. With my hand still in his pocket, I tickled him. He guffawed and playfully pushed me away.

"You fairies wanna let me buy some beer?" a tired-looking black guy asked, standing stooped behind me.

"Merry Christmas to you too, my good man," I sang to the black guy. I dug into my still-deep pocket and gently placed a ten atop the twelve pack he cradled against his gut.

"You're beautiful," he said solemnly.

"I'm in love."

"With him?" The black guy nodded at the Pakistani.

"With both of you. I love all the colors of humanity." I winked at him, grabbed my sherry and departed to search for chocolates.

The chocolates weren't easy to find. With Christmas only—what? twelve days away?—the stores couldn't keep up with guys like me who can think of nothing to buy their babes but chocolate. But it works out, really. Babes love chocolate. After trundling through Marshall Fields and elbowing past the fur-wrapped, sour-pussed old ladies, I found one last box of overpriced chocolate. I forked over the fifteen bucks, then stood for ten minutes in the gift-wrapping line. My last stop was at a florist, where I bought a bouquet of roses. Finally, with aching feet and joyous heart, I was back in the ol' Slug and on my way to Lydia's.

A bit of nervousness set in as I approached her condo, so I recalled the scene that inspired tonight's impulsive behavior. Yeah, there I am knocking on Lydia's door, clutching the sherry and chocolate and roses. Whoops. Hold on a minute. In this version, Lydia is alarmed to see me at her door with booze.

Okay. Fair enough. As I pulled into her driveway, I stuck the sherry, still snug in its brown sack, beneath the passenger seat.

I stood before her door—newly decorated with a Christmas garland—and sucked down several breaths. I hadn't been this nervous about a chick for quite a while. I must really love her. My heart was doing a terrific tom-tom imitation as I knocked and waited for the heartwarming welcome of an opening door.

Huh...I knocked again. No answer. Several more unanswered knocks convinced me that Lydia wasn't home. Or maybe she just wasn't home for me. After a few more half-hearted raps, I drove home.

Tell me.

Why do women do that? Get drunk with you? It just gives you the wrong ideas. I managed a bitter laugh—to think she'd be at home waiting for me! By the time I pulled into my driveway, I was whipped. My duplex looked forlorn, with no Christmas lights or door wreath or even fake windowpane snow. I just wasn't up to going inside. Not yet. Not without a little holiday cheer.

I rescued the sherry from beneath my seat and uncapped it. Poor bottle. It looked pretty dispirited. We kept one another company, the sherry and I. At one point, I was so grateful for its company that I treated it to my own rendition of "The Twelve Days of Christmas." Around the fourth day, I passed out. My chattering teeth woke me and urged me to my duplex. I fell several times on the way to my door, but I wasn't hurt. Of course, if I'd taken those falls sober...!

Once inside, I pulled of my shirt, kicked off my shoes, and revived myself sufficiently to make coffee and turn on the television.

Oh, terrific. The news. More corporate downsizing, and just in time for the holidays. A "reporter" stood outside the gates of a factory in...in where? Good old Flint! Oh man. Look at those shell-shocked shop rats, staggering from the weary factory for the final time. The cuts were getting deeper and bloodier. Not one of these men and women looked younger than fifty.

"You're laid off a week before Christmas during a so-called economic recovery," the reporter helpfully reminded them. "What are your feelings?"

The workers endured the morbid queries with a shrug or quick "What're you gonna do?" then escaped the mini-cam's glare. But all the news wasn't bad. An auto industry analyst cheerily noted that car factories were springing up in East Germany, with super-low labor costs. Corporate profits, he assured us, would continue to soar. The network thoughtfully devoted a half hour special to Flint, "The City Without Christmas." Seems the economic recovery didn't stick around long in Flint. The city's so broke that Christmas was canceled. Yeah, no Christmas: not a single city school had enough cash to put on a Christmas show; not a single city agency had the dollars to buy toys for poor kids; even the city's homeless shelters—for a while, Flint's only growth industry—were downsizing.

I couldn't endure ten minutes of this and killed the damned television with the trigger of my remote control. I stared at the heavily shadowed ceiling and wondered how long Mum could hold out up there. I mean, she's lucked out so far; no robberies in a year. But they're coming. The robbers, thieves, lowlifes, and ethically-challenged march inexorably through the city, block by block, an army cheered only by more booty and more blood. Why won't she move out? I've asked her a couple of times, but she insists that Flint is her home. It's that immigrant's roots thing, you know? Flint is her adopted home. Dad worked and died there, so she's decided that she's got to die there.

Nodding off, I mused that the rust belt is lucky to have people like Mum, people with genuine loyalty. But loyalty, it just doesn't pay off anymore. Don't they get it? They'll never escape working class level until they spurn that tender attachment to rust belt town and trade. I mean, look at me. Sentiment doesn't get in my way, and things are going just fine, thanks.

Chapter Twenty Five: Holiday Depression Syndrome

At work, a few reporters were trying to snag details about yesterday's campus chaos. One asked about trustee plans for a presidential replacement.

"I'm unaware of the trustees' plans."

"Rumor has it that Dr. Douglas will take over."

"Really?"

"Is he a good choice?"

"—Absolutely." He'd be a terrific choice, what with he and I doing the male bonding bit. Huh...you can't count out Douglas. He's way too clever.

"Why did both the President and board chair resign?"

"I really don't know what's going on."

"That's an understatement," the reporter complained.

I wondered...maybe Bruce had some inside dope about Douglas. Better call him immediately. As I entered my office, Barbara was quacking on the phone, her desk occupied by donuts and a behemoth mug of coffee.

"The dear's here even later than usual," she noted.

"Good morning to you too." I fumbled with the keys. Huh. Wrong one.

Jesus, I need glasses.

"Too much to drink last night?" she needled.

"Not enough." Again, the key wouldn't work. "Goddammit anyway!"

"Learn some new words?"

"What's with these keys?" I studied my key ring at arm's length.

"It's a new lock." She asked her gossip mate to hang on for a moment and, with a show of immense impatience, rose from her snack bar and inserted a key into the lock.

"Did you get a new key for me too?"

"You're welcome."

"Do you have a key for me?" I demanded.

"No."

"Fine," I boomed, banging into my office. "I do everything myself around here, and you can't even manage to—"

Then I shouted.

I really didn't want to shout like that, right in front of Barbara. But I did: I shouted. And she lumbered to her desk to bleat happily into the phone: "He just shouted! Shouted like an idiot!"

Like a *fired* idiot. No wonder my lock had been changed and I had no key. My office was no longer mine.

Steven D. Vivian

My desk was gone, my books were stacked sloppily, my disassembled computer sulked in a corner. My phone was gone.

"He just went, he just went 'Oohhh!' like he'd filled his drawers."

Some residual ego urged me to face my tormentor, to demand that she get to work. But of course I couldn't. I'd been demoted from flunky to fired flunky, a harrowing plummet into the societal sewer of unemployment. I recalled last night's story about the shit-canned factory workers. I imagined myself among them: shuffling, grunting, stubbled, avoiding the camera's glare. Sacked on national television. My fifteen nanoseconds of fame.

"—he's been here too long if you ask me." She paused to clamp her fat hand over the phone's mouthpiece. "The pink slip's on your desk."

The so-called pink slip was white, actually, and crowned with the crimson West Central College letterhead.

Pursuant to Section VI. of your employment contract and college board policies III a. and b., I have been directed by the Board of Trustees to inform you that your employment contract shall not be renewed upon its expiration.

Sincerely,
Jennifer Modine,
West Central Board of Trustees Attorney and Counsel

I clamped shut my eyes. The faces of my career—Boyle and Douglas, Bruce and Lydia—appeared before me. They formed a wheel that spun against a crimson background. The wheel spun faster, and its faces became a blurred ring of runny noses, watery eyes, and shouting mouths. The circle then disappeared into a dark hole like dishwater down the drain.

I don't know how long I stood there, grunting and twitching. Barbara's voice nagged me back to the unpleasant present.

"—glad they're all canned," she was crowing into the phone.

Well, it could have been worse. They could've sacked me and refused to pay off the balance of my contract. I mean, what could've I done? Hired a two hundred dollar an hour lawyer and litigated for three years? At least I had paychecks through April. I wondered who else was on the chopping block. The heads were rolling fast: Boyle, Rochinni, and now me. What about Bruce? And Douglas?

And Lydia?

I grabbed for the phone. Yeah, old habits die hard: the phone was gone. I turned to Barbara and asked if I might use hers.

"No."

"Please."

"Leave me alone."

"Just for a minute."

"Call you back," she sang. She slammed the phone into its cradle and faced me. My former secretary, this daft clock-watcher and gossip queen, was transformed into a gorgon, her oft-frosted hair writhing with supernatural static charge.

"You creep!" she barked, her big hot face inches from my own. "You mistreated me for, for years. And you ask..."

A fear, primitive and powerful, sloshed in my stomach.

"—to use my phone? *My* phone? It's not your phone anymore. Some nerve to—"

The old bag was pissed enough to split my skull.

"—you've done to me, condescended to me. You still owe me two hundred and seventy seven dollars in coffee money!"

Yeah, I often borrowed a couple bucks from the coffee club's tin can, which sat beside the office's brewer.

"I bought that coffee! It was my money!" Now she shook a yellowed sheet of paper in my face. At the top was scrawled Deyme: Coffee Account Payable. From there followed several dozen scrawled entries consisting of a date and a sum of money: three dollars, five dollars, ten dollars. It adds up over the years, doesn't it?

Barbara damned me as a bullying cheat. "I was always scared to ask for the money. Now I'm not!"

She slapped me.

"Pay me!" Another slap. "You've got a big salary!"

"I had a big salary."

"I never did." A very sharp slap made my cheek sting as if jabbed with a dozen needles. "I never will." She reared back for another slap.

"I'm sorry," I half-whispered.

Her hand—age-spotted, trembling, damp—slowly lowered, and tears dribbled down her crustily rouged cheeks.

I pulled out six crisp fifty-dollar bills and placed them on her desk.

She wiped away the tears with the back of her hand and gathered the money. She counted the bills once. Twice. Thrice. "I've hated you since the day you started here," she finally said.

Huh...she just won't shut up, not even after three hundred dollars. "I've hated you too," I retorted, my guilt instantly assuaged by coughing up three hundred bucks. "I should've fired you immediately."

"You tried." She abruptly turned on her scuffed triple wide black flats and left me standing in the empty room.

"I should've tried harder." Oh yeah...I returned to my rifled desk, but the skin mags were gone.

"In case you're interested," Barbara sneered. "Did you hear who the new President is?"

"It's Douglas! Big deal!" The snake. It hurt, really hurt, that he wouldn't keep me on. And he pretended to like me! I shouldered past Barbara and hurried for the nearest exit.

"Lydia Fairview."

I broke stride only momentarily. I mean, when you're making a grand exit, you've gotta keep marching. No hesitation is allowed.

"Did you hear me?" she happily bawled as I hurried down the hallway.

Lydia!

As I ran toward the parking lot, I mused that women have gotten as bad as men. They stick in the butcher knife as ruthlessly as we guys. Only a few blessed months ago, I was fucking Lydia Fairview.

How could she do this to me?

That question—How could she do this to me?—replayed in my head like a malicious tape-loop. I stopped at Ralph's for a lunch and a drink. But not a drink. Not alcohol. I ordered an innocent cola.

Yup, just soda. Circumstances reveal character, someone once said. Well, circumstances were pretty damned dire at the moment, and I was responding with that flinty core of character I knew I'd always had. Even in the midst of this little tragedy—no job, no prospects, in the street while Lydia ascended the college totem pole—even in the midst of all this, I didn't self-destruct with a pitcher and a carton of smokes.

Ah, that corned beef is good. I took my time, savoring the beef's decadent, pleasantly fatty texture and the toasted rye. Ironic, isn't it? I've gotta get sacked to enjoy my food. I'd always been in such a hurry, always rushing about, that I simply ate. I rarely dined, and so I rarely enjoyed all the subtle pleasures that the word implies.

"A beer?" the waitress cheerily queried as she took away my emptied plate.

"Not today," I begged off.

"Too much work to get through, huh?"

"—Not exactly."

"A diet, then," she said knowingly. "I'm trying to lose weight myself."

"I'm not on a diet." Man, the nerve of some people.

"I didn't mean—well, last time you were in, you mentioned you were on a diet." She smiled apologetically.

"I'll take that beer," I announced, eager to show her I was indeed free to eat what I pleased, calories be damned.

She patted my shoulder. "That beer's on me."

The waitress's beer greased my skids.

Hell, I thought, I'm doing okay. Just three—no, just five beers. But waiting for those little glasses seemed so inefficient. Circumstances reveal character, so I ordered a pitcher.

"It's two for one on pitchers," the waitress chirped.

"My lucky day," I grinned.

My head, it was really swimming. Well, swimming is too vigorous a verb. Dog paddling is more like it. Just to sober up, I had another corned beef before taking my departure. I was tired. More tired than drunk. No, more drunk than tired. The Slug, it was as tired as me. She refused to accept the ignition key. What is it with keys today? First the office key, now the car key. Finally, my patience frayed, jammed the key into the ignition halfway, then hammered it into place with my shoe. And the damned ignition still wouldn't turn.

Wrong key, of course.

After many sweaty heaves and hoes, I yanked the mangled duplex key from the ignition. The correct key slid easily into place and I was on my way. But to where? I didn't want to go home. I mean, walking into one's home after being fired is a painful moment, a high water mark of misery. I'd been through it before, as you know. At least now, I was divorced. At least now, my dearest ex wasn't waiting at home to make it worse. Nobody was waiting at home to make it better, either.

Goddammit, how could she do it to me?

"Why not ask her?" I heard myself ask. The time was nearly 4:30. Maybe she's home. Yeah. Catch dear Lydia off guard, and come on strong and indignant, demanding fair treatment.

Or if the situation demanded, I could grovel and beg.

And here we go again. Lately, I'm always on Lydia's doorstep. I heard a guitar twang the opening bars of "Jingle Bell Rock." Well, Lydia was home all right. I knocked firmly but politely on the door. I felt good about this. What did I have to lose? Nothing.

I knocked harder. Hmm. The door wasn't locked, so I gingerly pushed it open. I heard a little laugh, or was it a hum? Yeah, Lydia was humming along. I announced my entrance, then prudently took a step forward.

Now that cheesy saxophone was carrying the melody, and I couldn't help but smile. Suddenly, everything felt right. My feminine intuition must be attuned to the sensitive and sentimental pangs of the holiday season, when pain are soothed by gifts, song and gently falling snow.

After removing my snowy shoes, I took a few steps, again announcing my presence.

Lydia was still humming in the kitchen. A little off-key too. I padded across the room and turned the corner.

A naked guy was on top of Lydia.

The naked guy's ugly ass bunched up then flattened, bunched and flattened, and I deducted that Lydia wasn't humming to Peggy Lee. She was humming and groaning to the earthy rhythm of his, his...

There's nothing erotic about watching somebody fuck your beloved. Some guys, I've heard they really get off on it. They even pay other guys to do it.

Right on the cold tile floor, I mused.

I took a cat-like step forward to get a gander—whose ass is that? I paused, took a few deep breaths and advanced stealthily. Lydia's butt was squeaking on the bright tile floor, and her off-tune humming was transposed to a breathy keening.

Why hadn't Lydia done it with me on the tile floor?

Lydia's eyes bugged. "*Pig pig pig!*"

Her lover disentangled himself and scrambled to his feet, and before he even turned I knew. Him. Him!

"I'm going to beat your ass," Steve Luken roared.

I didn't talk back, not even as Luken's backfist flattened my nose. Not as his heel stomped my instep. The pain wasn't as bad as you'd think. I had that booze buffer, of course, but beyond that I was gripped by a curious resignation, a resignation to the fact that my life was a disaster. This noisy battering—dammit, kidney punches hurt!—was pretty logical, a suitable coda to these absurd last few days.

"—were you watching us?"

Sudden pain. Bleeding mouth.

"How long were you watching us?" Luken repeated. He wrestled me to the floor and, grabbing a handful of my hair, bounced my skull off the floor. This is real macho shit, I thought: an angry naked guy flogging me, an angry naked woman cursing me—and me, wincing beneath a downpour of punches and oaths.

Lydia, now decent in her terry cloth robe, stepped between Luken and me. "How long?" she demanded.

Luken reached around Lydia and slapped me. She ordered him to retreat to the living room. He did only after promising me a second beating. I pulled myself up and slouched into a kitchen chair.

"Why are you here?" she demanded.

She was beautiful.

"Why?"

I avoided her enraged eyes and held a napkin to my mouth. Hey, look at that: a sweaty imprint of Lydia's rear on the tile floor.

"Tell me, James!"

Let's get this over with. "I came here because—" I paused to gather my convoluted thoughts and motives. "Because I'm out of a job. Because you're the President now. Because I need my job back."

She shook her head.

"I really need it."

"That's quite impossible," Lydia explained, her tone suddenly and eerily officious. "You and Boyle, Douglas and Rochinni. You're all out. The second campus scheme is poison, and I need a clean slate."

"And because I love you."

"God you're a creep."

"Please."

Her face softened momentarily. "I'll give you a recommendation for another job. That's it."

"I'll work for less."

"That's it."

"I love you," I whispered.

"Good evening."

I rose as briskly as possible—Luken, he must've kneed my balls— and hobbled to the door, my snow-soaked socks squishing the whole way.

Steve the Conquering Stud had donned a silk smoking jacket and now lounged on the couch. "Told you I'd have your office," he reminded me.

Now I knew how our cave-dwelling ancestors suffered at the hands of plundering foes: your loathed enemy, the bastard you hate more than all others, kicks your ass out of the cave and screws your woman on your hallowed bed of twigs and leaves.

"You shouldn't rub it in," Lydia teased. "Steve is my new Vice President, though he'll probably take over the second campus site soon." She joined him on the couch and rested her head on his shoulder.

Warming to the task, Luken continued. "I took the liberty of keeping your computer. You won't be needing it. And those skin magazines? I threw them out.

"How could you do this to me?" I asked her.

"You did it. You were the leak."

Uh?

"That night you were at the bar?" Lydia reminded. "You called me, and you were so drunk?"

"—No."

"Bruce Herrig was with you. And Jo Ann."

Oh yeah...I'd called her from Stadia the night before my sabotage stunt.

"You told me everything you were going to do, and I thought you were just drunk. But when Boyle announced that he'd found the second campus site, well, I knew you'd really destroyed that property." She paused to sneer at me. "How pathetic for all concerned."

Soon after, Lydia explained, she'd had a business lunch with Rochinni. She hoped to get final approval on the new art gallery. The newly-cultured Rochinni made a great show of sampling exotic fare from the extensive wine list and got thoroughly soused. Soon he was boasting about the second campus shenanigans. "He even said he was the driving force, not Prescott or anybody else. Then he grabbed my boobs."

"Poor you," I mocked. "You had no idea that showing him dirty pictures would give him ideas."

"So I'd kissed his ass a little," Lydia conceded. "I had to get him interested in the art gallery."

After freeing herself from Rochinni's paws, Lydia demanded that he leave her alone. But the old dick, high on Eros and Chablis, declared her his secret temptress and read her an original love poem, scrawled on a cocktail lounge napkin. Quite a performance, too. The lunch crowd fell into stunned silence as Rochinni scaled the oratorical heights.

"Something about his mighty mast driving me far from the gentle shore," Lydia recalled, disgust wrinkling her forehead. "I slapped his face, and the cook threw him out. I was so embarrassed."

Lydia didn't hear from Rochinni for a while and figured he'd come to his senses. Then he showed up last night at Boyle's fete, fully pissed and fully drunk. Everything had gone to shit: Lydia had told him to sod off, and Boyle, Douglas, and Prescott were clubbing him with video blackmail. And some spoilsport had blown the whistle on the second campus.

"Rochinni is terrified. He just wants to get Boyle and Prescott before they get him," Lydia explained. "He actually called the state's attorney at 6:00 a.m. and told him everything. He's hoping for a plea bargain."

"Why couldn't you just keep quiet about it all?" I snapped at her. "Why'd you ruin it all for us?"

"You were the leak. Blame yourself."

"No, I mean you didn't have to call the governor's office, for Christ's sake." I recalled her teasing Douglas and me about a disgruntled citizen spilling the beans. What an actress. "Couldn't you just shut up?"

"Shut your mouth," Luken warned. "You've got nerve complaining about anything."

"She could've kept quiet," I insisted. Oh oh. Luken clenched his fists as if to punch me again. Then he grinned.

"I blew the whistle on everything," Luken announced. "You told Lydia, Lydia told me. And I told the governor."

"I didn't want him to. But he convinced me." Lydia's pronunciation of convinced was embarrassingly carnal.

"It was a pleasure to bury you and Boyle," Luken exulted. "And Rochinni, that old bastard."

"Thank God Prescott already cut a check for the art gallery," Lydia snickered. "He won't be feeling too generous from here on in."

Lydia cupped Luken's face in her hands, turned it toward hers, and kissed it. Twice. Three times...This lovey dovey act was sobering me up far too fast, and sobering up too fast really hurts. It's like getting the bends.

"Oh yeah," Luken added, struggling to speak as Lydia licked his ear. "I dropped your watch in the mail. Douglas had it—he got it from one of the state inspectors the morning after your little stunt. It was insurance, just in case you gave 'em any trouble."

"You're lucky," Lydia noted. "Without that watch, there's nothing to connect you."

"—Huh?" This was scary shit.

"No watch, no proof," Luken smirked. "You did it by yourself, so there's no direct witness at the college to fry you, either. We're being very kind to you, actually."

Lydia buried her face in his neck.

Nearly ill, I ran out of the house. I knew that in a few moments, Lydia would slip out of her robe, and Luken would slip his—

I'd forgotten my shoes.

My poor shoes. I pictured them abandoned on that "Welcome" doormat, their polish running like a chick's teary eyeliner. Welcome, the doormat had said. Uh...where am I welcome? Where are my shoes welcome?

By the time I'd pulled into my driveway, I was too demoralized to get out of the car. Why should I? What waited for me inside my duplex except a freezer-burnt pizza? Here I was in the driveway the second night running, unable to haul my sorry ass from the car.

A knock on the window startled me.

"It's cold out here," Kim exclaimed.

I opened the door and fell out of the car.

"You don't have any shoes!"

"I'm a karate master."

With a steadying hand, Kim helped me to my door.

"Thank you so much Kim." Christ, here I was trashed in front the neighbor's daughter. Certainly, Mr. Kwang's opinion of me would plummet.

She grinned conspiratorially. "I like to put on a buzz once in a while too."

"If you were of age, I'd offer you a drink."

She was saying something as I closed the door, but she cheekily reopened it and walked right in. I stood there tilting back and forth as she disappeared into the kitchen. She returned with two cans of beer.

I held up both hands. "Please. I've sworn off booze."

She shrugged and popped open a can for herself.

"And neither can, neither can you. Not here."

"Relax."

The hell with it. I sat on my couch as Kim turned on the TV.

"Great, you've got cable. Dad won't let us have it." Wielding the remote like a sharpshooter, she gunned through several channels, then settled on a movie: a sweaty guy with tattoos was balling a noisy Puerto Rican chick.

"Turn that off," I ordered halfheartedly.

"I've seen it already. That guy's a cop and she's his informant."

"Oh it's a romance."

"God, he's a hunk isn't he?"

Resigned, I stretched out and administered a post-traumatic event smoke.

"Hey great, cigarettes."

The cable-movie's romantic interlude concluded and segued to some crunchy pistol whipping. Kim kept yakking and smoking at teenage warp speed.

Oh no. She's talking. And talking. Why must people yap at such hours? When you're drunk and depressed and unemployed? I did my best to be courteous but was snoring in thirty seconds.

Chapter Twenty Six: Because I was Mad

My dreams were what you'd expect: that is, my dreams were nightmares. They found me driving desperately from house to house in search of a friend; at each stop, I was only laughed out of the house. Bruce, Lydia, Robobabe, even Mum: they all laughed at me.

Then the dreams took a darker turn and simply replayed, in documentary fashion, the humiliations at Lydia's house. Several times, I shook myself awake. And each time I woke, I realized that both my job and Lydia were really in the past, a past that already possessed the bittersweet gold and blue hues of nostalgia. Meanwhile, I kept suggesting that Kim leave. She ignored me.

Around midnight, I yielded to my bladder's stabbing and rose to relieve myself. The door was—the door was locked. Goddammit. I stood there clenching my prong and gritting my teeth. Rather gruffly, I asked if I too might have access to the necessary room.

"I'll be right out," Kim assured. But I heard the telltale squeak of the medicine cabinet being opened. What a snoop. Probably searching for a big bucks prescription narcotic. Hah! The most exotic compound in the cabinet was my Enforcer no-stain deodorant.

Arm extended, I steadied myself against the doorframe. "You have to get home," I said firmly. "Your family will be scared to death."

"I don't care."

"I'll call them myself."

"I can't go home."

"You're going."

The door swung open and she turned off the bathroom light. "I got kicked out. My father, he disowned me or something."

"Or something?"

"I shamed him."

Standing in the dark, I winced a bit at the palpable hurt in her voice. "What did you—"

"Nothing, practically. I slept with Brian."

My bladder was fully pissed, pardon the pun. It was practically kneeing me. I excused myself and, to cover the noise of my urine drilling the toilet bowl, asked who Brian was.

She opened the door and asked me not to shout. "They'll hear you," she whispered loudly.

Oops…that's right. They live on the other side of that wall. "Close the door would you?"

She obeyed. I washed my hands at a laggardly pace and, just to gather my wits, splashed cold water on my sore eyeballs. Finally, after a leisurely gargle, I turned off the light and opened the door.

"Go home and talk over with your father," I whispered.

"I shamed him."

Hmm...Mr. Kwang is really Old World. He's still straining under the burden of family reputation, a burden that plenty of American parents have long shrugged off as antiquated or exhausting or pointless.

"—Are you pregnant?"

"I'm not stupid," she retorted, indignant.

"Then there's hope," I suggested. "If you can—" Hold on here! I rubbed my eyes. I couldn't be sure, given the hallway's darkness.

"So what's the big fucking deal?" Kim asked matter-of-factly. "Everybody's sleeping together."

"Get your clothes on!"

She giggled.

"Do it!" I shouted.

She clamped her hand over my mouth.

"You're an idiot," I mumbled through the tiny hand on my mouth.

Her mouth replaced her palm.

I pushed her and retreated a step. My eyes had adjusted to the dark. Yes indeed. Kim Kwang was half nude. Now, I'd heard rumors that today's teens matured quickly, what with their fortified cereals and hormonally enriched cow burgers. The rumors aren't rumors. They're true.

"I slept with Brian, but..." She lowered her voice. "I thought about you." She kissed me. I kissed her back. I couldn't help it. Well, yes I could. But I didn't, and I followed Kim down the stairs. She was already disrobing, and tossed her clothes up and over her shoulder with giddy high spirits.

You know how long-time married women complain that their husbands don't engage in tender heartfelt foreplay? Well, I've got news: neither do teen girls. Kim, she just fucks, like me. Maybe I'm still young at heart.

She stretched out on the bed, popping and fizzing with youth's hormones and youth's stupidity. Her teenage skin was, I confess, a treat for my aged hands and jaundiced eyes. But given my state of mind and spirit, the sex grew grim as I threw my heft into this 110 pound kid. She thrust back at me, mistaking my crudity for passion. But I soon wore her out with sour machismo. I rolled Kim onto her belly, then ordered her to her hands and knees, then onto her back again. She collapsed under my weight, my anger, my acutely poor character.

"It's fucking good for you," I wheezed.

But it wasn't good for her, fucking or otherwise.

She was weeping.

And she wouldn't stop weeping. I'd immediately climbed off of her, of course, but my chivalric concern didn't help. She kept wiping at her nose and crying.

"Did I hurt you?" I asked dumbly. "Or—"

"Now I've really shamed my father!"

Uh?

"You're so old!"

"Why did you..." I held up my hands, bewildered.

"Because I'm so mad at Brian. And father. They won't let me just be."

Weepy Christ. Teen age angst.

"And what about you?"

Uh?

"Why did you do it with me?"

"—I'm mad at somebody too."

She studied me, reddening eyes rimmed with tears. "Father will kill you if he finds out."

"I'm not telling," I blurted. "Are you?"

"He'll kill you."

"Well are you?"

Finally, she shook her head with something less than conviction. The gross gravity of this act—John Deyme spooling the troubled neighbor kid—had struck both of us. Kim looked nauseous, with a disquieting green pall on her face.

"You should really go home," I finally whispered.

"I can't."

"Where've you been living?"

"With our minister. But he's cheap and won't give me any money at all. I was about to sneak into my house for money when I saw you pull into the driveway. I really need some money."

"How much?"

She chewed her lip for a few moments, calculating, then arrived at a figure. I balked, but she insisted.

"I got fired, Kim!"

"But I've got to have it!" That's all I needed: a nude teen squalling for more money. I rose and wrote her a check for three hundred dollars.

"Wait a minute." She did some calculating, eyes half-closed in concentration. "I need more."

Teenagers, they're like everybody else: they don't care about your problems, but they care passionately about their own problems. I opened my wallet and fished out a couple hundred in twenties and tens. The extra cash satisfied her and she dressed, hopping about lightly on one leg as she pulled on her top-tab tattered denims. She even offered a chipper

"Later" as she stealthily departed by the back door.

I woke at ten thirty. After a quick cup of instant java, I rolled up the bed, the scene of last night's shabby act...at least, I thought it was shabby. My moral compass sure needed recalibration. Sure, I felt filthy, but in a couple days or a couple hours, the filth would fade. Maybe in another week or two, I'd recall last night as one of racy romance, a bohemian rebuffing of Midwestern mores. In a few weeks, I'll call her and invite her over for another round of—no, I'm just kidding.

I'm a bastard. And I've got no job.

The first few days at home were not bad, actually. I half-expected Mr. Kwang to pay me a visit, red-faced and heavily armed. But nothing happened. Kim must've shut up about it. I was soon satisfied that Mr. Kwang and Mrs. Kwang were ignorant of Kim's grimy treatment at the mitts of the good neighbor.

In fact, they were gone nearly all the time. The restaurant obligated them to work sixteen-hour days. The restaurant is, by the way, doing pretty well. It sports a cheery red brick exterior and a sign that proclaims Kwang's Dragon Inn. It's right on the corner of Bridge and Sanderson, with a newly paved lot. I'm happy for them, I really am. I just can't...you know, I don't feel right about breezing in for fried rice and egg drop soup.

In three days, I'd hit my stride and fell into a slacker's routine: Rise and shine around 10:00. Turn on the TV and think about breakfast for a while. Then dress and go to breakfast. I'm still driving the Slug, by the way. My Sail rests glumly under snow and ice. The damned heater doesn't work.

After breakfast, I do—I do what? I drive around. I try to enjoy the bracing winter air and cobalt blue skies. Downtown is decked out in holiday garb, street lamps in red ribbons and shop windows filled with confetti snowflakes. Everybody's smiling, enjoying the bright days and bright moods. Funny, isn't it? Just last week, Boyle had predicted nothing but blue skies. In a very narrow sense, he was right: the sun's been shining every day.

After my drive, it's back to the duplex for a look-see at the soaps. I developed a liking for *Vengeance* pretty quickly. Lots of scantily dressed babes—several in their late thirties and early forties, but admirably preserved, and with a sly glint in their eyes that bespeaks vast sack savvy. After the soaps, I treat myself to a chocolate Sundae and/or video-inspired handjob. Then, all tuckered out, I nap until dinner time. Unlike the lunch hour, which regularly features plenty of solo diners, the dinner hour at restaurants features mostly couples and groups. I feel conspicuous by my solitude at dinner time, so I settle for fast food. Burger Stud's got a terrific holiday dinner deal: two cheeseburgers and bonus barbecue beef sub.

After dinner, it's off to a local bar. I don a moderate beer buzz then amble home to sack out on the couch with several cable porn flicks: by eleven, they're surprisingly explicit. By this late hour—after the barley malt and cathode ray porn panoply—by now, I'm pretty worked up. I watch without pants.

Two days before Christmas, I was pretty low. Mum called. I put on a brave front, talking loudly and longly about all the challenges at work. The challenges were coming so fast and furious, in fact, that I most regretfully could not visit over the holidays.

"—That's awful."

"Mum, I'm just busy."

"On Christmas Eve? Christmas day?"

I hate it when Mum's voice takes on that mournful, keening tone. She tries to make me feel guilty. She succeeds.

"On the day after Christmas, I'm—"

"For Heaven's sake, they work you terribly hard."

"—I'm flying out to San Diego for winter workshops on, on administrative leading. Leadership."

"No time for your family on Christmas."

"I'll be up just a little late. Around January."

"I'll be lonely."

"But I'll be there. And I'll send my presents in time for Christmas."

"Don't bother. Just bring them up with you when you visit."

"C'mon. Try to understand."

It went on like that, and I was pretty convincing. I tell you, I had myself believing that I really did have a conference in San Diego. Mom conceded that seventy-five degrees sounded fine. After a bit more small talk—including my repeated assurances that I'd visit sometime in January—we exchanged light hearted good-byes. I'd cajoled Mum out of her mood and even got her chortling about all the delicious "food" she'd prepare for me, like blood sausage and stale scones.

"All right then," Mum chuckled, "I'll see you in January."

"I'll send you a postcard from San Diego," I promised.

After I hung up, it hit me. San Diego...why not? I had checks coming in for another few months. In fact, my paycheck had arrived by mail yesterday. I hadn't rushed out to cash it because I'd been mightily depressed. In such a state, I might've done something brazen, something compulsive like—like jetting off to San Diego.

The hell with it. I'd earned a respite: bright hotel room, pool side with cocktails. I thumbed my way through the phone book and made all the arrangements through a local agency. The agent cautiously noted that I'd have to pay an extra couple hundred for such a quick departure. In fact, flights were filling very quickly: perhaps I'd like to buy them right now, over the phone. A marvelous idea, I agreed. I gave her my credit card number. After booking the flight, she made reservations for me at the Spa, a nice mid-level hotel with two pools, saunas, and a nightclub with a jazz trio. I praised the agent's prompt service and stated that I'd pick up the tickets this afternoon.

I felt better already. I was doing something. Then I thought: why not bring Robobabe along? She'd be a poolside inspiration as her Amazonian bod made mincemeat of an overmatched bikini. Before caution could rear its timid head—the tab would quadruple with Robobabe in tow—I called her at work. Tersely, the sales manager informed me that she'd been fired. Huh...not reaching the ol' sales quota, huh? She was a loser just like me. I called her apartment. She unconvincingly assured me that she'd been meaning to call me about paying for the Sail, then confessed that she'd been fired. "So I'll be a little late in getting you the money, but I really—"

"I'm here to help," I cheerily interrupted. "I'm going to San Diego. You're going with me."

"Wonderful!" she squealed. "What should I bring with me?"

"A bikini and a diaphragm."

"You pig," she laughed.

"You slut," I snorted.

"Hey, how about lunch? On you?"

I agreed and suggested we meet at the travel agent's office in a half hour. I called back the agent and breezily informed her that "my girlfriend" was accompanying me. The agent happily made all the arrangements. Such service!

With a marvelously light step, I hurried out to the Slug. The brightness of the day—cloudless sky, fresh clean snow—was a friendly omen: I'd certainly done the right thing. San Diego...a fresh start? Who knows? Nothing was stopping me, really, from packing up and heading west. California's still got that old magic, I mused as I pulled into the agent's parking lot. The land of limitless opportunity still might yield its riches to this immigrant's son.

Lauren, bless her, was waiting inside for me. She held out her hands for me to grasp. She was—Christ she's a dish. Her attire looked suitable for a westward journey: simple white cotton blouse with plenty of room for her assets, and stone-washed denims, the seat of which cupped her bionic buns like a D cup brassiere.

"It's wonderful to see you, James."

"And you're always good to see," I assured her. And she was. I noticed, though, a melancholy in her eyes. The New Year's been rough on her too, I guessed. For a moment, my gaze held hers, and we exchanged weary smiles. "God it really is good to see you," I half-whispered.

She gave me a hearty hug, then began chirping about how she had friends in San Diego. They'd be happy to put us up for a few days if we decided to stay longer, and—she clamped a hand over her mouth but the squeal still escaped.

"It's a sunny ditch!" somebody behind me roared.

I turned to see Mr. Kwang sprinting toward me, fists raised menacingly.

"It's the son of bitch!" he roared again.

Oh oh. He was animated with wrath, twitching and hopping and sweating. Mrs. Kwang was right behind him, swinging her purse like a deadly weapon. Kim cowered by the entrance, adrenals pumping for a fight or a flight.

"Mr. Kwang. Please. Take it easy." I held out my right hand in a gesture of reconciliation. "Let's talk about this."

"You ruin my daughter!" He grabbed my extended hand and twisted.

"You pay her for sex! I saw check!"

Delicate bones snapped and cracked. For a few nanoseconds, I thought, Hell, this isn't going to hurt so much. I mean, clearly he just broke some fingers and yet the pain isn't horrible, so—

I dropped to my knees. The pain of snapping fingers is—it's electrifying. It leaps through your entire arm, past your elbow and shoulder to your eyeballs.

"For three hundred dollars!" His scuffed shoe, spotted with cooking grease and soy sauce, struck my nose. "You buy her for three hundred dollars!" He kicked me again and, retreating to the fetal position, I took refuge on the floor. But something was tearing at me: a pen or pencil or—

"Monster!" Mrs. Kwang shrieked. She clawed my face, my scalp, my throbbing neck.

The blitzkrieg stalled as Lauren shouted and swore. God bless that Lauren. She's defending me. Resting my mangled mitt against my stomach, I cautiously regained my feet. Kim was still poised at the door, ready to bolt. She averted her eyes from me, as well she should. I mean, yeah, I spooled her. But I didn't pay for it!

"—so that's how we found out!" Mrs. Kwang screeched. "Our minister found the check and confronted Kim, and she confessed that you pay her for it!" She pointed a quivering forefinger at me, like an avenging Mum about to pull the trigger of her Dirty Harry hand cannon.

"There's a big mistake here," I protested.

"Back on the floor, dog!" Mr. Kwang warned.

"There's a big mistake here," I continued from the floor. "I gave Kim a check, yes. But not for, not for that."

"Then what was check for?" Mrs. Kwang wailed.

"For—I don't know. She said she needed money, so I wrote her check."

"So you *did* sleep with her?" Lauren wailed, incredulous.

"But there was no money involved in the, in—"

"Pig!" She kicked my head like a football. The terrified travel agent yelled at somebody in the back to call the cops.

I leaped from the floor like a sprinter out of the starting blocks. Mr. Kwang's fist just missed my face. I was moving so fast and frightened that the other's faces were distorted, oval-like and gape-mouthed. I was instantly out the door, slipping and scrambling up the poorly salted sidewalk.

The Kwang lynch-mob was whooping and cursing right behind me. Even Kim had joined the tribe to give chase. My pulse, amplified to speed-metal volume, blocked out all other noise as I ran. And ran. As I rounded a corner, I glimpsed over my shoulder and saw Mr. Kwang lose his footing, then crash against a parking meter.

I thanked huffing Christ and ran several blocks further, my sides paining me and my bouncing belly exhausting me. Finally, I ducked inside Annie's Dump and calmed myself with a pitcher. Then another. Around six, I asked a chain-smoking codger to give me a lift to my car.

"Looks like you been fightin'," he observed on the way out.

"I'm even getting good at it." I slid into the passenger seat and thanked him for his courtesy.

He regarded me with cheerful exasperation. "I've got a boy about your age. He's always fightin'. What a fuck-up he is." The codger yapped contentedly as he trolled his way north. "All the money he's cost me, and he still don't—"

"Hey, there's my Slug," I directed.

"Somebody busted your windshield."

Indeed. The windshield had suffered a three-crack concussion. Mr. Kwang must've shattered it with a karate chop or spinning double-axle heel kick.

"As long as it gets me to the airport," I laughed, happy that the Slug, and not I, endured the blows. It's great to be alive! I mused. I gave my friend a five for his trouble and wished him a Merry Christmas.

The Slug, she's as faithful as any dog. Unconditional love and obedience, no matter the depths of my neglect or abuse. She started immediately and belched only minimal blue smoke; I reminded myself that the Slug, running on the same oil for over 13,000 miles, had really earned a lube job.

I reached into my shirt pocket for the airline tickets.

No tickets.

I pulled over to a curb and checked each pocket. I searched the car floor and under the seat. Then I re-checked my pockets, anxiety making me sputter like an over stressed teapot. Some wanker at the bar probably lifted them. Maybe the old prong who gave me a ride!

Then I remembered: The Kwangs had stormed into the travel agent's office before I actually claimed the tickets. The office was now closed, so I drove around the corner to a phone booth and looked up the agent's home phone number.

"Your fiancé took the tickets," the agent snapped.

"She's not my—"

"Fuckin' a high school girl for three hundred dollars! She was humiliated!"

"Merry Christmas, moron!" I slammed down the phone.

"Merry Christmas, moron," said a familiar voice behind me. Mr. Kwang punctuated his glad tidings with a ram-rod punch.

"Enough already!" My *nose*. It was all over my face, like red bean dip dropped on the floor.

Mr. Kwang tossed a balled-up fifty at me. "I curse day I took any money from you."

"So do a lot of others." I clutched my head with wary hands, resigned to yet another blow, but Mr. Kwang was already gone.

I spent Christmas day watching those moronic parades: plenty of has-been and never-was show biz types, grinning idiotically into the cameras. I called Mum around noon, pretending to be in San Diego. The weather was marvelous, I assured her

"Really? The news said it was rainy today."

No, it really was wonderful.

"What's wrong with your voice?"

"Uh—a little sinus infection." My nose is held together by several layers of white tape and baling wire. For a little guy, Mr. Kwang can sure punch.

People like me have trouble making use of time. Sure, I can kill time. But how to use it? I mean, what should I do? Read? Think? I made a real pest of myself with Herrig, calling every other day ostensibly for gossip, but actually for the sound of a human voice other than soap actors, TV pitch men, and strangers at restaurants and grocery stores. Herrig, he really holds out on me, makes me almost beg for good gossip. But the other day he passed on oodles of prime inside dope.

Boyle has returned to his Irish Catholic roots by scoring a consulting contract with the Chicago diocese. He's been hired to organize super high-stakes bingo nights. With Jesus and his flock now hardwired into the new century, the computer screen replaces the bingo board, and thousands of players in hundreds of Chicagoland churches shall compete against one another via the Internet, with some churches even setting up Internet kiosks. I suspect—and don't you, really?—that the Church has gone high-tech because, well, all those suits against pervert priests. At any rate, rumor has it that some Cardinals may join in the gaming fun from Rome. The whole scam kicks of next month. The first winner gets a guaranteed take of one grand, plus an authentic replica of the Pope's big spangled hat. Drock supplied the computers, of course. Boyle and Drock are going into business, with church networks and ecclesiastical software a specialty. Better yet, Boyle tracked down some of his favorite troubled stars from *Homeboy Video* to tearfully testify for the Lord on monthly TV specials. Born again thugs are pretty persuasive, I guess.

Dr. Douglas, not surprisingly, continues to prosper at West Central. Lydia hired him back. Despite his shadowy, conspiratorial mind—he's just wrapping up his book about the JFK thing—Douglas is more dependable than your Dad's Timex. He's every tyrant's Godsend, and Lydia knows he'll take a bullet for her if need be.

Dr. Olsen? She's not doing too well. Her husband dumped her for adultery, and apparently she's the manager of a senior's trailer court.

Boyle refused to answer her phone calls or letters, and she's pretty down.

Oh yeah. Lydia and Luken. They're still an item, the new West Central tag team. Lydia's got the board of trustees eating from her fragrant hand. Luken—I knew it!—is a breath-taking turncoat, using his new administrative position as Endowed Vice President to beat the spirit out of the faculty union. See, he knows all the union tricks and knows exactly who the weak sisters are. Luken's defection is a strategic masterwork that'll keep Lydia in power for years. Former comrades Farella and Pouris are shocked and demoralized. But as I told you: *I told you so!* Luken's a blow-hard hypocrite, happy to turn on his union buddies for a big bonus and shiny office.

Ironically, Bruce can't enjoy Luken's traitorous intrigue as much as he'd like. His squeeze Jo Anne is gone. Yeah, Lydia canned her. Turns out that she's George Prescott's niece. Lydia sanctimoniously declared that all vestiges of Prescott's corruption had to be cut. Sounds good, but I'm suspicious. Lydia would deny it—she'd call me a sore loser—but I just think she wanted to be the only big woman on campus.

Yeah, Jo Ann was just another patronage hustler. Pretty funny really, what with her fevered rants about patriarchal rapist sexist logocentric Eurocentric capitalists. That's the thing about Eurocentric capitalists: they're villainous scum until they toss some cash your way. Then they're not so bad.

Kwangs moved out on January 2. A couple burly guys from a moving company—one bald, the other bald with a pony-tail—threw all the furniture and clothes and appliances into trucks. I kind of miss the Kwangs' shouting and squalling: the holiday silence was really deafening.

Around mid-March, I couldn't endure any more call-in radio shows, freezer-burnt pizzas, and cable porn. I watched *The High Hard Ones* seven times in a month.

I had to get a job, even a junk job. On little more than a whim, I answered an ad for a "Director of Personnel Education" for Burger Stud. Seems that fast-food emporiums are having trouble finding employees who can—who can what? I mean, what's to think about at Burger Stud? You don't have to count change. You don't have to know the prices. There's nothing to think about.

A Mr. Langdon interviewed me. His own office, barely the size of a closet, was too small for us so we sat in the back of the Burger Stud, right next to the giant Jungle Gym erected for the youngest customers. Langdon was pretty friendly. He smiled easily enough and kept sweeping a longish lock of still youthful blonde hair from the top of his bifocals. I told him about my recent stint at West Central and explained that campus politics had forced me out. When I casually mentioned that I was from Flint, he looked at me with new interest. Turns out he was born and raised in Flint and worked in the engine plant on Van Slyke road until the bottom dropped out. He lucked out and got a "management" position at Burger Stud—making sure the teenage crew didn't spit in the French fries—and eventually moved up to regional manager.

"Hell, you got the job if you want it," Langdon grinned.

"—Terrific." Huh. That was easy. "What are my duties?"

"There won't be much to the job," he confided between long pulls on a chocolate shake. "And the pay's not that bad. Twenty nine K plus benefits. Two week vacation."

Welcome to the bright springtime of the private sector service economy!

"All you gotta do, basically, is have weekly meetings at each of your Burger Stud locations. Train the youngsters in basic skills. Help with their homework at school. Some of 'em are dropouts. With your background in education, no sweat."

What the hell. It was all very vague, and the pay was heart-breaking, but I'd wing it.

My territory was pretty big: Twenty Studs sprinkled throughout the suburbs. I hit five of them a week. Basically, I sit in a back booth with three or four employees at a time and check their math and spelling worksheets. Yeah, you heard right. Math and spelling. I'm no mathematician or grammarian, but I feel like Aristotle incarnate beside these kids. It's sad, really. They're pretty decent, once you get past their fragile facade of arrogance, their studied indifference. I review the homework, I fill out my no-brainer reports. I drink shakes and I smoke and, after the last tutorial, I sag into one of the ugly yellow plastic booths and read a paper. Or a book. Yeah, I'm reading. Seems I'm in the education racket, in one way or another, for the long haul. I might as well get comfortable with books, yes? I'm even cutting down on the TV. My head, it's clearing a bit. At the moment, I'm reading *Lolita*. It's about this pervert prig professor who's hot for a twelve year old. *Lolita* is oddly comforting. I mean, if Humbert Humbert could hump his lovely Lolita, can I be forgiven for fucking age-of-consent Kim Kwang?

Spring gave way to summer, and I'd gradually quit calling Bruce. I was tired of his condescension and detailed descriptions of Lydia's string of successes. Then, one muggy Sunday evening, Bruce called with bedazzling news: Lydia had broken ground on a second campus at the now-razed Garrison apartments.

"Wonder if I'll get a thank you note from her?" I sneered.

Luken will be the Provost of the second campus. His Provostial rest room will, Bruce claims, make Boyle's look like an Arkansas outhouse.

But the real news was about Jo Ann Staulen. "We're back together," Bruce gushed. "She's really changed."

"What, she gargles?"

"She's really changed."

"How so?" I demanded.

"And it's all because of your old girlfriend. Robobabe."

"What is?"

"I've got my own Robobabe now."

Yup. After Jo Ann got sacked, she happened to run into Lauren. They got to talking and ended up having lunch at a local restaurant. They enjoyed a few feminine cocktails, and their talk turned serious. Liberated by the booze, Jo Ann blurted that she was sick of her life. Of her job failures. Of herself.

That very evening, Jo Ann consulted with Lauren's on-again, off-again plastic surgeon husband. She demanded loud and proud tits, a high round butt, and a smaller nose. The capper: her post-job golden parachute allowed for discretionary surgery, so she got a new face and bod for free.

"That's, uh--that's *incredible.*"

"She is so stacked," Bruce enthused. "She made me dinner the other night. Then Lauren came over and we watched a movie." He sighed with deep satisfaction. "It was porno."

"Bullshit."

"*The High Hard Ones.* Then we had a threesome."

"Bullshit!"

"Yeah, it is." Bruce confessed. "Lauren's living with her husband this week, so it was just me and Jo Ann." He paused meaningfully. "Maybe next week."

"Did she mention me?"

"Yeah," Bruce taunted. "Jo Ann still thinks you're an ignorant asshole. Did I tell you? She's got a big contract as a model for romance novel covers—you know, she's the chick getting ravished by a long haired weight lifter, and—"

"No, I mean Lauren."

"Oh. No, but she still thinks you're an asshole too. But she did say that she had a great time in California, courtesy of your travel agent."

"Bruce, this is not the kind of gossip I want. I wanna hear that Lauren misses me. That Lydia misses me. That everybody misses me."

"I miss ya, buddy." Then Bruce laughed to show he did not at all miss me. "One more thing. Douglas finished his book about JFK, and he's already got a publisher. It's quite a sensation, I guess. There was a reporter on campus last week to talk with him."

"So who killed JFK this time? The CIA?"

"Guess again."

"Castro?"

"Uh uh."

"The mob?"

"Close."

"I give up."

"The killer was indeed Italian."

"I said I give up."

"Brace yourself, my friend: it was the Yankee Clipper!"

My mood wasn't the best, as you can understand, and I didn't really feel up to Monday's tutorials. I hurried the kids through their division and spelling and was done by one thirty. I flipped through the paper. I'll be flogged. There was a story about Douglas's book. And Bruce was right: Douglas's book presented allegedly "ground-breaking research–including just released CIA documents and other strong evidence" that Joe DiMaggio pushed for JFK's murder. Douglas conceded that DiMaggio hadn't actually pulled the trigger, but he insisted that DiMaggio appealed to a mob-connected uncle to arrange the hit. The Yankee Clipper was furious at the Kennedys for their cavalier treatment of the former Mrs. DiMaggio, treatment that DiMaggio was convinced led to her untimely death. The CIA and mob were already upset at Kennedy, and DiMaggio's anger sealed JFK's fate. He contributed tens of thousands to set up Oswald in Dallas with the help of old friend Guy Bannister. Furthermore, DiMaggio often met with Clay Shaw in business dealings and—"

A familiar voice diverted me from the story—Kim Kwang! Or more precisely, Kim and her new husband. And infant. Kim waved at me as if I were merely a friendly ex-neighbor. Then the trio violated all sense of decorum by joining me at my booth.

"I heard you worked up here," Kim remarked. "Oh. This is my husband Brian, and this is our son, Tim." She nodded at the sleeping baby in Brian's arms.

I nodded at Brian and pretended to show interest in the baby. Brian balanced the baby in one arm and wolfed down food with the other. He was a thick-haired, wispy-framed ragamuffin of eighteen or nineteen, a requisite trio of rings dangling from his earlobe.

"So, where are you working, Brian?" I asked.

"I'm not, like, working at the moment."

"Can you get him a job?" Kim asked.

"I'm not in personnel, exactly."

"Could you, like, get me a job?"

Hearing-impaired Christ. "Where'd you work most recently?"

"Huh." He looked at Kim for help, but she only shrugged. "Oh yeah, I know. It was at, uh—No, it wasn't there."

The baby burped.

"Yeah. It was the mall. A flunky job at the skate shop."

"Brian's an excellent skate boarder."

"Yeah, I'm pretty good."

Kim apologized for her father. "He regrets all of it. He was just so pissed off at you."

I touched my nose, which still sometimes ached.

"You know," Kim laughed, "we thought Tim was yours."

"—Mine?"

"My father was fuming! But I had a test, and the baby was Brian's."

"And your old man got mad all over again," Brian recalled with a daft grin. "Your old man, he sure gets pissed off a lot." Brian faced me. "Kim was, like, glad it wasn't your kid."

Kim punched Brian's shoulder to silence him, but he blithely continued.

"If Tim was yours—Dammit, Kim, stop hitting me!" He swatted back at her until she stopped. "Kim was afraid that if Tim was yours, he'd really be, like, really fat."

"I didn't say fat!" Kim protested.

"Oh yeah. You said, like, obese."

www.ingramcontent.com/pod-product-compliance
Lightning Source LLC
Chambersburg PA
CBHW030446250626
47154CB00003BA/1147